Scalping Columbus
and
Other Damn Indian Stories

AMERICAN INDIAN LITERATURE AND CRITICAL STUDIES SERIES

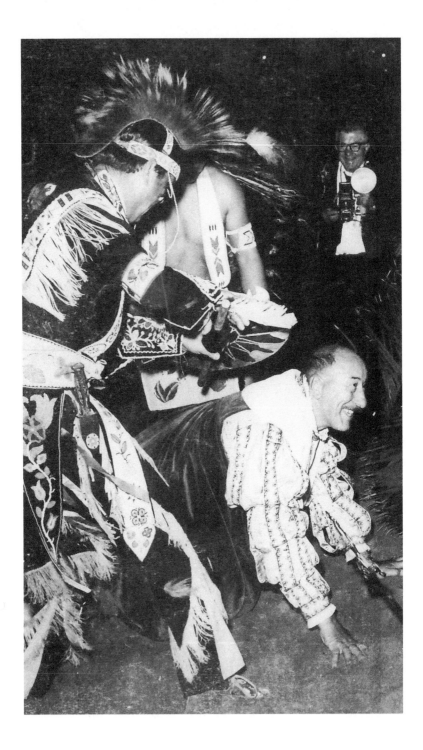

Scalping Columbus

and

Other Damn Indian Stories

Truths, Half-Truths, and Outright Lies

Adam Fortunate Eagle

UNIVERSITY OF OKLAHOMA PRESS / NORMAN

Also by Adam Fortunate Eagle
Heart of the Rock: The Indian Invasion of Alcatraz (Norman, Okla., 2002)
Pipestone: My Life in an Indian Boarding School (Norman, Okla., 2010)

Library of Congress Cataloging-in-Publication Data

Fortunate Eagle, Adam, 1929–
[Short stories. Selections]
Scalping Columbus and other damn Indian stories: truths, half-truths, and outright lies / Adam Fortunate Eagle.
     pages cm.— (American Indian literature and critical studies series; v. 60)
ISBN 978-0-8061-4428-3 (pbk.: alk. paper)
I. Title.
PS3606.O7489A6 2014
813'.6—dc23

2013024936

Scalping Columbus and Other Damn Indian Stories: Truths, Half-Truths, and Outright Lies is Volume 60 in the American Indian Literature and Critical Studies Series.

The paper in this book meets the guidelines for permanence and durability of the Committee on Production Guidelines for Book Longevity of the Council on Library Resources, Inc. ∞

Copyright © 2014 by the University of Oklahoma Press, Norman, Publishing Division of the University. Manufactured in the U.S.A.

All rights reserved. No part of this publication may be reproduced, stored in a retrieval system, or transmitted, in any form or by any means, electronic, mechanical, photocopying, recording, or otherwise—except as permitted under Section 107 or 108 of the United States Copyright Act—without the prior written permission of the University of Oklahoma Press. To request permission to reproduce selections from this book, write to Permissions, University of Oklahoma Press, 2800 Venture Drive, Norman OK 73069, or email rights.oupress@ou.edu.

1 2 3 4 5 6 7 8 9 10

Contents

List of Illustrations IX

Acknowledgments XI

Foreword XIII

Preface XV

Moose on the Loose 3

Three Hole Outhouse 5

TP 10

Grandpa's *Gebic* Bag 11

How Poor Were You? 16

Ancient Ojibwe Recipes 17

Amos Gets a New House 18

Damn Hippies 23

Hurling With Luci 26

Shared Sorrows 28

Scalping Columbus 30

The Curse of the Totem Pole 47

Now That's Brave 49

Farts Among Many 50

Evil Spirits of Alcatraz 57

General Fremont's Cannon 76

How I Saved Patty Hearst's Father from the SLA:
  The Untold Story 81

Never Let a Good Deed Go Unpunished 86

The Saga of the Lahontan Valley Long-Legged Turtles 90

Mark Your Territory 99

Sonny Mosquito and the Chicken Dance 106

White Man Sweats Him 117

Tell Me Another Damn Indian Story, Grandpa 124

Alcatraz Is Not an Island 127

Onward Christian Soldiers 134

Good Medicine 135

Brokeback Boulder 136

Filipino Gold 139

Good Medicine II 144

Italian Mill House 146

Peace and Friendship 156

The Goose Hunter 164

Going Back 166

The Nickel Hunter 169

Medicine Gift 170

Newt 174

Walking Eagle Nation 176

Jewish Indian 184

Don't Take Chances   185

The Four B.C.s   186

Twelve Disciples   186

Two Tents   186

This is a Mini-Joke, So You Give Me a Mini-Ha-Ha   186

Spiritual Leader, Shaman, Almost a Messiah   187

Indian Health (You're Gonna Die!)   190

The Nine Lives of Fortunate Eagle   193

Glossary   197

Appendix: Percentage of Bullshit per Story   199

Illustrations

Adam Fortunate Eagle presenting Luci Baines Johnson with
    necklace, 1964   27

Dancing for Luci   27

Scalping Columbus actors, 1968   32

Adam and Bobbie in Rome City Hall, 1973   41

Adam and Pope Paul VI   44

Cartoon of Adam in Alcrataz from *San Francisco Chronicle*, 1969   64

Acknowledgments

Gloria "Whip Woman" Meyers, my local editor, received all my handwritten manuscripts and entered them on her computer, editing and spell-checking as she labored along. It was a major challenge to arrange all the chaotic and often bizarre stories into a semblance of order, and I owe her my thanks.

Thank you, my friend Professor Magoroh Murayama, who offered me the brass ring of opportunity and made it possible for me to make history with my discovery of Italy for the American Indians and my audience with Pope Paul.

A special *mii gwitch* to the University of Oklahoma Press for keeping an open mind and having the courage to publish this book, and perhaps for realizing that some of these stories are destined to become legends retold by future generations.

Finally, there is no way I can properly express my gratitude and appreciation to my Shoshone wife, Bobbie, for enduring sixty-four years of marriage to me and having the patience required to support my efforts for the fifteen years it took me to finish these stories.

This book is a compilation of short stories that can only be described as truths, half-truths, and outright lies. One cannot dismiss one of mankind's oldest oral art forms: bullshit.

Foreword

Mark Twain, Will Rogers, and Vine Deloria held a meeting on Sitting Bull's grave, discussing who should write the foreword to this book. Sitting Bull was the unanimous choice, as he knows more than all of them put together about the sacred and profane, and he, more than anyone else, understands the ways of Fortunate Eagle.

* * *

Mitakuye Oyasin, I am honored by your request to sing Praise Songs for my old friend, Fortunate Eagle, who is a member in good standing of the Teasing Clan. As a matter of fact, I would call him a Contrary Warrior, in that he joins the ranks of shamans, skinwalkers, shape shifters, sacred clowns, *heyokas*, contraries, republicans, and evangelists.

To many he is a badass Indian who sees another reality, who dances to the beat of a different drum, who uses satire and humor to call attention to the inequalities of our society. Or, he can be a bumbling coyote, who can screw up the best of intentions, crap on it, kick some dirt over it, and then walk away with his tail held high. He has the guts to write a book this bad and thinks he can get away with it, and if he hasn't offended someone with his stories, he is not doing his job.

Hecetu (So be it),
Sitting Bull

Preface

Some of these stories are so outrageous they appear to be pure exaggeration, when in actual fact they are true, only the author knows which are fact and which are fiction.

Other stories are based on facts, which begged for embellishment. I will stand by the facts until someone accuses me of fibbing. At such time, I reserve the right to accept or reject that challenge based on my assessment of the level of intelligence and knowledge of my accuser. After all, liars have the greatest flexibility of all storytellers, except when they are on the witness stand, where they have no flexibility. The exception to this rule being politicians and lawyers, who are, as everyone knows, the masters of bullshit.

Prevaricating allows one to expand his or her oral storytelling or literary horizons; in fact, they become unlimited. Some of my stories are total fabrications disguised as the truth. These tales test not only the literary creativity of the author but also the gullibility of the reader. Personally, I find it impossible to distinguish the difference between outright fabrications and bullshit. You, gentle reader, must decide. But don't you agree that bullshit is the fertilizer of the mind?

Scalping Columbus
and Other Damn Indian Stories

Moose on the Loose

It was always a special treat for me to go back and visit my reservation at Red Lake, Minnesota.

As a five-year-old, me, my four older brothers, and my older sister were shipped off to Pipestone Indian Training School for the next ten years.

I felt robbed of some of the traditional and cultural activities which took place on the reservation, such as tapping maple sap in the early spring, netting walleye pike in our great lake, harvesting wild rice in late summer, and hunting snowshoe rabbits in winter.

Our tribe was famous for its wild rice and its variations—river rice, paddy rice, lake rice, long grain, and short grain—all were tribal delicacies.

I was determined to participate in those tribal events in spite of my inexperience.

Late one summer I arrived at the reservation just in time for the wild rice harvest. Uncle Charlie had a cabin near the river, where the shallows were filled with large stands of wild rice. He loaned me his beautiful aluminum-hulled boat equipped with oars, canvas, beater sticks, and rope. I shoved off downstream at dawn. *Ho wah!* I felt just like those old-time Indians.

However, gathering wild rice is not as glamorous as it may seem. In the rice paddies, I bent the rice stalks with one stick and then beat them with the other stick. The rice then fell onto the canvas. The chaff of the rice flew high in the air; it clogged my sinuses and made my skin itch. Being uncomfortable and itchy was the price one paid for tradition.

Rounding a bend in the river, I came upon a bull moose with his head underwater, feeding on the succulent stalks of water lilies.

Ho wah! Not only was I gathering wild rice, I now had a chance to catch a moose. I quietly formed a lasso out of the rope, and deftly looped it over his horns as he raised his head.

That was when I discovered moose do not stand still when they are roped. In fact, they run like hell! And, I found out something else—moose are huge! Mine was seven feet high at the shoulders and must have weighed twelve hundred pounds. That enraged moose charged up the riverbank and headed straight for Uncle Charlie's cabin. I desperately hung on to the oarlocks as I experienced the most terrifying ride of my life. That aluminum boat was rattling and banging like a load of tin cans tied to a dog's tail. At times like these, some people find that their lives flash before their eyes—I saw my obituary, "Indian boy killed in a dry-land accident in a rowboat being towed by a bull moose."

In spite of the bumpy ride and the fact that we were rapidly approaching Uncle Charlie's cabin, I had the presence of mind to holler, "Fresh meat! Uncle Charlie! Get the gun, I'm bringing fresh meat!"

Hearing the commotion, Uncle Charlie grabbed the .30-30 Winchester rifle next to the door and rushed out of his cabin, only to be confronted by a charging bull moose.

"Shoot the moose!" I hollered to Uncle Charlie, "Shoot the moose!"

Uncle Charlie dropped the rifle and took refuge behind a pine tree as me and the moose came flying by, knocking over the outhouse with Aunt Jane still inside.

The boat hit a large bump in the ground, and flipped sideways. It was caught between two trees, causing the rope to break. The liberated moose trotted off into the deep woods—its dignity was still intact.

Uncle Charlie surveyed the damage: his rifle broke when the moose stepped on it; his prized aluminum-hulled boat laid crumpled like a tin can; wild rice was scattered all over the landscape; and above it all we could hear Auntie Jane, cussing and screaming over the indignity she had just endured. Uncle Charlie tried to maintain his composure. He looked me straight in the eye and said, "Nephew, next time you come back to the reservation, don't you ever try playing Indian again!

Three Hole Outhouse

In these modern times one rarely concerns themselves, or even thinks about, how humans dispose of bodily wastes. I'll bet you haven't given this subject even a passing thought in the past week, unless, of course, you happened to be in a crowded shopping mall when nature called. Your only concern then was not the "how of it" but the "where of it." In a growing panic, you finally locate that haven for elimination of human by-products. Truly a "pause that refreshes."

If you come from a rural background, you can still remember the indispensable outhouse. Old-timers like to tell the modern youngsters about how difficult those "good old days" were—tales of walking five miles, through knee-deep snow in subzero weather to go to school, of going down the bush-lined path to a pure water stream to fetch water, of shoveling snow to clear the path to the outhouse. When real bad weather prevented trips to the outhouse, the reliable "thunder mug" was used. This was often a large stoneware pot with a lid. The lid was very important, as it served to hold down the awful odor inside.

But, even the outhouse was considered a modern advancement in technology at one time. Only four generations ago, on the reservation, when nature called, it really meant that we simply went behind a bush, tree, or rock and relieved ourselves. My Great-grandpa Amabese was a more forward-thinking man. He dug a deep hole in the ground and put two planks over the top. He spaced the planks so a person could squat over them and everything would simply drop between the space into the hole below. How clever, eh?

His son, Amabese the younger, was a more worldly person, and after he was grown up and had a family of his own, he built a real outhouse. Actually, it was quite pitiful—a small one-holer. Grandpa Amabese cut the hole with a keyhole saw and didn't think to round off the edges with a file. Everyone who used that little one-holer ended up with a red ring around their butt caused by the sharp edge of the seat. The longer a person sat, the deeper the red ring became and, of course, the longer it took for it to go away.

Our family was readily apparent at the nearby waterhole, where everyone liked to swim or to bathe. That red ring around our butts was a sure giveaway. People referred to us as their ringed-ass neighbors for as long as that little one-holer survived.

Halloween is a white man's celebration that the young Indians were quick to pick up on. None of that door-to-door trick or treating. No sir, it was all trick. Like stealing pantaloons off the clothesline, then hanging them high in a tree next to the road for all passersby to see—to the great embarrassment of Gramma. Or, the boys liked soaping up the windows of houses. But the all-time favorite was tipping over outhouses. That little one-holer was a real target, for all it took was two boys running down that short slope, jumping, and pushing at the same time. That little one-holer flopped flat on its back, and the boys hardly broke stride as they dashed off into the woods before Grandpa could come out and shoo them away. The dastardly deed had already been done.

The next year was the final straw. The two boys showed up again at the site of their favorite target. They let out a war whoop and charged down the slope, jumping and flopping the little outhouse flat on its back with a loud bang. A loud roar of profanity erupted from within as Grandpa had been sitting inside, heeding the call of nature. The two boys quickly vanished into the night. Everyone inside the main house heard the commotion and knew right away what had happened. It was difficult to keep from laughing as Grandpa came stomping into the house, still livid with rage. His pants had come off during the flip-flop of the outhouse, and he had a red ring around his ass. He looked nothing like a respected elder should look.

That was the end of the little single-hole outhouse, for the next day Grandpa went out and chopped it into kindling with his big double-bladed axe. He threw quicklime into the pit and then filled it in. A few yards away, Grandpa dug a huge deep pit and built the largest, most sturdy outhouse any of us had ever seen. Five full-grown men couldn't tip this one over. This was truly a deluxe model—a sporty three-holer. He even filed down the edges of the holes, making it almost a delight to sit on. Best of all, the ringed-ass look was gone!

The little boy's section had no seat—just an opening. This way we could pee without splattering all over the seat. The girls and the women hated to sit down on a splattered wet seat. Grandpa sternly instructed the boys never to use the other side. The two holes were reserved for the men, the women, and the girls.

The next year at Halloween, nobody bothered that formidable three-hole outhouse and Grandpa was very proud at having outwitted the pranksters.

American Indians found a way around the government's ban on certain ceremonies and feast days by adopting the white man's days of celebration. The kids loved Halloween, but the adults were more favorable to celebrating Thanksgiving, for it was, in fact, a feast day. The entire clan—aunts, uncles, and a whole passel of children—had our annual Thanksgiving dinner at Gramma and Grandpa's house. Early in the morning the womenfolk started preparing the foods to be served at the feast. In no time at all the air was filled with the delicious aroma of roasting turkey, moose meat, or goose. Then it was the smells of marvelous home-baked bread and pies, taking their turns teasing the nostrils of the children. Even though they were constantly being shooed out of the house, the children couldn't resist sneaking back in to lick the leftovers of delicious frosting that still clung to the bowls and spoons.

Like Thanksgivings everywhere, everyone enjoyed a sumptuous feast. Full plates of food were quickly consumed by the children, for at times like this they were always anxious—anxious to eat, anxious to play. After dessert and before the boisterous children got out of hand at the table, Gramma shooed them all outdoors to play so that the grownups could leisurely finish their desserts, washed down by steaming cups of coffee.

Well, has anyone ever been able to figure out why little boys like to play around outhouses? Maybe it's some kind of primordial urge, like a dog that smells something awful out in the yard and can't resist rolling in it. Human logic cannot explain it, they just do it. That Thanksgiving,

Jimmy and his little four-year-old brother, Charlie, were there at the outhouse, swinging the door shut with a loud bang. They tore up the Sears and Monkey Ward catalogs just to be shredding paper. Jimmy jumped up on the seats of the outhouse, walked around the holes, then started marching around the pee-splattered ledge of the little boy's side. The wetness of the ledge caused Jimmy to slip and fall into the deep pit, almost half-filled with a year's accumulation of human waste! No amount of struggling on Jimmy's part got him free, as a matter of fact, he was slowly sinking deeper into the sludge. Little Charlie realized Jimmy's dilemma and he ran up the slope to get help. The first person he saw was his cousin, my sister, Myra.

"Jimmy fell in the shit house! Come help Jimmy!" he hollered at Myra.

She was twelve years old and had more sense. She told Charlie, "You go on up to the house and tell the folks. I'll try to help Jimmy." She ran down the slope to the outhouse while little Charlie made his way to the main house.

"Help me!" Jimmy hollered when he saw his cousin above him, looking down into the darkness trying to find him. "Help me!"

"Grab my hand," yelled Myra as she bent over the ledge to grab hold of her stricken cousin's outstretched hand. Clutching, grasping hands finally found each other and Myra started to pull.

There is an old saying among the old-timers and that is, "Don't be a shit disturber." There is a truism there, for, once disturbed, all the pent-up gasses are allowed to escape. It is a choking, gagging stench that overwhelms and nauseates you.

Myra found this out the hard way, for the more she pulled on Jimmy's arm, the more noxious gasses were released from his odorous tomb.

It was more than a full belly could stand. Myra threw up all over Jimmy, adding to the absolutely obnoxious and disgusting scene. She still had the presence of mind to hold onto Jimmy's hand. He was crying at this new outrage. His head and shoulders were covered with offal. Myra, courageous and determined, pulled again. The suction of the gooey mass held Jimmy tight as Myra pulled even harder, releasing a whole new volume of that putrefied gas. Her overwhelmed stomach once again discharged another load of its contents over hapless Jimmy's upper body. Then Myra started crying at the outrage of the moment. She pulled and pulled again, releasing more of the gagging, noxious fumes. Her poor stomach emptied its remaining contents over the countenance of her beloved cousin.

It was at that moment that the men arrived at the incredible scene. They quickly pulled little Jimmy to freedom. Once he was safely standing on the ground outside the outhouse, everyone immediately backed away. Jimmy was the worst looking, gosh-awfullest-smelling little boy anyone could ever remember. He was a true slime ball that no one dared approach. Grandpa ordered all the men to fetch buckets of water. Jimmy was stripped naked and bucket after bucket of water was thrown on him to wash away the sticky gooey mess.

Gramma warmed up water on the stove, while the other women got a washtub and put it out on the lawn. Jimmy was washed and lathered down with strong lye soap and every other kind of cleansers the women could lay their hands on. After repeated rinsings, Jimmy still reeked with a putrid odor. It took two weeks of washing and scrubbing before Jimmy could eat at the table with the rest of the family.

He never played around the outhouse again.

TP

My Uncle George had a notorious drinking problem. There was no form of alcohol he wouldn't drink.

He found a bottle of rubbing alcohol in the tribal gym and chug-a-lugged it before anyone caught him. That rubbing alcohol put him in a life-threatening coma.

The stomach pump in the emergency ward helped bring George back to a sense of reality. The doctor said, "Chief." They always like to call old Indians chief. "Chief, you go on one more drunk like that and you're going to be one dead Indian."

George responded, "Well, Doc, I've been drinking all my life. I can't just suddenly up and quit."

The doctor suggested an alternative. "Next time you get an urge to drink, have a cup of tea instead."

Now, Uncle George was in a cultural dilemma. He had not followed the traditional ways enough to believe he would go to the Happy Hunting Grounds after he died, and his Catholic upbringing told him about Heaven, Purgatory, and Hell. He was told by an Indian convert, "Thanks to progress, Indians can go to Hell just like anyone else."

At the next Fourth of July celebration beer, whiskey, and wine flowed in the teepees circling the powwow arena. True to his word, Uncle George stuck to his commitment. Avoiding all the temptations of alcohol, George drank his tea. In fact, he drank seventy-two cups of tea in one night.

The next morning they found Uncle George drowned in his own tea pee.

Grandpa's *Gebic* Bag

Amabese was the name of my grandfather, his father, and his grandfather. When I was born on the Red Lake Reservation in Minnesota, I inherited the hereditary name of my ancestors. Old Amabese was very proud of his young *weh-eh* (namesake), and as I grew older the honor of carrying on the hereditary name became more and more important to me.

Now that he had a weh-eh, his name was changed to Amabe, the elder. So the two of us, Amabe and Amabese, became very good friends.

When Grandma Mahnee died at eighty-seven, it was a very pleasant kind of expiration. She was a woman who enjoyed a fulfilled and contented life. Sure, life was hard on the reservation, sometimes even brutal. But, if your life was full of love and happiness, you could just about cope with anything. They were married Indian-style when she was seventeen, and she bore Amabe's children year after year, until she quit having them at age forty-five. She had a total of twelve children. By that time, their older children were married and having kids of their own. As a result, Grandma Mahnee and Grandpa Amabe had a number of grandchildren who were older than their aunts and uncles.

After Grandma's passing, Amabe went into mourning for an appropriate time, and even though he was getting well along in years he turned out to be surprisingly popular with the ladies of the reservation. One could even say old Amabe was downright in demand by them.

I was very puzzled by this phenomenon of a man in his late nineties continuing to be very active with the ladies. Sometime, with great patience and determination, I would find out Grandpa's delightful secret.

Grandpa turned out to be surprisingly candid and open with his weh-eh. It was interesting to watch him talk. When something appeared really funny to him, he would tilt his head back and laugh a most enjoyable laugh. But when he talked about his prowess with the women, he had a more mischievous laugh. He would simply lower his voice down an octave or two and laugh, "Heh! Heh! Heh!" So it was rather easy to tell the different kinds of moods he was in by his laughter. It was hard to figure out how this old man could exude such joy in life when his environment hardly seemed suitable for such levity.

His house was pitiful by modern standards. The clapboard siding on the outside walls showed only traces of paint. I could only guess what the original color was. The hinges of the weathered front door were somewhat loose and caused the door to drag noisily across the threshold when it was slowly opened or closed. The wood-planked floors sloped downward toward the heavy stove that kept the house reasonably warm in the brutal winter months that seemed to go on forever. The windows had little flimsy curtains, and the pull-down window shades were tattered along the entire bottom edges. In the wintertime, old blankets were hung over the windows to help hold out the chilling draft. Even though the gaps were chinked with rags, the cold air always penetrated around the double-hung windows.

But there was old Grandpa, sitting there in his equally old rickety chair. He seemed oblivious to the poor condition of everything around him. Even the spit can, alongside his chair, could amuse him, especially when he missed.

Of course, Grandpa was equally rickety-looking in his advanced age. By now he was 103 years old. His frame was rather slight. "Sinewy" might be a good description of his physique, for he had been an outdoorsman all his life. Most of the time he wore dark glasses. This way the people didn't know the pupil of his left eye was almost pure white in sharp contrast to the black pupil of his right eye. People said if you got an opportunity to stare into that white left eye, you could see into another world. This spooked the Indians that saw Grandpa without his dark glasses, and they discretely averted their gaze away from him. Many people said they were curious about seeing what the other world looked like, but they were afraid to look Grandpa in the eye.

As Grandpa talked, he waved his hands for emphasis and his old chair squeaked right along as if it understood. And sometimes, when he leaned forward, a small buckskin pouch hanging by a thong around his neck would dangle out of his shirt. This was something very few people got to see, because most of the time Grandpa kept himself pretty well covered.

Many old-time Indians carried small pouches like that around their necks, or they slung them crossways so the bag was suspended below their armpit, completely out of sight, because those little pouches carried powerful medicine to protect the wearer. Exposing their personal medicine to curious eyes could diminish their powers, or in some cases they would even lose their powers altogether.

Mustering up my courage, I asked Grandpa if he could tell me what he kept in his pouch. He stopped rocking and carefully looked around the living room and then into the kitchen to make sure no one was there to overhear the words he had to share with me. Satisfied that only the two of us were in the house, Grandpa spoke, "Amabese, my weh-eh, this little buckskin pouch I wear around my neck I call my *gebic* bag and it is filled only with a powder, no other amulets or charms, just powder, but what a powder." He broke out in his low laugh, "Heh, heh, heh."

I knew right then that he was about to share something unusual and delightful with me. Grandpa continued, "It's my woman medicine, my love medicine. If I know I'm going to be with a woman, I open my gebic bag and then I wet the tip of my finger with my tongue and stick my finger into the powder. Just a little bit, not too much, and then I put the powder on my tongue. That wondrous love potion makes me feel like a young stud again to the delight of the women, who have gentle smiles on their faces." Grandpa laughed, "Heh, heh, heh," just thinking about it.

Naturally, the news of Grandpa's prowess on the mattress spread far and wide, due to the women's inability to keep such connubial marathons secret. Grandpa could have made a fortune if he would have sold the secret hidden away in his little gebic bag. His formula, however, was well kept.

"Get me that long package under the bed," he said. I crawled into the dusty darkness under his bed and retrieved a long package wrapped in buckskin. I handed the package to Grandpa, who blew off the accumulation of several years' dust. The small fibers of goose down that had sifted out of his mattress caused me to sneeze uncontrollably, much to Grandpa's delight.

Very gently, Grandpa untied the buckskin thongs that secured the package. He slowly, almost reverently, unwrapped the buckskin and revealed a hand-carved board made of white ash. The thin little board was about four inches wide and a foot and a half long. On it was incised, or carved, a series of small figures.

"There you see the secret of my gebic bag," Grandpa proclaimed, in a rather grandiose way for him. He had a right to be proud and he showed it at this time. I carefully studied the figures with growing puzzlement.

"What are they?" I asked.

Grandpa laughed his uproarious laugh, and leaned back in his squeaky chair in sheer delight. "That's another secret." He went on, "Several years ago my other board like that was stolen. We heard the thieves were working for Fong Wang, the famous Chinese herbalist in San Francisco. It didn't do him any good. Even with his great knowledge of herbs he was completely baffled. He was looking for the physical plants, but what the board showed represented the spirits of the plants, that's what confused them. They were looking for another reality, and I drew the spiritual reality."

I sat there in numbed silence, trying to comprehend what Grandpa had just revealed to me. During this moment of silence, Grandpa slowly rewrapped the board, and then tied it with the thongs. He handed it to me without a word. He simply pointed toward the bed in the Indian way, with his lips puckered out. I carefully replaced the treasured package back into the dust print where it originally was. I crawled back out, sneezed a couple times, and sat back on the wooden fish box I had been sitting on, still trying to comprehend.

Grandpa continued his escapades with the women. One was a good-looking eighteen-year-old girl. This dalliance was going on for several months, and it looked like it was developing into a heavy-duty romance, much to the growing concern of the other tribal elders.

One of the elders was appointed to talk to Grandpa about their concerns. "Amabe," he said, "we hear you are seeing an eighteen-year-old girl."

"Yuh, that's right," replied Grandpa.

"We hear that things are getting pretty serious between you two."

"Yuh, that's right," responded Grandpa.

"We hear talk that you two might even consider getting married."

"Yuh, you might say that."

"Well," said the elder, "you know there's quite an age difference between you two. Something like this could prove fatal."

Grandpa blinked his eyes in surprise at this remark and thought about it. Then he shrugged his shoulders and said, "Well, if she dies, she dies."

Grandpa went on to live a delightful 104 years. The debate surrounding his death was interesting as some people maintained he died prematurely, while others held the attitude that anyone who lived over one hundred years could not consider his or her death to be premature.

"But Amabe was shot by a jealous husband," proclaimed the first group. They reasoned that since his life had been cut short by a bullet, and he had not died of natural causes. Therefore, his death was certainly premature. Debates of this type have a way of going nowhere, and the more important matter of arranging for the funeral had to be attended to.

A shallow grave was dug out by the fence by the road. The hole was only four or five feet deep and kinda short because Grandpa was going to be buried in a sitting position, facing to the east. At his feet was a small cast iron pot that was filled with food to accompany his spirit on the four-day journey to the Spirit World. His favorite hunting rifle was placed alongside him, along with his medicine bundle and pipe bag.

Other men were busying themselves building a small Spirit House to be placed over the grave. It looked like a rather long doghouse, only there was no door. Small openings on the east side were made in the shape of a crescent moon and stars. These were made so that people could bring food offerings to Grandpa's spirit when they came to pray for him.

The women were busy preparing food for the feast to be held after the wake. They made a delicious variety of Indian foods: deer meat, moose roast, ducks, geese, turtle meat, wild rice, vegetables, berry preserves, fry bread, and feast pies. Those feast pies were something special, as they were extra plump, just loaded with fruits or berries, and their flaky crusts were sprinkled with maple sugar.

Funerals of this type were both sad for the loss of a loved one and a celebration of life for the living. The children were impatient to get the wake over with so they could gorge themselves on all the tribal delicacies. The focal point of all this activity, however, was Grandpa. He was laid out on a wooden platform covered with Pendleton blankets. Even in death, he looked elegant in his beautiful beaded buckskin outfit. People approached his body and said goodbye to Grandpa and wished his spirit well on his journey to join his ancestors. The men had tears in their eyes at the loss of a special friend and comrade. The women, however, were much more demonstrative. Their plaintive wailing seemed capable of penetrating the thickest walls. Some hugged Grandpa for the last time, then placed little tobacco offerings for his Spirit Gift. Some acknowledged there would never be another man like Grandpa.

While this sad scene was going on, the men of the family were off to one side. "Has anyone seen Amabe's gebic bag?" "Whoever gets his medicine is going to be one lucky guy."

The women were also curious. "Who is going to carry on where Amabe left off?" "Is this to be the end of another tradition?" "We've lost so much already."

They started to look around the assembled throng of people for the possible answers to their questions. The answer became readily apparent, for his grandson Amabese was the only one at the wake who was smiling.

With the persistence of medical science, traces of powder from Grandpa's gebic bag were found, analyzed, and a scientific potion was created—Viagra.

How Poor Were You?

We were extremely poor, living on the remote Red Lake Indian Reservation in the deep woods of northern Minnesota.

"How poor were you?"

Why, we were so poor, when my grandpa died at the age of 104, I had mixed emotions of sadness and joy: sadness because I missed my grandpa and joy because I inherited his toothbrush.

Ancient Ojibwe Recipes

By Chef Boogit

Snapping Turtle *Naboob*

Catch one snapping turtle, preferably washtub size. Cut off legs, head, and tail. Save the main part of the body for a later dish, such as snapping turtle sausage. Wash turtle parts thoroughly and place in Dutch oven. Add three quarts of water from Chimagon Creek, add salt and pepper to taste. Cook over an open fire for three hours. Remove turtle parts and skin them, and set them aside. Save turtle claws to be used later as toothpicks. Add *manoomin* (wild rice), Ponemah mushrooms, and wild onions to the broth. Cook another hour, then add the turtle meat and cook until the meat falls off the bone.

Fry turtle skin in bear grease until crispy, like pork rinds. Salt to taste, and use as an appetizer.

Serve snapping turtle head to tribal elder, its tongue and eyeballs are an ancient delicacy.

Serves four.

Other Award-Winning Recipes by Chef Boogit

Moose Nose Stuffed With *Manoomin*
Boiled Sucker Heads
Waboose (Rabbit) Meatballs
Squirrel Kabob
Fricasseed Pig Nipples

Amos Gets a New House

One of my older brothers, Curtis, was working for the Bureau of Indian Affairs in Sacramento, California. Working for Indian housing for California tribes was his principal duty. He called me one day and said, "Adam, I have just met an Indian who is one of the most amazing people I have ever seen. He said he lives way out in a little remote *rancheria*. He is the only one living there. He doesn't speak English. He doesn't know about World War II. He doesn't know who various prominent people are, including the president of the United States. He seems to be in a sort of time warp. He is someone comparable to Ishi, the last of the Yahis. You guys ought to do a story about Amos."

So, I called Tim Findley, and he got hold of Curtis, and my brother told him about Amos, who had no knowledge at all about anything that had taken place in the outside world. All he knew was his native language, which was Miwok, and no English at all.

Of course, as a TV reporter, Tim was quite excited and he made arrangements with the TV station to investigate. This sounded like a fantastic story. They had found a man who didn't know World War II had happened, or who was president—he didn't know who President Nixon was. Anyway, the prospect of finding an Indian who was so isolated that he knew nothing about the world outside was very thrilling to Tim and the TV people.

So, Tim got a TV crew and we all met near the airport north of Sacramento, and from there we met Curtis, and then Curtis led us to a little town north of Sacramento and then off the road. When the pavement ended, it turned into a nice, fairly decent dirt track that ended at a fence, where we had to open a gate. As a matter of fact, there were a total of five gates we opened and shut. The farther in we went, the worse the dirt road got, until we finally got to a place where we had to ford several little creeks and streams. And then we arrived at the rancheria.

There were two little cabins, little tiny cabins. We called out hello. Nobody showed up, and then a guy came out and we asked him if he was Amos.

"Amos? No. I'm Cowboy. Amos is my brother. I'm here visiting for a while." He spoke a little English, but very little.

We asked, "Where is Amos?"

"He went up the mountains looking for wild pigs." Amos had a little old single shot .22 rifle and he was up there trying to shoot himself a great big wild boar with that little old rifle.

Cowboy pointed toward the mountains. "He went up that way."

Well, here we had the TV crew and the reporter all primed for this story, but no Amos. So we decided we better go and find the guy. Curtis and the rest of the men stayed at the cabin, and I headed up along a little stream up a canyon looking for Amos. There were little ponds that were very beautiful. But as I proceeded up there, it got steeper and steeper and then I saw tracks, human tracks. Well, they could only belong to one man—Amos—and I followed those tracks. And the canyon just simply pinched off. No one could have continued up that way unless he was a mountain goat.

And I decided to go around an area which was so steep that it was easy to start sliding downhill, because it was a forty-five degree angle. Instead, I had to get through the underbrush and thicket to get to the other side of the mountain where the climbing was much easier.

I went all around the mountain and down a sort of drop, and after about an hour I heard a sound. I looked up and there was a man holding his rifle in his hand, looking at me. I called out, "Amos!" I was looking at him with his rifle and all sorts of thoughts went around in my head. Whether I had invaded the man's territory here and he might not want me here; he might just point that rifle at me and go bang! I could die right up here in the mountains. I yelled, "Hey!" and I smiled and smiled, because smiling is good medicine. I tried to show no fear. "Amos!" I yelled, "It's me. My name is Adam. I want to talk to you."

He looked at me and then he disappeared in the bush. But I could hear the sounds of him going downhill, and I followed those sounds downhill, too, but at an angle, figuring that in time our paths would intersect.

I went down, and sure enough, there on his little saddle on the hillside was Amos. I approached and said, "Amos, my name is Adam," and stretched out my hand. He shook my hand and he grunted a greeting. I continued, "My brother is Curtis, Curtis Nordwall, and you have been talking to him."

He said, "Aha." He started off down this ridge and I saw he was a very old man. He was in his late sixties at least, and this man walked off down that steep mountain ridge with a stride I couldn't believe. I had to hop and skip behind him just to keep up with him, and I was twenty years his junior. It was amazing to me that this old man carrying his rifle could walk so fast. And I was getting winded—I was not used to that at the time. I was an urban Indian and I found myself in the mountains with this man who walked with such spirit. So I hollered, "Amos!"

He turned around, and I reached inside my jacket and pulled out a can of beer and I yelled, "Coors?"

He broke out in the biggest grin and said, "Yes."

I gave him the can and he took it and appreciated it, and we continued down the mountainside.

By that time, Curtis, Tim, and the TV crew spotted us up there on the mountainside. I hollered down that we were on our way down. The cameraman, who was a Frenchman, a very handsome Frenchman, shouldered his camera and started hiking up the mountain as fast as he could to get to an outcropping overlooking the route that we would be taking on the way down. And Tim shouted, "Adam, stay where you are." Because, of course, this was a story about Amos, and they wanted to film him alone on that mountain.

So I held back, and the cameraman filmed Amos walking down the hillside through the bottom of the draw and up the slope, and then as Amos passed him, the cameraman swung around and followed. It was a beautifully conceived shot. Anyway, we got back to Amos's camp and started talking.

Later we found out the film was shown on Bay Area TV, not once, but several times. They talked about drawing water from a well, and the little shack—the one-room cabin, just wide enough for a bed. Everything was very neat, extremely neat, in that little cabin. They talked about hunting for deer and rabbit, and how when Amos needed things like basic staples, he walked the entire distance to get them in town, and then walked back. It was sixteen miles to town and back. Sometimes he stayed overnight and walked home with his load the next day.

You might have guessed by now that all this information wouldn't have been possible for Tim to get if Amos hadn't been able to speak English. It turned out that Amos could speak English; not very well, but he could speak enough for Tim to communicate with him, and they had a beautiful interview.

They talked about the way he lived. This is where Curtis came in, because since Curtis worked with the BIA he could arrange for better housing for old Amos. He had to sort of manipulate the funding guidelines for a single person, because under existing guidelines, Amos should have had a family to qualify for BIA housing. Curtis put it under the rubric of a community center, because Amos was the custodian of the tribal cemetery, and Amos knew all of the people that were buried there. He talked about different places and events down the wash, where Indians used to live and camp, and how people used to flee up into the mountains to get away from the hunters who were looking for them in the old days. Amos himself was living right up against the mountain. People lived up there in a little band, and now most of the old people were gone, all except Amos who remained as the caretaker of the burial grounds.

So, through Curtis it was arranged to build a home there for old Amos, and the following year it was done. And then we were called to have a dedication. By that time, because the TV had done his story, all the neighboring Indians from other bands and tribes, Miwok, and Maidus, and Pomos had heard about it. When the time for the Dedication Ceremony came, Indians from these other places all congregated at Amos's new place.

I was to lead the Dedication Ceremony, and so we went up the day before to help make the preparations. Everything was pretty much as we had left it before, but there, over to the left of the old cabin, was the brand new home—way out there in that isolation. It was very exciting.

We got there early, and that day I went out hunting. I shot a small buck and I brought it in. Old Amos, he was a real Indian, and he was really excited. He went to work at once, and every move he made was so graceful and practiced. It was a joy to see that the old skills were still very much alive in this old Indian. He had that deer nicely skinned in moments. That night we went out again to hunt for meat for the ceremony, and as I remember, we killed about eight rabbits. We brought the rabbits back and the women took care to prepare them for the feast. People had come from all over, and one of them was Essie Parish. She was from Kashaia on the Pomo reservation or rancheria. It was like a little Valhalla—high in the mountains, overlooking the Pacific Ocean. And, because it was close to the ocean, it was enveloped in fog a lot of times. When we traveled up there, we drove up a little winding road, in the fog, and then as we approached the village, we emerged out of the fog, and there before us lay this little village—on the uppermost part of the mountain.

In the little Pomo community, Essie Parish was the Medicine Woman, and she was the one who was in charge of the old traditional Round House at Kashaia. So, on the day of the dedication of the new home for Amos, she was there. I went up to talk to Essie, and she was talking politely enough. But when I told her that I had been out in the night hunting rabbits, and how many we had brought back, she changed completely. She became real animated because now she knew that I wasn't just some urban Indian and part of the BIA with Curtis, but that I was very much a part of what was going on. She became much more outgoing.

We had a very nice feast and Dedication Ceremony for Amos's new house. We used sweetgrass to purify all the rooms. And everyone ran all around the house—going from room to room. It was a way of having an open house for everybody—a beautiful Dedication Ceremony. They all followed along and everybody got to see Amos's new house, inside and out.

It was a wonderful occasion, and afterwards everybody enjoyed the feasting. People came from Kashaia and everywhere, and everybody brought food. In fact, most people brought native foods: acorn mush, acorn soup, acorn bread, fried seaweed, fried fish, and, of course, rabbit stew. So that was the story of Amos's new house.

Damn Hippies

Being an Indian leader in the San Francisco Bay Area in the 1960s made me a target of all kinds of special interest groups, from religious organizations trying to convert me from my heathen, savage ways, to the newly created hippies of the Haight-Ashbury District, who appeared to be looking for a red guru.

Out of a sense of hospitality and curiosity, I invited a group of them over for dinner. Their apparent leader and spokesman was Stewart Brand, who later became the successful editor of the *Whole Earth Catalog*. I had just returned from a visit to my home reservation at Red Lake, Minnesota, and decided to treat my new friends to a special Indian-style meal.

The hungry hippies loaded their plates with fry bread, corn on the cob, green beans, and the secret main course. In no time, everyone was scarfing up the tribal delicacies.

While chomping a mouthful of food, one woman asked between bites, "What is this dish?"

"Moose nose stuffed with wild rice," I replied.

She stopped chewing. I saw her roll her tongue around her mouth as she thought about it. She started chewing again. "Man, this stuff is really delicious." The entire group obviously agreed, as they all helped themselves to seconds.

Stories had long circulated that hippies would smoke just about anything, from dried up banana peels, to ground-up leather shoe soles.

After dinner I inquired if anyone would like to smoke some *dawsa*. It's an Indian medicine root with a wide variety of uses. It can be made into a powerful tea to settle an upset stomach or to thin blood. Or, it could be shredded and rolled up like a cigarette to relieve a sore throat or head cold congestion.

In no time they were all toking up, taking long pulls on the smoke, holding their breaths to give the dawsa time to grab their lungs and sphincter muscles. Letting the smoke out slowly, they uttered, "Far out man!" "This shit's really cool!" "Way to go!"

My wife and I stole knowing glances.

Stewart Brand was not through with me, as he invited me to be his guest at the notorious improv theater staged by The Committee in San Francisco's North Beach.

Entering that theater was like entering another world—a world of choking smoke, colorful flashing lights, and throbbing music—Moog synthesizers, didgeridoos, and Indian sitars. The affair was as free-spirited as the people. There were colorful tie-died shirts, braless women, and a phenomenon of those times, long-haired men.

We watched the stage in amazement. I cannot describe those events in a coherent way, so all I can do is call them performances.

Stewart Brand took the stage, I thought to introduce the next act. Instead, he called me out from the audience. I stood next to him as he introduced me to the crowd. I took the microphone to voice an acknowledgement and thank you. I turned around to return the microphone to Stewart, but that long-haired, lily-livered bastard set me up. He walked back to his table. The audience started stomping and clapping.

"Speech! Speech! Speech!"

There I was, on stage like a deer caught in the headlights. *Ho wah!* I was surrounded by a howling, screaming tribe of hippies. I figured the only way to settle down this mob was to tell them a damn Indian story.

"In the early 1950s, a circus train traveling through Arizona was hit by a flash flood. The boxcar containing the monkeys was washed down a ravine.

"The following day a hunting party of Navahos came across the body of a dead monkey.

"They had never heard of monkeys or seen a monkey before.

"They carried the dead monkey back to their village where they placed the monkey before the hogan of the chief. The chief had been many places and seen many things and was the logical person to explain this strange creature.

"The chief proceeded to examine the dead monkey. Rolling it over, he studied it some more. Finally, standing up and addressing his fellow tribesmen, he intoned, 'Judging from the silly look on his face and the calluses on his ass, he must work for the Bureau of Indian Affairs.'"

The audience, being antiestablishment, cheered the story, and I staged a hasty retreat. Stewart Brand laughed as I returned to my seat. "That's what you get for serving moose nose to my friends."

"Touché! You damn hippies!"

Speaking of hippies, what ever happened to this subspecies of man? Anybody seen one in the twenty-first century? Did they die out like the Neanderthal? Or perhaps, as many suspect, they went "straight." Rumor has it some even became Republicans. Who says there ain't no such thing as evolution?

The hippies were so far down the evolutionary ladder they survived only one generation. The flower children of the early 1960s lasted only three years.

The Bohemians have morphed over and over again. It's impossible to identify one today. Could be a ragged homeless guy spouting poetry at Fisherman's Wharf with a tin cup at his feet.

Hurling With Luci

When President Lyndon Johnson officially announced he was running for reelection in 1964, the Democratic Party political machine shifted into high gear.

A wealthy democrat hosted a Texas-style barbeque on his San Francisco peninsula ranch for the leaders—kinda like an adult pep rally. To give it an Old West flavor, they hired the Intertribal Dancers of Oakland to stage Indian performances to entertain the group.

In the photo op, I presented a beautiful beaded necklace to the president's youngest daughter, Luci Baines Johnson. That picture appeared all over the country. It was even published in *Ebony* magazine. This was before Oprah.

I then presented Senator Birch Bayh of Indiana with a traditional war club to symbolically beat the ass of their republican rivals. The logic being if Sampson could beat the crap out of the Philistines with the jawbone of an ass, the democrats could do it with an Indian war club.

I guess the California barbeque must be different from the Texas barbeque, because shortly after eating, Luci Baines took sick. She was immediately surrounded by Secret Service agents, while she noisily wretched and wretched on their highly polished shoes.

The republicans were not to be outdone in the barfing department. The first President Bush upchucked his meal on the lap of the prime minister of Japan during a state dinner.

I realize this may be an inappropriate story, telling of the weak stomachs of the political parties; however, can you imagine how the public feels when the news reports feed us the bickering, corruption, and scandals in Washington?

Barf!

Adam presenting Luci Baines Johnson with necklace, 1964. Author's collection.

Dancing for Luci, 1964. Author's collection.

Shared Sorrows

In the Bay Area, when I was very involved with all the Indian programs and people, I was hurt from time to time by the statements of a few Indian people. They'd say, "How do you know how we feel? You never had it bad." Or, "You never went through struggles like we did." Those words were hurtful to me, because the people who said them didn't understand the kind of things I had gone through.

Their starting point was where they perceived me to be at that time—a businessman in a leadership position. And, what they didn't know was that I had gone through some of the same personal turmoil, grief, and frustration that they experienced. And there is no point in replying, "Oh yes, I know what it is to grieve and to suffer." So, I retreated into my shell, but the words stuck and they hurt. Indians have a way of retreating into a shell, and not letting anybody know what we have gone through.

Indian people can hurt me worse than the words of a white man. But when I sat down and talked it out with some of them, they would say, "Hey, Adam, you really shared a lot of similar problems."

I remember once in the early days of my relationship with Sy Williams, we started to compare notes about our wanderings at a very early age. He was just trying to find some place or somebody to care for him, to take him in, at night especially. He had no place to go but there was one place that always had an open door. He always knew he could go and spend the night there. He used to sleep in people's outhouses. It seems a strange place to spend a night, but he had nowhere else. They were refuges for him.

It's like the time I was in Sioux City, Iowa. I roamed all over that city looking for a place to spend the night indoors, and I ended up sleeping in jail. So, I can understand what Sy went through.

So when we made comparisons about our younger days, I understood the problems Sy had. His were different from mine, but not really all that different. And, as I talked to other Indians, I found so many similar stories. For various reasons, there were a lot of broken families and shattered lives among the young people. And sometimes, when I did say something about our own fragmented family, somebody would say, "Adam, how could you go through that and maintain yourself the way you have? You have a good home, a beautiful wife, beautiful children, everything around here is beautiful. How did you do that when so many who came from broken families ended up hardened criminals, or narcotics addicts, or dead from exposure?"

Well, my sister died by her own hands. Oh, she may not have intended to, but she did. She overdosed on some kind of aerosol spray. She sprayed it into a plastic bag she put over her head, and she breathed the concentrated fumes. And then somebody went into the room and found my sister's body on the floor with that plastic bag over her head, and a can of spray on the floor beside her.

That is the ultimate unhappiness. I know it is necessary to think about this for the book, but it is not easy to talk about.

Scalping Columbus

It was early October 1966, and our council members were sitting around the tables at the Intertribal Friendship House in Oakland, California. We were discussing the upcoming Columbus Day celebration scheduled to take place in San Francisco. None of us had ever witnessed the celebration, and the negative attitude the Indians had for that event was obvious. However, curiosity got the best of us and several families agreed to check it out. Mead Chibitty, Comanche, and his family; Sy Williams, Chippewa, and his family; Wilson Harrison, Navaho; and, as United Council chairman, I, Chippewa, my wife, Shoshone, and our three children rounded out the Indian war party.

On Columbus Day we scouted out the territory of Aquatic Park and selected a grassy knoll on the south side where we could see the grandstands, stage, beach, and the bay itself. We spread out blankets like we were having a picnic. The grandstand was rapidly filling up with a festive crowd, as three fishing boats decorated to look like old-time sailing boats approached Aquatic Park.

"Well, here comes the Niña, the Pinta and the Costa Nostra," quipped Mead Chibitty sarcastically.

The ships anchored offshore and a rowboat was put over the side of one. Christopher Columbus, played by Joseph Cervetto, rode to shore along with four sailors. Columbus, standing in the bow holding the Spanish flag, looked kinda like the painting of Washington crossing the Delaware. After Columbus went through his routine of discovery, a group of Indians portrayed by Sea Scouts went out on the beach and performed a Welcoming Dance. They were dressed in the worst versions of Indian costumes I had ever seen. They clapped their hands over their mouths and shouted "Woo! Woo! Woo!" At the same time, they jumped up and down like a flock of ruptured chickens. Other boys beat the hell out of drums, without any rhythm.

Sy Williams growled, "Oh damn, damn, damn! Those clowns are supposed to represent our people. We've got to do something about this, Adam."

"Okay, okay," I replied. I was also upset at the spectacle we had just witnessed.

Our crew of intrepid warriors walked down to the beach, where we met Mr. Cientelli, the director of the event. We told him we were insulted by the Sea Scouts' performance.

After more discussion, Mr. Cientelli suggested, "Why don't you folks perform the re-enactment next year? I'll give you $50.00"

"Each?" inquired Mead.

"No, that's all we can afford out of our budget," said Mr. Cientelli.

I figured we had our honor at stake, and the others of our group agreed. "We'll take it!"

The next year a group of us from the United Council got together and called ourselves the Intertribal Dancers. We were Comanche, Nez Perce, Navaho, Sioux, Shoshone, and Chippewa. Our dances and Presentation Ceremony were greeted by an enthusiastic audience.

Someone in the crowd said, "We have real Indians joining us." But, not quite, because we had not been invited to attend the other civic activities such as the Columbus Day Parade or the banquet. They didn't even invite us to observe the selection of the Columbus Day Queen Isabella.

"Damn, we're just being used by those Italians!" exclaimed Sy Williams disgustedly.

"Yah! We're being treated like black performers, who were not allowed to eat at the place where they performed. And, by the way, they had to use the back door," said a frustrated Wilson Harrison of the Navaho tribe.

My appeal to be invited to participate in the other events went unheeded by the Italian American Heritage Foundation.

1968 proved to be a turning point in the history of the San Francisco Columbus Day reenactment, as this time, after Columbus planted the flag of Spain and kissed the sand of the New World, he came forward to me, expecting his annual pleasant greeting. I took my coup stick and made an exaggerated blow to the back of his shoulder—I pulled my punch because I did not wish to hurt old Joe.

"Get down! *Get down!*" I urged him in a stage whisper, as I pushed

Scalping Columbus, November 7, 1968. *From left to right:* Adam Fortunate Eagle Nordwall (Chippewa); Columbus, played by Joseph Cervetto; an unknown photographer; Cheri Nordwall (Shoshone/Chippewa); Shirley Harrison (Navaho). Photo by Peter Breinig.

him down onto his knees. Sy Williams rushed up and pulled off his wig. Joe Cervetto was bald!

The audience was stunned. Someone said, "Oh my God! The Indians have scalped Columbus!"

The scalping of their hero did not sit too well with the Italian American Heritage Foundation. In fact, they were damned pissed off, and we were told we were not invited to attend the next year's festivities.

Not to be outdone by this banishment, the United Bay Area Council on American Indian Affairs declared Columbus Day to be a National Day of Indian Mourning. The line was drawn in the sand of Aquatic Park between the Italian American foundation and the American Indians.

The retreating fog of San Francisco Bay gave way to a beautiful day in October 1969. Since Aquatic Park is a public facility, we erected a teepee on the east end of the beach. We tore black cloth into strips and made armbands for our members, and to our surprise we were joined by a whole bunch of non-Indians. This was the era of civic unrest—from civil rights protest marches, to farm workers' strikes, to antiwar demonstrations that were occurring throughout the country. And then we had the counter-culture movement in the Haight-Ashbury District of San Francisco.

As I secured a black armband on a bearded hippy, he said, "Way to go man! You dudes are far out, and I'm with you!"

"That's cool man, that's cool," I responded in my best version of hippy talk.

We could talk the talk, but we still had to walk the walk.

The Italian American Heritage Foundation officials watched our rapidly growing numbers with great concern and alarm. And, despite my offer to one of their officials for a modified ceremony, it was rejected.

I returned to the east side of Aquatic Park to join the rest of our group sitting on the warm sand and we watched what was to be Columbus's return to the court of Queen Isabella, announcing his discovery of a New World.

With that, I stood up and started walking toward the stage holding my peace pipe over my head with both hands. I was followed by the Indians and hundreds of supporters. As we made our way down the beach, the great doors under the grandstand swung open and out marched dozens of San Francisco policemen dressed in riot gear. They created a blue line of cops stretching from the bleachers all the way to the water's edge. With their riot clubs at port, their boots firmly straddled that stretch of public land.

As we got within fifty feet of the long blue line, the lieutenant shouted an order and all his men leveled their head-chopping batons to a double-handed combat grip. I dug the heels of my moccasins into the sand, but I was pushed along by the Indians behind me. Marvin Bob of the Nez Perce tribe whispered in my ear, "C'mon, fearless leader, let's go!"

Here I was in full tribal regalia, holding my peace pipe, and being pushed into what would be a strange confrontation with the police. The police lieutenant positioned himself in front of me and our procession came to a screeching halt.

"If you go any further, you will be charged with trespassing and causing a disturbance with intent to create a riot," the lieutenant snarled.

I knew this was a total overreaction to a peaceful protest. I turned to the crowd behind me and shouted, "Sit down. Please, everyone sit down." Hundreds of us sat on the beach as we watched Columbus and Queen Isabella's court clear the stage. The grandstands soon emptied, and the long blue line of police slowly marched into the shadows of the grandstands.

Hundreds of us quietly sat on the beach. Sunset was not too long in coming. We listened to the squawking seagulls and the gentle lapping waves on the sandy beach. We quietly gathered our belongings, broke camp, and headed home.

Later, a reporter asked the chairman of the Columbus Day Committee, "Why was there such a great show of force against the Indians?"

The chairman responded, "How did we know he wasn't going to hit somebody with that pipe?"

That culturally ignorant son of a gun!

I thought that was the end of my adventures, but I was wrong, really wrong. For that summer of 1969, I was summoned to a meeting at California State University at Hayward where four professors questioned me about my knowledge of the culture, tradition, history, and even the spirituality of the American Indian people. I did not understand their motives; however, by July 1969 I was notified by California State Superintendent of Public Instruction Dr. Max Rafferty, that I was awarded a lifetime teaching credential in higher education. It's called an Eminence Credential, and they gave it to me despite the fact that I had never attended a college or university. Professor Snow of the Sociology

Department soon hired me to teach in his department, with emphasis on American Indians. This paved the way for a Native American Studies Department.

My wife, Bobbie, grew increasingly concerned that I was taking on too many responsibilities: chairman of the United Bay Area Council of American Indian Affairs, acting director of the California Intertribal Council, a seat on the Board of Directors of the California Indian Legal Services, founding member of the California Indian Education Association, owner of the First American Termite Company, and board member of the Hayward Chamber of Commerce Promotion Committee. In addition were my monthly visits for twelve years to the American Indian Cultural Group at San Quentin Prison.

In life you have to go with the hand you are dealt. Only I was able to deal myself additional hands that added to the fullness of my life. When you see the brass ring of opportunity, you grab it.

Professor Magoroh Maruyama taught sociology at the University of California and offered me another brass ring of adventure. He had been following my years of activism in the Bay Area with special interest. We became friends through our shared interests.

In the spring of 1973 Professor Maruyama paid us a visit at our house in San Leandro, and surprised my wife, Bobbie, and me with an amazing offer. He asked, "How would you and your wife like to go to Rome, Italy?" He went on to explain that he was on the planning committee for the upcoming World Futures Research Conference to be held in Rome in September. Then he told me, "I would like you to be an official delegate at that conference."

Ho wah! That was an offer I could not refuse, because Bobbie and I had never been out of our country before, and now was our chance to go international. I hit the books in earnest, studying the history of Italy, and to my delight I found no historic reference that Italy had been discovered by anybody. My sense of logic and reason kicked in. If an Italian can lay claim to discovery of the Americas, with a native population estimated at eighty million in North, Central and South America, then an American Indian should be able to discover a land called Italy.

Francisco de Vitoria is considered to be the father of international law. He wrote a legal opinion early in the 1500s stating that "if the act of having discovered and inhabited it, the world gave the Europeans the option of taking it (the Americas) into possession, the Indians would have just as much right to extend their sovereignty over Spanish or other European lands."[*]

Ho wah! Now I had international law on my side, and I started to plan my next adventure.

I announced my plans to the United Council and was surprised at the negative reaction.

Sy Williams became concerned and said, "They might shoot you!"

"They could arrest you and throw away the key," chimed in Mead Chibitty.

Marvin Bob said, "Maybe our fearless leader has lost his mind! After all, look at how the Italians treated us in San Francisco. They even called in the riot squad to bash our heads in with their billy clubs."

I decided to go the diplomatic route by contacting the Italian Consulate in San Francisco, where I was ushered into the consul-general's office. Sitting behind a large ornate desk was a chubby little man, Consul General Giuseppe Squadrille. After formal introductions, I went directly to my reason for being there.

"Who discovered America? I asked.

Clapping his chubby hands together, he proudly proclaimed, "Christopher Columbus, 1492."

I pressed on to make my point. "Who discovered your country of Italy?"

"Remus and Romulus," he responded.

"No," I countered. "According to legend, they were twin boys who were suckled by a she wolf and they were credited with the founding of Rome. However, they did not discover your country of Italy. So, who did?"

---

[*] "Indigenous Renascence: Law, Culture and Society in the 21st Century: III. Scalping Columbus." *St. Thomas Law Review* (Fall 1997).

Mr. Squadrille raised his hands in frustration and said, "I don't know."

I replied with a smile, "So what you are saying is that your country has never officially been discovered by anyone? That being the case, Mr. Squadrille, I am going to lay claim of discovery to your country in the name of the American Indians."

Mr. Squadrille laughed and clapped his hands at the idea that his country was about to be discovered by an American Indian. "I will personally contact my country's news services and tell them about our impending discovery."

Mr. Squadrille was a man of his word. As the people of Italy awaited discovery, Rome television ran a special documentary about American Indians.

As Bobbie and I transferred from American Airlines to Alitalia Airlines in New York City, their newspapers were already carrying the story of impending discovery. On that large jumbo jet 747 we were treated as celebrities. We never had it so good in San Francisco.

After we were airborne over the Atlantic Ocean, we were moved up to first class and, to my surprise, the captain invited me to tour the cockpit. As I looked around I told him I had christened his aircraft "The *Chief Joseph*."

Back in first class they served us champagne and hors d'oeuvres. All the while fellow passengers ambled over and engaged us in conversation.

I had forgotten about the nine-hour time difference between San Francisco and Rome, and as I pulled up the window shade I could see dawn breaking in the east. It was obvious there would be no sleep for Bobbie and me tonight.

Our first stop was at Milan on the north side of Italy, where many of our passengers disembarked. Our final leg of the trip was into Rome itself, about one hour away. The flight crew was very helpful and allowed me to change into my Traditional Grass Dance outfit. My beautiful but shy Shoshone wife, Bobbie, refused to put on her traditional buckskin dress because she was not sure what to expect in Rome. Or, perhaps, it was our earlier reception by the tact squad at San Francisco's Aquatic Park. She chose instead to wear her regular street clothes.

As I walked into the main flight deck of the *Chief Joseph*, it seemed like a pep rally before the main event, for all of the passengers were involved with the historic discovery of Italy by an American Indian. *Ho wah!* After a smooth landing at the Leonardo de Vinci Airport in Rome, our aircraft did something else out of the ordinary. Usually planes park way out on the tarmac, where shuttle busses transport the passengers to the terminal. Instead, the *Chief Joseph* taxied to the edge of the tarmac near the main terminal.

The captain came on the PA system: "Ladies and gentlemen, welcome to Rome. Due to the special nature of our flight and the presence of the news media to greet us, all passengers will exit the plane first. Then 'Chief' Fortunate Eagle and his party will be the last to depart."

I looked out the window to the tarmac below and was surprised to see about a hundred news people, including Walter Cronkite's *Evening News* crew and photographers from *The New York Times* and *Time* magazine. Two rows of police officers formed a protective shield against the onrushing media.

"Captain, would you be so kind as to escort my wife and me down the steps?" I asked. The big smile on his face told us he was more than willing to do the honor.

As we walked down the steps, we were confronted by a firing squad of all types of cameras. It seemed like everyone was shouting instructions. "Raise your spear!" "Look this way!" "Injun!" "Injun!"

I knew we were Indians, but I was puzzled by them shouting "Injun!" over and over. Then my wife yelled, "They're calling 'ENGINE!'" She said they wanted me to pose in the large engine of the 747 jumbo jet. Perhaps there was something symbolic about that picture—primitive man enters the modern age.

While I held my spear over my head, Bobbie and I walked to the edge of the tarmac followed by the swarm of news media. "In the name of the American Indian and pursuant to the Doctrine of Discovery, I hereby lay claim to the land called Italy." With that I plunged my spear into the soil of Italy. This act of discovery, in keeping with international law, now placed me in a very exclusive group of men credited with the discovery of lands of the New World, starting with Christopher Columbus, Ferdinand Magellan, Ponce de León, Vasco Balboa, Hernando de Soto, Henry Hudson, and John Cabot. And, as I write this account, I am the only living discoverer of any country.

To my surprise, the people of Italy loved being discovered. There were so many smiling, happy faces. This was nothing like the dire warnings of the members of the United Indian Council or what we had experienced in San Francisco.

As they escorted us to the VIP reception area of Alitalia, we stopped several times to shake hands and pose for pictures with airline officials. A beautiful young lady dressed in an Alitalia uniform introduced herself as being our escort and translator for the upcoming press conference.

She was a remarkable woman, who fielded the questions from reporters in many languages besides English and Italian—from German to Japanese. She interpreted their questions into English for me, and then gave my answers back in the language in which it was asked. I found that to be amazing and, for that reason, the press conference lasted an incredible hour and a half—despite the many naive questions about American Indians, such as, "Do you still live in teepees?"

As a contrary warrior, I took this opportunity to continue turning the tables on history. "According to the Doctrine of Discovery, the land becomes mine and the people become my subjects," I bravely announced. "Therefore I will establish a BIA, Bureau of Italian Affairs, and appoint Gina Lollobrigida as titular head." Most of the journalists got the humor of that proclamation, while others shook their heads not understanding the laughter of the others.

"I will not impose a change of your government, even though you have changed your government forty-five times since World War II. And, finally, I will not attempt to change your belief system and make you worship Native American Spirituality. If you are happy with your beliefs, I will not interfere!"

I was using satire and humor to make my point; however, my declaration was extremely mild compared to what the Europeans actually did to the American Indians for the last five hundred years.

We concluded the press conference. Our interpreter and the Alitalia officials escorted Bobbie and me out of the airport and toward a waiting Mercedes limousine. We heard shouting and saw an old man in frumpled clothes waving his arms and yelling in Italian. Our interpreter told us that the old man had driven over a hundred miles and wanted to meet the Discoverer of Italy and get his autograph. *Ho wah!* How could I refuse such a request?

Our driver took us through the streets of Rome as we made our way to a monastery located on one of the Seven Hills of Rome. The traffic was terrible! It was as if all the drivers were in a demolition derby where pedestrians had to play dodge 'em since the cars had the right of way. I noticed ancient ruins still existed in many parts of Rome. Broken marble columns littered many sites, even the Colosseum had seen better days. If these conditions existed in the United States, urban renewal projects would have removed all that old stuff and replaced them with high-rise apartment buildings. I guess the Romans like to live in the glory days of the past, when they ruled the world.

"You did it, Adam! You really did it!" A grinning Professor Magoroh Maruyama greeted us as we arrived at the monastery. "You have given our conference international publicity. Let me sign you and Bobbie in for the conference, and check you into your room. You must be exhausted after that long trip and the reception at the airport."

We entered a small elevator that must have been built by Otis himself. It was a small steel cage that clattered and slowly crept upward to the third floor. Our room was as Spartan as anyone would expect in a monastery. In fact, it reminded me of the single-wide iron bedstead with thin mattress, hard pillow, and single thin wool blanket I had at the Pipestone Indian Boarding School. It kinda felt like being home. The large shower head was seven feet off the floor and had no shower curtain—just like the boarding school.

After a two-hour nap Bobbie and I rode that rickety little elevator down to the lobby where we met Professor Maruyama, who could hardly control his glee when he introduced Bobbie and me to the international delegates. They were a wide variety of intellectuals and scholars from all

Adam and Bobbie in Rome City Hall, 1973. Author's collection.

over the world. All of them, it seemed, understood the statement I was making about our approach to global history.

Dinner that evening was a new experience. Our plates were stacked up, one for each course. The servers took away the first plate and then served the next course on the next plate. What's that old saying? "When in Rome do as the Romans do!"

This conference was the most incredible event I had ever attended. The sponsors made certain there would be no "dead time." Even the spouses were looked after. Bobbie and the others were given an extraordinary tour of the historic catacombs of Rome.

The following morning the conference sponsors announced to the delegates, "After lunch we are all to board busses to tour the city hall of Rome."

Maruyama whispered to me, "You and Bobbie should pack along your traditional outfits. You never know when they may be needed."

He was right! When we arrived at Rome City Hall the media and paparazzi were out in force. Bobbie and I were given a private room to change into our outfits. Bobbie looked fabulous in her buckskin dress with beadwork decorations and her high-top beaded moccasins.

Once again it was a media frenzy. The paparazzi swarmed around us like bees around honey. On the marble steps of city hall we posed for pictures next to a large statue of a nobleman on a horse. Everywhere Bobbie and I walked the media followed us, despite the fact that we wanted to tour city hall.

The mayor of Rome stood in the hallway watching the activity. And, as we approached him, he slipped out the back door. He was probably worried that I might try to scalp him. Before coming to Italy, I thought the highest-ranking official we would meet would be the mayor of Rome, and now he ducked out on me.

The next day the sponsors of the conference informed us that the next field trip that afternoon would be to the Quirinale Palace to meet the president of Italy, Giovanni Leone. That exceeded my wildest speculation. I would meet the president himself, so the snub by the mayor now meant little to me.

The marble steps leading to the palace were flanked by huge guards dressed in white uniforms with shiny helmets. As we approached the steps, the first two guards snapped to attention and saluted us. I wasn't sure of the protocol; however, I weakly returned the salute. The next two guards repeated the salutes, and now my confidence was growing, so I snapped back a sharp salute. One of the guards gave a sly grin as I did so. After more salutes from the palace guards, I looked around and discovered that Bobbie and I were the only ones being saluted—we were receiving a royal reception.

Our group gathered in the great hall of the palace where President Giovanni Leone greeted us with a short welcoming speech. Then I presented him with a peace pipe, symbolic of our friendly relations between the American Indians and the people of Italy. After the formalities, we were all invited to enjoy a culinary feast of delicious finger foods, along with a selection of fine wines and champagne.

During our visit to Rome, Bobbie and I enjoyed the outpouring of friendship and hospitality. All of this was in sharp contrast to our treatment in San Francisco where we could not receive an invitation to a Columbus Day cocktail party. Or where, during the reenactment at Aquatic Park, the riot squad stood ready to bash our heads with their night sticks if we dared to cross their line.

After breakfast the next morning, Professor Magoroh Maruyama excitedly ran up to me shouting, "HE wants to meet you! HE wants to see you today!"

"Who wants to see me?" I asked.

"The pope! The pope wants to meet you!" Professor Maruyama smiled broadly and could hardly contain his excitement.

Instead of wearing my traditional Chippewa dance outfit, I decided to wear my beaded buckskin shirt and all the trimmings, along with human hair scalp locks. (I had acquired the hair at a local beauty shop.) As usual, Bobbie looked fantastic in her buckskin outfit. We were dressed fit to see the pope.

The ride from the monastery to the Vatican took us through the heart of Rome with all its ancient glory. In my wildest dreams I never knew I

Adam and Pope Paul VI, 1973. Author's collection.

could go so far in representing our Native American people in Italy—first I met their political chief, and now I was about to meet with the spiritual leader of the entire Catholic world.

I was surprisingly calm as our driver approached Saint Peter's Square, with the giant Egyptian obelisk dominating the central area of the Vatican. Bobbie and I were escorted to the right side of the Vatican, where the Swiss Guards had turned out in full force. They were resplendent in their uniforms, designed by Michelangelo almost five hundred years earlier. As we approached the first guards they pounded their pikes on the marble floor and saluted. The pounding of the pikes alerted everyone in Saint Peter's Square that someone important was on their way to see the pope. My experience at the Quirinale Palace paid off, for now I returned all salutes with confidence. Bobbie remained somewhat embarrassed by this exchange.

The inside of the Vatican was everything I expected of a royal palace. Masterpiece paintings and artistic treasures of the Christian world adorned the walls. Marble sculptures mounted on pedestals seemed to watch us as we went by. The fancy ceiling moldings were covered with gold gilt, a silent reminder of what happened to some of our Indian gold.

The second large room was just as ornate; however, a large throne was at the far end for the pope to sit on. He entered and made a short welcoming address to all the delegates, and then stood up to greet us. I watched the proceedings with great interest, and soon it was my turn to be introduced to the pope. I walked forward in measured steps, and as I did, Pope Paul slowly raised his hand with his big, beautiful ring for me to kiss. As he did so, I slowly raised my hand revealing a large Navaho silver and turquoise ring for the pope to kiss. There was an audible gasp in the Vatican as all the pope's aides, cardinals, and bishops feared an international incident was about to take place. The pope blinked a couple of times and grasped the humor of the moment, and then he broke out into a big happy smile as he reached out to hold my hand. We talked, and then he told me, "I have read a great deal about the American Indian and I know what you are doing."

I smiled and replied in a low voice, "Thank you, my son."

I had never experienced such attention from political and religious powers before. And everywhere my wife and I appeared in Rome, the paparazzi were there, even as we enjoyed the fantastic food around the city. I especially loved the large scampi cooked whole like a lobster. Unfortunately, something in the food or water made me urgently ill with diarrhea—the craps—the shits. And that single roll of toilet paper in our bathroom didn't last long.

I took the rickety elevator down to the main floor where I confronted a young assistant to the conference by the name of Diego Neutzo. He didn't understand a word of English. I tried everything. "Toilet paper?" "Pay per?" "Crapper?"

Diego looked at me with a blank look, and did not understand my request. A graphic pantomime of wiping my ass helped him get the message, and he scurried off to return a few moments later with several rolls of toilet paper.

For two days I considered myself the "Splatter Ass of Rome," and I referred to it as "the Pope's Revenge." Some medicine provided by a doctor from New York who was a delegate to the conference ended my intestinal ordeal.

Once on my feet, my friend Magoroh introduced me to the Japanese delegation. He told me, "They want to open negotiations for the sale of Italy." The delegation and their media called me a samurai warrior, a very high honor. In my tribe, the Chippewa, a warrior is called *ogichida*.

My friend, Professor Gerald Kitzmann of New York State University at New Paltz, organized a committee of Indians to welcome Bobbie and me to LaGuardia Airport in New York City. The loud booming of the drums echoed throughout the terminal and surprised the other airline passengers. The drum group sang Honor Songs and Victory Songs. We were officially welcomed back home to the United States.

On our return flight on American Airlines to San Francisco, Bobbie and I were surprised to find the same airline crew that had brought us to New York. They bumped us up to first class and served little complimentary bottles of champagne. It appeared as though our notoriety in Italy had spread to America.

Friends and members of the United Bay Area Council on Indian Affairs showed up at the San Francisco Airport to welcome us home. The Mocking Bird Singers gave us a hero's welcome as they sang Honor Songs over the booming of the big drum.

A representative of the Italian American committee approached me and said, "We are inviting your people to join us at the next Columbus Day banquet. And, as the discoverer of Italy, we will provide you with a float in the Columbus Day Parade."

It took us over five years to go full circle in our relationship, and now we finally made it.

The Curse of the Totem Pole

Even as a little boy in the Indian boarding school at Pipestone, Minnesota, I always loved to carve. Being too poor to buy toys, I simply carved my own: airplanes, boats, cars, and slingshots. My little sharp-edged pocket-knife was my ticket to boyhood happiness. In reality, I was carrying on a tribal tradition.

When the expedition of Jean Nicollet, the famous French explorer, reached northern Minnesota, he came upon a clearing by a beautiful lake where the Indians were chipping and carving huge basswood logs into all kinds of implements: spoons, bowls, etc. Turning to his aide he exclaimed with great excitement, "*Mon dieu,* Pierre. I do believe we have discovered the famous Chip-a-way Indians."

Sorry about that, I just couldn't resist a little Chippewa pun. With that little bit of levity aside, I will continue the story.

In 1968, for the one hundredth anniversary of the city's founding, I was commissioned to carve a totem pole for a new shopping center in Livermore, California. I designed and carved a beautiful eighteen-foot totem pole out of a huge redwood log.

After a large civic celebration dedicating the new shopping center, their executives gave me the bad news. Leases of the new units were going slower than expected, and they could not pay me the two thousand dollars we had agreed upon for that custom-made pole. *Ho wah!* After all that time and expense, I was stiffed by the white guys.

Stuck between the proverbial rock and a hard place, since the pole was impossible to sell any place else, and in the spirit of community, good will, and racial relations, I decided to give that totem pole to the good people of Livermore. The city's park and recreation department took possession of the pole.

Months went by before they told me that the pole had been installed in Centennial Park, in beautiful downtown Livermore. What an honor it is for any artist to have his or her work recognized by a city and installed in a public park for the entire community to share and enjoy.

With eager anticipation, I drove from my home in San Leandro to

Livermore. I visualized that eighteen-foot pole supported on a four-foot concrete base, soaring twenty-two feet into the sky. The large erection I had anticipated turned into a crushing disappointment, for as I arrived at Centennial Park I beheld a stubby ten-foot pole! The city fathers had "Bobbitized" my pole. They had cut off four feet of the lower pole and buried another four feet in concrete. (Those of you with a good memory will recall John Wayne Bobbitt, who had his penis cut off by his wife, Lorena. I feel his pain.)

Outraged, I demanded to be heard at the next city council meeting, where the mayor patiently told me they didn't know where the four-foot cutoff was and the rest was buried in concrete. In addition, there was no budget to get a contractor to dig it out. It was obvious I was getting a political run-around and I knew the old adage, "You can't fight city hall." The hell you say! You just have to change the tactics. I shouted to the assembled city council, "If you cannot or will not make things right in the restoration of the totem pole, I will put a curse on your sewer system!" With that I turned on my heels and stalked out of city hall to the sound of nervous laughter.

The following week, one of the city councilmen was in his bathroom using his old reliable plumber's helper to unclog his toilet, which refused to empty.

Hearing noises out on the street, his wife went out to investigate, only to find a city maintenance truck parked by an open manhole.

"What's going on here?" she asked.

"Well, ma'am, the city sewers are backing up."

"Oh my God! *Oh my God!*" she exclaimed and she ran back to her house.

"Honey, the sewers are backing up. The curse is working! You've got to get ahold of that Indian!" she cried.

The mayor called an emergency meeting of the city council and invited me to be the special guest.

The mayor reported, "We found the missing four feet of your totem pole in the city's corporate yard and we're going to reattach your member—er ah, your pole. We have a contractor willing to excavate the other portion of the pole in Centennial Park. We have prepared an artist's rendering of the reconstructed pole to be mounted on a concrete base. Attached to the base will be a bronze plaque telling the story of the pole, listing you as the maker and carver."

A round of applause erupted from the council, and to my surprise members of the city council volunteered to donate their own money to pay for the bronze plaque.

A few months later, along with a group of Indians, I returned to do a Blessing and Dedication Ceremony of that beautiful pole, which stands proudly erect to this day, forty-five years later.

POSTSCRIPT: In these days of international terrorism, if the secret of the curse were to get into the wrong hands, the people of American cities would be up to their hips in shit. In the interests of national security, I flushed the recipe of the curse down the toilet, which promptly backed up!

Now That's Brave

On November 9, 1969, a two-masted barque loaded with fifty Indians circled the island of Alcatraz.

To everyone's surprise, Richard Oakes, a Mohawk, dove over the side and desperately swam to the island. Soon, four other Indians joined him in the frigid waters.

We watched one of them prepare to go overboard by taking off his shoes.

The man standing next to me exclaimed with pride, "That's the bravest son of a bitch you will ever know!"

"Why is that?" I asked.

"He can't swim."

Farts Among Many

Once upon a time there was a young Indian who went by his boyhood name of Short Feathers. He and his people lived in the beautiful rolling foothills nestled below the great purple Rocky Mountains that loomed skyward to the southwest of their village. The tall grasses and sedge provided lush feed for the buffalo, elk, antelope, and deer that ranged in great profusion in these hills. Short Feathers and his people lived a peaceful and contented life in their land of great bounty and beauty.

Short Feathers was not tall and angular like the rest of the young men of his tribe. As a matter of fact, he was kind of chubby, like he had never outgrown his baby fat. He was a warm and friendly young man who was always generous to others. In spite of his warm personality, people seemed to avoid him because of a physical condition he could not understand. All the green things he loved to eat—wild turnips, onions, camas root, etc.—all produced great amounts of intestinal gas. After feasting, his anal explosions sent his closest friends running for cover.

During ceremonies no one wanted to sit near him, because his sporadic outbursts always interrupted the eloquent narration of the spiritual leader or the quiet moments of silent prayer. A loud "*pfoom!*" drove everyone to distraction.

Short Feathers was somewhat saddened by this tribal shunning, but he refused to let this destroy his positive outlook on life. He decided to try to make the most of a bad situation.

He went to the nearby mountains to be alone, and there he practiced creating different sounds with his gaseous emissions. In time he could sound something like a love flute—*toot-twee-ooohh,* or he made staccato blasts—*pfoot-pfoot-pfoot.* When he entertained his young friends, his grand finale was a huge baritone blast that made their braids flap in the wind. He also discovered that if he held a burning branch next to his anus and then passed gas, a beautiful bluish-red flame belched out two to three feet, to the great surprise and delight of the children. Short Feathers was no longer an outcast! The range and variety of sounds he created were amazing to those witnessing the exotic event.

Almost all tribes enjoy a variety of competitive sports and games. Most events are for sharpening hunting skills, like spear throwing, shooting an arrow through a rolling hoop, running, and jumping. However, Short Feathers' friends challenged neighboring tribes to fart contests. No one could even come close to the variety of sounds or the range of volume created by Short Feathers. Gifts and prizes were heaped upon their gasified hero. They sang Praise Songs for him when they returned to their village.

As the time of manhood approached, Short Feathers celebrated a Sweat Lodge Ceremony, and then went up the mountain for four days without food and water. It was at that time he would seek his vision, his medicine power, his spirit helper. After he came down from the mountain, Short Feathers' parents and relatives hosted an honoring feast, during which he would receive his manhood name.

Tall Bull was his clan uncle. A year earlier, Short Feathers' parents had given Tall Bull a brand new Pendleton blanket as payment for him to find a name for their son.

Tall Bull stood at the end of the willow branch–covered arbor and addressed all the people:

> Today is the day that a young man is to receive his manhood name. I have been honored by his parents to find an appropriate name for him. We have several ways in which to select a name—a clan name, a hereditary family name, an exploit name, a dream name, or an earned name.
>
> A name is important to a person. It must be appropriate and it must fit the person. This young man sitting before you has earned his name! From this day forward, unless he earns a greater name, from this day forward, his name will be 'He Who Passes Wind Among People,' or 'Farts Among Many.' There is no direct translation into English, but it means those things. Farts Among Many may sound obscene and disgusting to the white man, but I believe war is obscene and disgusting. I believe what they have done to our people is obscene and disgusting. I believe what the white man is doing to our Earth Mother and the Sacred Circle of Life is obscene

and disgusting! This young man has a condition that is different and because of that special difference, he has a right to call himself Farts Among Many.

All the people at the honoring feast were joyous, and tradition dictated they must shout the name of the young man four times so no one will forget it. "His name is Farts Among Many! His name is Farts Among Many! His name is Farts Among Many! His name is Farts Among Many!"

Everyone applauded, and loved ones threw blankets and shawls around the shoulders of Farts Among Many and they hugged him warmly. Farts Among Many erupted almost continuously, as the feast contained many green vegetables and the hugging forced out more blasts. It was a very noisy naming reception, as laughter, conversation, and farts abounded.

Every year the tribe hosted a huge powwow in the third week of August. Tribes came from miles around and set up their teepees in circle after circle, radiating out from the powwow arena located in the center. More than five hundred teepees were set up in a great grassy valley area surrounded by low, rounded-top mountains. Each clan has its own area that they maintain year after year. The Little Big Horn River winds its way across the valley. The people swim or bathe in its cold waters, and they bring their horses down for a much-needed drink every day.

Every night the arena is crowded with dancers resplendent in buckskins, beadwork, and colorful feathers. The audience and spectators are packed in the arena surrounding the dance ground.

There are more than twenty huge drums, each with four to eight singers around them. The singing and dancing goes on until around two in the morning. The weary dancers go back to their teepees, where they take off their outfits and hang them on ropes stretched between the teepee poles like a clothesline. After crawling into their beds, they listen to the night sounds of the camp, the laughter of the young people out visiting, and the music of serenades or doorway singers. The serenaders are a group of men forming a line, each pounding their own hand drum and singing special Serenade Songs. The beautiful singing gives everyone a feeling of bliss as they drift off to sleep.

It is during this time that the Teepee Creepers quietly move into action. These young men know where the teepees occupied by pretty girls are located. It's a kind of dangerous game, for the guys have to figure out which side of the teepee the girl is sleeping by. They cautiously and quietly lift the edges of the teepee flaps and carefully reach under in the hopes of finding receptive young ladies on the other side. Sometimes it's the mother of the girl—or worse yet—the grandmother, who screams "Teepee Creeper! Teepee Creeper!" She'll grab anything handy she can use as a club to pummel the unfortunate Teepee Creeper who's caught in the act. Worst of all is the Teepee Creeper who misjudges the sleeping arrangement and gropes the father of the girl instead. A bloody nose, a black eye, or broken fingers or arms can result from such an encounter. Teepee Creepers are a resolute bunch, for the amorous rewards they may occasionally receive makes the risk-taking all worthwhile.

Farts Among Many used a different approach to snag a girlfriend. Off to the side of camp, dozens of young people were doing the Circle Dance. This is a social dance where everyone locks arms or holds the person next to them around the waist. As they sing their joyous songs they dance in a circle and, just like the teepee village, there can be several circles of singing and laughing young people at the same time.

Farts Among Many had been dancing next to a good-looking girl for most of the night. Timidly, he started by laying his arm on her shoulder. A little while later it was around her waist, and since it was dark and nobody could see what he was doing and the girl offered no resistance, his hand slid down to her ample buttocks. Farts Among Many sang all the louder in his happiness, as he rubbed and fondled his willing dance partner in the darkness.

As dawn started to break over the celebration, so did the circle of dancers. "Your teepee, or mine?" Farts Among Many asked the girl.

"My parents are in my teepee. Let's go to yours," whispered the girl.

They walked slowly through the half-light of dawn, a Pendleton blanket clutched around them to protect them against the cool morning breeze. The row after row of teepees looked like silent spirits of the past.

Several elders had already started their campfires. The smell of freshly brewed coffee would soon fill the air.

Farts Among Many and his girl, Pretty Paint, were oblivious to all this. Their minds and their eyes were only for each other and the delights they would share in his teepee. Their actions didn't pass unnoticed by several of the elders, and by mid-morning the efficient moccasin telegraph got word to Pretty Paint's parents.

Her parents stuffed all her belongings into cloth sacks, saddled up her favorite horse, and trooped off to Farts Among Many's teepee. They didn't just burst inside the lodge and embarrass the couple, instead they stood outside the teepee door flap and loudly announced, "You have kept our daughter in your lodge. She is your woman now! Take good care of her." They dropped her possessions next to the door, tied the horse to a stake, and then left. The people in adjoining teepees heard the announcement and agreed, "Farts Among Many is now a married man."

After the powwow, Farts Among Many and Pretty Paint packed up the teepee and loaded it on a one-eyed Ford pickup and drove off to his place to set up home.

A few months later Pretty Paint's appearance was going through a sad change. Her once-fresh and sparkling appearance gave way to a drawn face and large dark bags under her eyes. She was haggard from lack of sleep. Farts Among Many did not stop his anal explosions at night, as a matter of fact they became worse, to the great distress of Pretty Paint. "You keep that up and you're going to blow your guts out," she admonished him. When he had an especially blasty night she would plead with him, "Honey, please, one of these nights you're going to blow your guts out!" Farts Among Many tried to laugh it off, but I could tell it was beginning to worry him.

One day he returned to the house with a couple of fat rabbits he had killed. He handed them to Pretty Paint and said, "We are going to have a good rabbit stew for dinner tonight." He then went out to tend to the horses in the corral.

Pretty Paint took the rabbits into the kitchen and picked up a braided sweetgrass bundle along the way. She laid the rabbits on the table, lit the sweetgrass, and as she smudged the rabbits with the smoke of the sweet-grass she prayed, "Oh, Great Spirit, bless the spirits of the rabbits that provide us with dinner and please help us, oh Grandfather. Farts Among Many is a good man, but his condition is getting to be too much for me. I can't sleep or rest and something has to be done or else I will have to leave this man." She then skinned out the rabbits, removed the guts, and put them in the sink, where she washed and cleaned them with a cloth. Pretty Paint then went on to finish fixing up the rabbits.

As was their custom, Pretty Paint got up one-half hour earlier than Farts Among Many. She lit a fire in the wood-burning stove to warm up the house and to start the coffee. She got the rabbit guts from the porch and put them on the stove to warm up. Then she very carefully and qui-etly took the warm rabbit guts into the bedroom where Farts Among Many was still snoring away. She slowly lifted the blankets behind him and rolled out the warm guts below his buttocks. She slipped out of the room and started to cook breakfast.

Pretty Paint was softly singing a happy little song and thinking how she hoped she would teach Farts Among Many an important lesson. Her song was interrupted by a low groan. She looked up from the table and there was Farts Among Many standing in the bedroom doorway, lean-ing against the doorframe. He was hunched over and as white as a ghost. "You were right, honey!" he moaned. "You were right! Last night I farted my guts out!"

Pretty Paint stifled a laugh and continued her best to look surprised, serious, and concerned.

Farts Among Many continued, "That was not so bad. The hard part was stuffing all my guts back in!"

Pretty Paint had to laugh out loud at this ludicrous situation.

As it turned out, when Farts Among Many was jamming the rabbit guts into his anus, he stretched or ruptured his sphincter muscle. That muscle was no longer taut and resilient, no longer springy. It was now soft and pliant, and it could hardly hold back the smallest amount of gas. No longer could it contain the thunderous explosions of yesterday. The only kind of fart he could make was a quiet, almost silent "*phfooooo*." A new and wonderful silence settled over the house and Pretty Paint once again got a good night's sleep.

Word quickly spread among the village, and another feast was called for in celebration of the event. The clan uncle, Tall Bull, once again told the assembled throng, "This man no longer deserves the name Farts Among Many. He has now earned himself a new name. From now on his name will be Soft Wind!"

Four times the people shouted, "His name is Soft Wind! His name is Soft Wind! His name is Soft Wind! His name is Soft Wind!" It was a joyous feast and a great celebration with many giveaways. The village was once again a peaceful and quiet place to live.

Soft Wind and Pretty Paint lived happily ever after.

Evil Spirits of Alcatraz

Three men pushed homemade rubber rafts from the rocky shore into the black, cold waters of San Francisco Bay. Under the cover of darkness, the three dangerous convicts made their escape from America's most notorious federal prison, Alcatraz Island, AKA the Rock.

A sharp-eyed guard in the east tower spotted movement in the water barely two hundred yards from the island. The searchlights were quickly turned on and the sirens screamed out the warning that an escape was in progress.

A quick, standing check of the prisoners in their cells revealed three missing inmates, indicated by three dummy heads in their beds that acted as decoys to cover their escape. The escapees were brothers Clarence and John Anglin and fellow bank robber, Frank Morris. The sound of rifle fire echoed across the water of the bay. Despite poor visibility, Clarence Anglin and his raft were hit. The slug from a .30-06 rifle penetrated the fleshy part of his upper arm and, at the same time, let the air out of his raft. Clarence shouted, "John! John! I've been hit! I've got to go back or I'll drown right here. You guys keep going."

While all eyes and searchlights were scanning the bay water, they failed to see the small swimming figure approaching the base of the rocky cliff on the west side of the island. The outgoing tide helped desperate Clarence Anglin make the perilous swim halfway around the sixteen-acre island. As Anglin dragged himself over the rocks at the base of the cliff, he spotted a small, half-submerged cave. Once inside, he found the shaft sloped gradually upward. The rising tide soon covered the opening, preventing discovery by the search boats. Clarence Anglin totally disappeared.

Inside the shaft, Anglin was soaking wet and nearly hypothermic. The searing bullet wound only added to his discomfort. As a farm boy from Georgia, Anglin learned survival skills: hunting, fishing, and trapping. He had prepared for his escape by taking along a small bag of emergency supplies that he had secreted away from the mess hall and dispensary. Matches from a waterproof tin soon provided dim light in the darkness of the shaft. Approximately thirty feet from the entry he discovered a small room cut out of solid bedrock. To his amazement it was loaded with barrels and boxes of supplies.

Making a torch out of old rags, Clarence Anglin explored his new accommodations, which measured approximately twelve feet by twenty feet, with vaulted ceilings. It was a mansion compared to his eight-foot by four-foot cell on D Block. Finding a large chest full of wool blankets, Anglin swiftly stripped off his cold wet clothes and wrapped himself in layers of warm comfortable blankets. Exhaustion overtook him, and he was soon sound asleep.

United States Attorney General Robert F. Kennedy ordered the closure of Alcatraz as a federal prison citing a variety of reasons, such as the high cost of maintaining the prison's population. The reasons not stated for the closure were the riots, the escape attempts, and the embarrassment of the still-missing Frank Morris and the Anglin brothers. Their disappearance and the mystery surrounding their escape became an obsession to author and freelance investigative reporter Chad Turner, who felt he could make journalistic history if he could crack the case. The media was invited to attend the removal of the last twenty-seven inmates from the island fortress on March 21, 1963. Chad took this opportunity to interview any inmates who would agree to talk to him.

"Those three guys were weird, man, especially Clarence Anglin. He was a piece of shit, man. He was starting to spook us when he told us he was talking to the spirits of the island," said one convict.

Another inmate said, "Most of us guys think this island is haunted. At night we hear things and sounds that we can't explain."

One inmate reported to Chad, "Clarence Carnes, everyone called him The Choctaw Kid, tried to escape the Rock in 1946. That damn Indian freaked us out when he told us the Little People and spirits came to visit him here. They told him the island was inhabited by a lot of evil spirits. If we don't get off the island we're all going to die. That's why The Choctaw Kid tried to escape the island and the evil spirits, who would either kill him or make him insane!"

Chad was stunned by this information, because it did not conform to publicized reports surrounding the escape by Morris and the Anglin brothers. Now Chad could report that the convicts tried to escape the evil spirits on the island! He wanted to know if the spirits wrapped their arms around Clarence Anglin and made him do their bidding as Carnes had confided to other inmates.

"That guy, Clarence Anglin, with his ranting and ravings about evil spirits on the Rock, was beginning to freak us out. We were damn glad when they made their escape," said a convict. "Even after they were gone, shit still happened. You know, weird things. Could those guys have been right about the evil spirits?"

After a long sleep in the storeroom far below the main structures on Alcatraz, Clarence awoke in the darkness of his cavern with no concept of time. It was low tide, so light came through the escape shaft to the bay. With the dim light, he had the opportunity to further explore his surroundings. That Georgia farm boy only had a schoolboy's understanding of history. His torch revealed things he did not understand. The barrels and boxes were marked in a language he did not comprehend. However, he assumed it was Spanish, as similar writings were on the prison itself. Eight large oak casks were full of whale oil. A nearby box contained oil lamps, which soon filled the damp cavern with a warm glow. Other boxes were full of candles. There was no need to hurry, so Anglin methodically examined each item in his miniature rock warehouse. Even after a hundred years, most of the items were in remarkable condition, especially the barrels and bottles of wine. Anglin stopped his exploration and decided to celebrate his good fortune. It took less than half a bottle of wine to get Clarence totally snockered. His singing, shouting, and maniacal laughter created bizarre echoing in the stone chamber. In a drunken stupor, he continued to make macabre guttural sounds.

After the convicts' revelations about the Anglin brothers, Chad Turner was more determined than ever to learn everything he could about the mysterious disappearance of the three inmates. He obtained permission to examine the bag the Army Corps of Engineers patrol boat found floating in the bay four days after the escape. The bag had a six-inch tear, but some of Clarence's items were still in it. Upon close examination of the tear, Chad concluded a bullet had caused it. After four days in the water, all traces of blood had been washed away. However, a tiny bit of something was still attached to the bag. With the permission of the captain, Chad carefully scraped the tiny piece into an evidence bag for analysis. It was human flesh. Clarence Anglin had been shot. But, where was the body?

The bodies of drowned victims of earlier attempts to escape Alcatraz floated out of the bay, and went as far west as the Farallon Islands. Chad concluded that if Clarence Anglin's wounds were fatal, by now someone would have found his body. A check of all hospitals in the Bay Area for shooting victims during the time of the escape revealed nothing. Chad came to another dead end.

Clarence Anglin spent most of his adult life in prison. No one knew the prison routine better than him and his brother John. He no longer had to conform to the routine of wake-up at six-thirty in the morning, roll call, and lineup before breakfast, work details, shakedowns, and all the demeaning practices of the federal penal system. Now, in the confines of his rock sanctuary, he enjoyed an isolated and comfortable lifestyle. The provisions conveniently stashed a hundred years earlier could sustain him for several lifetimes. Among the cases of wine, Anglin found a small cask marked "*La Absenta.*" It was filled with a bitter green liqueur he found strangely attractive, since a small drink sent him into a dreamlike state. What he did not know was prolonged use of absinthe resulted in the deterioration of the brain, and he could become a mad man.

Anglin's explorations of the booty continued to amaze him. In a wooden rack along the left wall he found ten flintlock muskets, a chest contained flintlock pistols, and nearby were miniature oak casks filled with gunpowder. Swords and knives were stashed under blankets next to them. Anglin figured out that he had stumbled upon an ancient Spanish fortress, or at the least, a hidden warehouse. He found a large brass or copper plate etched with "Francis Drake 1579 *Nova Albion.*" What Clarence didn't know was he unwittingly found proof that Francis Drake had declared discovery of Northern California almost two hundred years before Spanish Navy Lieutenant Juan de Ayala arrived on August 5, 1775.

Upon his arrival in San Francisco Bay, Ayala found Francis Drake's claim of discovery posted on the rocky outcropping of a small island we now call Alcatraz. Ayala was a claim jumper of history. Under the Doctrine of Discovery, by hiding Drake's claim to the region Ayala could claim Spanish rule over Northern California.

Anglin could not have known the historic background of the plate he held in his hands. In order to keep himself occupied, he cut the metal sheet into sections and methodically pounded out a total of eight bowls. Unworked pieces contained portions of Drake's name, *Nova Albion*, and the date 1579.

The constant pounding of rock on copper attracted an unwelcome visitor. Suddenly out of the dark water of the shaft emerged a huge, five hundred–pound sea lion. Clarence panicked as the enraged bull charged him, bellowing loudly. Pinning Anglin against the wall, the bull pummeled him with his large chest, and slashed at him with his teeth. Anglin's body quickly turned into a bloody mess as he was knocked to the floor, where he desperately crawled toward the hatchet he had used to cut the metal plate. Anglin fumbled and grabbed for the hatchet. The bull continued his brutal attack. After what seemed like an eternity, Anglin grabbed the hatchet and savagely struck the head of the sea lion. A lucky blow split the sea lion's head, killing it instantly.

"You big bastard. I can't let you stay here!" Anglin shouted at the dead sea lion. He drug the bulky carcass down the tunnel. The water turned red with the blood of both man and beast. Anglin gave the sea lion a final shove so it was free to drift into the bay. Weak, wet, exhausted, and wracked with pain, Anglin stripped off his wet clothes and rolled himself into the warm comfort of his wool blankets, where he soon fell into in a deep sleep.

As was his custom, Chad had his police scanner on when he heard a strange report from a Coast Guard cutter that a dead sea lion was found drifting in the bay near Alcatraz. At the San Francisco Marina, he hurriedly jumped into his speedboat and headed for Alcatraz, where he found the Coast Guard cutter and several other private craft full of curious onlookers.

"From the looks of it, it's been dead less than twenty-four hours," the officer of the cutter explained to Chad.

Chad asked, "Where do you think it was killed?"

"From the tidal flow on our charts, it could only have been one place—the Rock."

Chad suddenly got cold shivers, as he quickly speculated about the possibility of an Anglin brother still hiding out on the island. It had been months since the prisoners escaped, so where could he be hiding?

As Alcatraz was still under the jurisdiction of the Federal Bureau of Prisons, Chad had to get permission from them to search the island. The Bureau of Prisons had a vested interest in solving the mystery, because the escape of the three convicts continued to be an embarrassment to them. Chad went to the island armed with three sets of plans and documents. One was from the time of the Spanish garrison in 1853 to 1861. The second was from when the United States government took control of the island and made it a military prison. The third set of documents was created after 1933, when Alcatraz became a federal penitentiary.

After Alcatraz was shut down as a federal prison, they left only two caretakers to guard the island: Joe Hart, and his sidekick, Glen Hobson, who appeared five cards short of a full deck. At a scrawny five feet tall, Glen became hyperactive when excited. He was given the responsibility of guiding Chad around the island, which was laced with a number of tunnels, as well as cisterns. Most tunnels had steel bars to prevent inmates from using them. After two days of fruitless searching, Chad found no indication that anyone, with the exception of the two caretakers, was on the island.

During those two days, Chad had plenty of time to question Glen Hobson. Yes, he knew of the Anglin brothers. He also knew of the inmates' statements that there were evil spirits on the island. Hobson also believed what The Choctaw Kid had said about the Little People, and he confided to Chad that he was part Indian. "It doesn't matter that all the prisoners have left the Rock, Alcatraz remains a haunted, spooky place," said Hobson.

"Can you explain what you mean?" asked Chad.

"Two times each night we are required to do a full patrol of the island. We hear voices around a corner of the building. I quietly sneak up on the voices, and there is no one there. Or, we hear metal clanging and there is no wind that night. The freakiest of all is the screams, which echo through the cellblocks and other buildings on the island."

Even though the dead sea lion provided no new information about Anglin, Chad received a most comprehensive understanding of the layout of Alcatraz, and carried away with him a gnawing feeling they had overlooked something.

It took almost three weeks for the horrific wounds to heal on Anglin's face and body. He had no idea his face had been so badly disfigured by the mauling he endured. He could not risk another attack, so he set about to determine if there was another access to the tunnel. He filled his whale oil lantern, and carrying his trusty hatchet, he followed the upward sloping shaft for two hundred feet, where it forked off into two shafts. Both ended at brick walls.

"There's got to be more than that," Anglin muttered to himself.

A close examination of one brick wall revealed the bricks were installed with packed sand, not cement mortar. Using his hatchet on the packed sand, Anglin exposed a small, two-foot by two-foot hole in the wall. Crawling through the small opening he found himself in another brick chamber, with a vaulted ceiling. On one end he found pulleys, wenches, and chains attached to a section of brick wall. The chain connected to the counterbalance had been broken. Nobody had been through that wall in over one hundred years!

Anglin was overjoyed with the prospects of another access to his sanctuary. Among the supplies in his warehouse were ropes and chains. As he worked to replace the broken chain, he figured out how the contraption worked. He knew about the drawbridge over the moat that provided access to the island. The drawbridge was raised and lowered by a series of pulleys. This one was different. A two-foot by three-foot section, weighing no more than four hundred pounds, was connected to pulleys holding a counterbalance. Once he cleaned out the joints of the framework, Anglin could open and close the opening with one hand.

November 30, 1969   ©Chronicle Publishing Co. 1969.

"When you see most of the reservations in this country, Alcatraz looks pretty good."
—Adam Nordwall, an Indian on Alcatraz

Cartoon of Adam in Alcatraz from the *San Francisco Chronicle,* November 30, 1969, Sunday Punch, p. 1.

"Damn those clever Spaniards," he said.

His heart pounded as he crawled through the opening into the next space. It was the Citadel—the dungeons of the old Spanish fort. The Americans had built the main cellblock of the prison right over it. Now Clarence Anglin knew where he was, because he had seen the stairway leading from the cellblock down to the Citadel on many occasions.

As Anglin approached the bottom of the stairs, he blew out his lamp and listened. There wasn't a sound to be heard; it was eerily quiet. He thought it must be night and the inmates were sleeping. Quietly, he climbed up the steps to find it was daylight, and all the inmates were gone—no guards, no anything. Stunned into disbelief, Anglin couldn't understand how so many people simply disappeared. He went around all the familiar places in the cellblock, only to find them all empty. The kitchen fixtures, the dining hall tables and benches were all stripped clean. Not a single book remained in the library. All the cellblocks were open, along with the main security doors in the outer hallway.

"What happened to the world while I was gone?" he muttered.

Stepping outside the main cellblock, Clarence encountered bright sunlight for the first time in many months. Slowly his eyes grew accustomed to the light and he saw the entire island has been abandoned. In shock and grief, he howled out a loud and long lament like a wolf.

Down below in the guard shack, Glen Dodson heard the scream. "Oh shit, now the spirits are coming out in the daytime!"

The fact that Alcatraz Island had been abandoned as a federal prison was not overlooked by mainland Indians of the Bay Area. As chairman of the United Bay Area Council of American Indian Affairs, I saw an opportunity to make a bold and dramatic statement about the deplorable conditions of Native American Indians. Our plan was simple: seize the island of Alcatraz! The plan quickly circulated among Indians in the Bay Area. Young Indian men longing for the days of the warrior were quick to join. Chad knew about my activities in the Bay Area, and with rumors circulating, Chad made a special point to meet and befriend me.

I was very direct with Chad. "I can tell you our plans only if you agree not to tip off the media beforehand. And, if you honor your commitment, you can join us."

Chad was as happy as a young puppy, for he realized he was on the verge of a national story. At the same time, it might help him solve the Anglin mystery.

In the pre-dawn hours of November 20, 1969, eighty Indians occupied Alcatraz, and by Thanksgiving, four hundred Indians were on the island.

We used satire and humor to justify our takeover, and the liberal public of the Bay Area was quick to seize upon another cause they could get involved with. The Nixon White House was not too happy with the Indians and directed the FBI to "expose, disrupt, misdirect, discredit, and otherwise neutralize the groups, activities, and individual names of nationalist hate-type organizations and groupings, their leadership, spokesmen, membership, and supporters" in order to "prevent the rise of a 'messiah' who can unify and electrify the nationalist movement." Chad knew about the secret and covert action of the government. As a professional journalist, and having been with the Indians from the first day of the occupation, he saw certain individuals who didn't seem fit in with the Indian movement. He wondered if the Indian occupation of Alcatraz was being compromised by covert operatives of the United States government.

I was always accompanied by two of my most devoted followers: Rosemma Teton, was a beautiful Lakota woman. She was articulate and knowledgeable about Indian history and the governmental injustices against her people, as well as other tribes. Her boyfriend, Jimmy Blue Thunder, in spite of being a strong advocate for the Indian cause, had the running hots for Rosemma.

With so many comings and goings on the Rock, it was impossible to keep track of every Indian. When Joyce Small Thunder, an attractive twenty-year-old Assiniboine girl failed to show up at her sleeping quarters, it was assumed she had gone to the mainland to be with her friends in San Francisco. Two days later, a female body was found floating face down in the bay. Autopsies revealed she had been tortured, raped, and murdered with a blow to the head.

In the next three weeks, two more female bodies, murdered in a similar fashion, were found. The government was quick to blame the murders on the Indians. Chad arranged with the San Francisco Coroner's Office to see the autopsy photographs of the victims and made a startling discovery. Each one was killed with a sharp blow to the head! The same type of wounds were found on the dead sea lion. The Indians were distraught with the horrible turn of events. This was no way to stage a protest, for now we were being victimized more than ever. Everyone was told the haunted legends of the island. The ghosts of Indians who had been held prisoner on the island and others who had been chained and tortured in dungeons were the spirits The Choctaw Kid had talked about seeing before he was paroled from the Rock. Legends also talked about a horrible cannibal spirit, called Weendigo by the Chippewa, who could frighten his victims to death with his horrific screams.

Despite the terrible events taking place on Alcatraz, the movement and the protests had to go forward. The Indians on the island did not want the public to know what was going on. When Creedence Clearwater Revival asked to do a concert on the Rock, the Indians quickly accepted the band's offer. For the first time in the long history of the island, Alcatraz echoed with the magnified sounds of contemporary music. Alcatraz was rockin'.

Rosemma and Jimmy were dancing in free abandon to the music, which gave Jimmy the hots. The concert was in the dining hall and only forty feet from the entrance was the stairway leading down to the Citadel. Wrapped in a blanket against the cold night and carrying a flashlight, the two made their way into the foreboding darkness. A brick panel in a nearby wall slowly opened. Clarence Anglin saw that a make-out session was going on. In the dim light of the flashlight, Rosemma sensed the appearance of a hairy figure emerging from the darkness. Her scream alerted Jimmy and he whirled around to confront the danger. Anglin swung his hatchet, hacking and chopping at Jimmy's hands and arms.

A blow to Jimmy's head stopped the struggle. Rosemma was knocked unconscious from a crushing blow to the jaw. The next day we found Jimmy's bloody body; however, Rosemma was nowhere to be found.

A sweat lodge was constructed on the island and I summoned a shaman, a medicine man, and the Sun Dancers to participate. The shaman was an Alaskan Eskimo whose frail, bent features were classic to his shamanic calling. He requested articles of clothing or any objects owned by Jimmy, Rosemma, and the other women who were unaccounted for.

As Chad watched the preparations for the ceremony, he desperately wanted to participate.

I warned, "This will not be easy for you and if you do come in, you will have to prepare yourself spiritually." I continued, "You will prepare tobacco ties as gifts to the spirits. Spotted Horse, the medicine man, will prepare a potion of black water that you will be required to drink. It will cleanse your system and purge you of any bad medicine."

As the stones were being heated in the large fire, the men busied themselves with preparations for a special sweat. All the men lined up, each one had only a towel wrapped around him. The Eskimo shaman smudged them with sweetgrass and cedar. Spotted Horse approached Chad with a small bowl of black liquid. After drinking the vile stuff, Chad tried to maintain a proper demeanor, only to have his eyes bug out and his face distort from a challenge to his gut.

He suddenly whirled around and retched into the nearby shrubbery. The medicine man looked at the offal, and said quietly, "I see you had bacon and eggs for breakfast. You know, you should not eat before a sweat."

The other men smiled, as they understood the sacred and the profane in the balance of life.

As the red-hot stones were brought into the lodge, the men offered sweetgrass and tobacco to the Stone People. The lodge plunged into darkness as the door flap was closed. The shaman then threw *dawsa*, a medicine herb, on the hot rocks. It created a shower of sparks and a beautiful aroma. Then Spotted Horse poured water on the Stone People, and soon the lodge was full of steam. The men beat hand drums or shook their medicine rattles. This was the beginning of a Spirit Journey sweat.

The shaman and Spotted Horse called the spirits to join us. Soon the sweat lodge was filled with the sound of the beating wings of an eagle, The Messenger. The singing and drumming intensified to welcome the spirits.

"Help us spirits! Help us! We have to know what is happening to our people on this island," chanted the shaman.

Mystical spirits glowed in the darkness and swirled around as if guided by the eagle. Chad was mesmerized. He ignored the great heat and the sweat dripping profusely from his body, and to his surprise, he called out "Anglin!"

Suddenly the lodge was full of screaming, the agonizing screaming of women who appeared out of the darkness, turning and turning among the sweat lodge participants. Their long, beautiful black hair flowed with a hidden breeze, their faces were bloody messes, and all had deep wounds in their heads. Rosemma was not among them. The shock of this grisly sight caused us to become suddenly silent.

Then Spotted Horse, the medicine man, started to sing a Death Song. The shaman called to the spirits of the women to communicate to him how they left the physical world and entered the Spirit World. Among their screaming and wailing came eerie voices only the shaman understood. The lodge was suddenly filled with shooting lights and rainbow colors as the spirits made a sudden departure. The lodge was in total silence. The reflection of red-hot stones vaguely showed agony on the sweaty faces of the men. Chad had never had such a powerful, mystical experience in his life. It gave him a new sense of humility and respect for the spirituality of the Native Americans. Some of the Indian men were quietly sobbing, as they had known some of the women who had been brutally murdered.

As the evening fog rolled in from the Golden Gate, the men sat around the fire used to heat the rocks for the ceremony. The talk was subdued. Others, still in the spiritual dimension of another world, remained silent. None of the other people on the island dared to come near, because they knew that powerful medicine was taking place.

The Eskimo shaman knew it was Chad who had shouted out the name "Anglin" in the sweat lodge, which started an immediate response from the spirits. When Chad came to the shaman with an offering of tobacco, the Eskimo accepted it, knowing there would be questions to follow. Instead of being asked, the shaman said, "The spirits say there is an Evil One far below. He lives among the Stone People and desires the young women of our people."

Chad had researched Middle Age castles and forts of Europe and found all of them had clever escape routes. The king of France had one in a deep kitchen well in his castle, seventy-five feet below the surface. The king's men dug an escape tunnel extending one-half mile from the castle with the outlet hidden in a nearby woods. Chad wondered whether the Spaniards prepared an escape route from the island, in case they found themselves overrun by enemy forces.

What the spirits related to the shaman appeared to confirm this suspicion. Somewhere in the bowels of Alcatraz lived an Evil One.

Medicine Man Spotted Horse busied himself grinding powder in a stone bowl. "Tracking dust," he explained. "Tonight we will scatter it around the dungeon area. The spirits will not disturb it, but any living creature will."

Spotted Horse led the shaman, me, and the ever-present Chad into the dungeon. Carefully and quietly, the four of us went from chamber to chamber while the medicine man blew the dust out of the wing bone of an eagle. The last place dusted was the base of the stairs.

The memory of the visions and sounds of the screaming, bloody women kept Chad from a restful night. I gently tugged on his blanket at dawn. Four men—Chad, Spotted Horse, the Alaskan shaman, and I—stood at the entry of the main cellblock. We were joined by two Sun Dance warriors. We greeted the rising sun with upraised palms and a Morning Prayer. When we finished we pressed the rays of the sun against our bodies, asking for guidance and light for the upcoming day.

The small caravan of men entered the main cellblock and made our way to the right rear corner of the building containing the stairwell to the dungeons below. Laying his flashlight on the floor, Spotted Horse saw that something had crossed the tracking dust. They did not appear to be human tracks. In fact, the prints were nothing any of us could identify. What we didn't know was that after Anglin wore out his shoes, he wrapped his feet in the torn strips of Spanish wool blankets. The strips also served to quiet his footsteps.

Puzzled, but undaunted, we continued to follow the mysterious tracks through the maze of the labyrinth straight up to a brick wall.

One of the men said, "We must be dealing with a shape-shifter. No human could simply walk through a brick wall."

Remembering the stories of the European practice of preparing secret escape routes, Chad used his flashlight for a closer examination of the two-foot by four-foot recessed niche before him. Something was not right about the edges. Before Chad could say anything, we were startled by the stabbing rays of flashlights.

Two men approached the group and identified themselves as Officers Tinsley and Osgood of the FBI. "We are investigating the deaths of several young Indian women and we want you upstairs for questioning," declared Officer Osgood.

I introduced Chad as being, "Indiana Jones, our resident archaeologist. He is teaching us the ways of our recent history."

Office Tinsley responded, "You Indians have a warped sense of humor."

I retorted, "You white men have a warped sense of history."

The other Indians found it hard to stifle their outright laughter. After all, the FBI represented the government, which was responsible for the destruction of Indian Country. In fact, it was the very reason why Indians were occupying Alcatraz. We did not believe the FBI claims that they only wanted to solve the brutal murders of Indian women on the Rock. At the same time the FBI was committed, by federal policy, to do everything in their power to destabilize and disrupt the Indian occupation of Alcatraz.

Chad was shocked with the bluntness of my statement to the FBI agents, whose only response was, "We have the rules and the laws of the federal government to carry out."

My reply was forceful, "You agents have blown your cover with the Indians of Alcatraz. We outnumber you over one hundred to one. If you don't want to see a modern version of Custer's Last Stand, I will personally escort you gentlemen to the next boat to San Francisco."

Agents Tinsley and Osgood realized I was right and agreed to my offer of safe passage to San Francisco.

As the two FBI agents left Alcatraz, a cheer from the Indians let them know it was good riddance. After the FBI agents left, I confronted Chad. "Agent Tinsley said they have reports of you being connected to the Communist Party. If that's correct, you stand to ruin everything we've worked for by occupying Alcatraz!"

Chad was stunned by my confrontational challenge.

"I am not a communist!" yelled Chad.

I could not take a chance and ordered several of my warriors to escort Chad to the dock to be deported to the mainland. As we walked down the winding road to the dock, Chad continued to plead his case.

Chad's Jewish grandfather was captured by the communist forces and shipped to Moscow, where Stalin ordered his execution. His grandmother was killed during the Jewish uprising in Warsaw. At that time his mother was just a teenage girl, and was spirited out of Poland by the Resistance. As Chad, the warriors, and I walked through the tunnel containing the drawbridge, Chad continued to make his case. "My father, Stanley Turner, was a master sergeant in the Eighty-Second Airborne, you know, the paratroopers. At the end of the war he met my mother at a processing center outside of Berlin. And, as the old saying goes, 'It was love at first sight.' As you can see there is no one in my family who has any love for the communists or the Nazi Party."

"Your people suffered the brutal effects of tyranny, just as my people continue to suffer," I replied. "Chad, You have proven yourself to be a friend and ally of our people, and for that we won't deport you to the mainland. You're welcome to stay."

Clarence Anglin became more and more aware that the Indians were trying track him down. He decided the best defense was a good offense. After dark, when he figured the Indians were settling down for the night,

Anglin carried out his diabolical plan to burn the "red bastards" off the Rock.

He made his way out of the dungeon area and up through the main cellblock. Anglin was on the top of the island. Lighting his Molotov cocktails full of whale oil, he torched the Warden's House and other wood structures all the way down to the recreation building.

Laughing with maniacal glee and hopping up and down with excitement, he watched panic-stricken Indians futilely fight against the raging inferno, which continued to engulf the island. In the chaos, no one noticed the furtive figure sneaking into the main cellblock to his safe haven below. He celebrated his victory with a cup of absinthe.

"We have a brutal killer on Alcatraz," I told everyone. "We are warriors without weapons. And now we are caught in another dilemma. How are we to fight him?"

For the next two days, the Indians fashioned weapons in the old ways. We made crude knives and war clubs out of every conceivable material we could find.

On Tuesday evening the Indians lit a large bonfire and, just as in the old days, we sang, danced, and thought about the upcoming conflict with an unknown, unseen enemy.

The next morning, all the Indian men assembled in the prison parade ground. The Dog Soldiers and Sun Dancers organized six- to eight-man war parties, which were instructed to fan out all over Alcatraz, covering the shoreline, docks, power plants, and shops. In other words, we went to search every possible area that could be used as a hideout.

Chad found the scene unbelievable in the twentieth century: Indians were out looking for the enemy wearing war paint, stripped to the waist, and carrying handmade weapons. I led my war party straight to the main cellblock. Chad quickly followed.

"Hey, Adam, don't forget your white puppy," joked a laughing Indian.

Chad smiled with the irony of the situation.

We arrived at the brick wall in the dungeon where the mysterious tracks disappeared. A metal blade wedged into the bottom course of bricks caused the panel to move upward. Eager fingers reached under the

brick wall and slid it up, until it revealed a two-foot by three-foot opening. We peered inside with our flashlights and saw the next chamber with
another hole in the wall.

Chad barely contained his excitement. "We've found a hidden passage."

I turned to one of the warriors and said, "Go out and tell four of the
war parties to stand guard over the cliffs on the west side of the island.
We have a rat trapped in his hole."

I started crawling through the opening, when suddenly the brick panel
started sliding downward. Shouting out warnings, Chad and the warriors
desperately struggled to stop the panel before it crushed me. A makeshift
tomahawk was used as a doorstop and I squeezed through.

"That madman has this place booby-trapped," said Chad.

Single file we cautiously made our way down the tunnel, the beams
of our flashlights stabbing through the darkness. A piercing scream of a
woman in distress hurried us along the shaft to the chamber below.

Clarence Anglin saw the oncoming beams of light. Grabbing a Spanish
flintlock musket, he pointed it at Chad, who was at the front of our group.
There was a sudden flash of light, but no explosion as the old black powder misfired. Angrily, Anglin threw the musket at us and scurried down
the tunnel exit toward the bay. Because it was low tide, the light from
the entrance silhouetted his body. Rosemma was chained to a wall in the
chamber, her half-naked body was covered with blood from the effects of
the brutal, sadistic torture she had just endured.

I told a warrior to loosen her shackles, so we could continue our pur-
suit of Anglin. The warriors on the cliffs above were shocked by the sight
of the creature that emerged from a hole in the base of the cliff. It had
long unruly hair and beard. Its clothes were a ragged combination of old
denim pants with a shredded blanket poncho draped over its shoulders.
Looking up the cliffs, Anglin saw the line of warriors. Then he saw me
and my party emerging from the tunnel.

Clarence Anglin gave a bloodcurdling scream of rage as he realized
he was trapped. He turned and plunged into the bay—his last hope of
escape. His scream frightened a small herd of sea lions, which had been

sunning on the rocky cove. Their shimmering bodies splashed into the water, seeking safety in the bay.

The herd bull saw the frantic Anglin and took him as a threat to his herd. His angry bellowing was quickly followed by a ferocious attack on Anglin. We heard screams and bellowing from their mortal combat. The sea lion was in his element. His small but deadly fangs slashed Anglin's body, turning the churning waters blood red. We watched in awe as Anglin's screams subsided and his body sank into a watery grave.

Even though Anglin had been the enemy, we sang a Memorial Song in recognition of his death. Others threw tobacco offerings into the water of the bay and gave Thanking Prayers to the spirits for their help.

Two days later, Chad sat on a small bench next to the prison parade ground, writing the final chapter to the historic event.

I approached him and said, "Well, my friend, it looks like we will be going our separate ways soon. You have your story, and the United States government agreed to our terms. They will not close down our reservations, and as our part of the agreement we will all be off Alcatraz in another week."

After a moment of deep thought, Chad responded, "You know it will be supremely ironic that you and the warriors of Alcatraz saved the reservations of America from being abolished by the United States government, and the Indians will never know it."

I responded, "But we know it, and that's all that matters."

General Fremont's Cannon

Ever since I was a little boy on the Chippewa Indian reservation at Red Lake, Minnesota, I have had a fascination with guns. They were a necessity for our tribe, whose major source of meat was deer and moose. A good rifle meant meat in the pot for a hungry family. With side dishes of wild rice, vegetables, and homemade bread, we enjoyed veritable feasts.

My uncle was a bootlegger on the reservation. Most reservations are closed reservations, which means it's against the law to serve or sell alcoholic beverages on them. So, the bootleggers did quite well, unless, of course, they got caught and found themselves spending time in the slammer. My uncle, however, was one of the more clever ones who eluded arrest. It was a treat for me to visit him when I was just a little boy, because leaning in a corner of the living room was a bunch of rifles that other Indians hocked for booze. At that early age it was the greatest collection of guns I had ever seen, and it helped stimulate a life-long interest in firearms.

My first rifle was a brand new Marlin 336 in .35 caliber. I figured that heavy 200-grain slug could drop just about anything on this continent. It was a beautiful carbine with a pistol grip stock, and with it I got my first buck in the East Gate Range of Nevada back in 1952. My Shoshone father-in-law, Bodie, was very proud of his new son-in-law for showing interest in the same things he had enjoyed for many years. We both loved hunting and the great outdoors. His main interest was prospecting, and he taught me a lot about the various minerals and how to find them. My wife, Bobbie, and I were living in California and every time we visited her folks on the Stillwater Reservation in Nevada, Pop and I would go hunting, prospecting, or both.

First published in *In Focus* 5, no. 1 (1991–92): 42–47, Churchill County Museum Association, Fallon, Nevada. Revised 2009 and 2013.

Pop used to tell me about lost mines or about a cave at Silver Peak where gold nuggets glittered by the light of a carbide lamp. The two guys alleged to have found this incredible cave had their base camp in Austin. After their discovery of the cave, they went back to Austin and got new supplies. They shared the story about their exciting discovery before they left town. The two were never seen alive again.

The next spring a search party left Austin and headed toward Silver Peak. In the vastness of the high desert, they came upon the remains of the small wagon the prospectors used to haul their supplies. In the litter, they found a couple of small pouches full of solid gold nuggets! The secret of that fabulous cave died with those prospectors. Despite repeated efforts, their friends found no trace of the prospectors; they suspected the miners froze to death when they were overtaken by a brutal winter storm and their wagon broke down on the return trip. That little cave entrance is believed to have been sealed up before the prospectors left on their final journey to town, because no one has ever found it since.

Pop used to tell this and many other stories to his fascinated son-in-law; however, it was the story of General Fremont's cannon that always grabbed my attention the most. In 1844, General Fremont came through northern Nevada with his troops, looking for an easy way to the California territory. They also dragged along a bulky, two-hundred-twenty-five-pound cannon on a three-hundred-pound carriage that often got stuck in the sand and mud. After several skirmishes with the fast-moving Paiutes, General Fremont found his cannon to be more of a damn nuisance than a help. So he stashed the cannon in a safe place until he could return and retrieve it at a later date. His troops dragged that cannon up a rock-strewn slope to a strategic outcropping overlooking a valley and left it there.

To this day, no one has ever found General Fremont's cannon, and it was my dream that one of these days Bodie and I would find it. Bobbie and I had three children to raise in California and, during that time, I continued my interest in guns. Every time an old pistol or rifle was added to my developing collection, I also added a book or a magazine to expand my understanding and knowledge of the gun world. My collection grew to include virtually every model Winchester of the last century, starting with a beautiful and extremely rare iron-frame Henry rifle from 1860. The Henry was the first successful repeating rifle to use a self-contained cartridge and was the immediate precursor to the Winchester rifle of 1866. The Winchester Repeating Arms Company developed its fame and fortune on the western frontier. I added Colt and Smith & Wesson pistols to my growing collection, but always in the back of my mind was the ultimate acquisition—General Fremont's cannon!

After raising our children and seeing them all married off, complete with Indian ceremonies, Bobbie and I moved back to her Shoshone reservation in Fallon, Nevada. Again, my quest for the old or unusual gun continued. I took a temporary job as tribal building inspector while we built a ceremonial-style round house that became our art gallery and museum. In the mornings, the men employed by reservation programs hung around the coffeepot swapping yarns or (heaven forbid!) gossiping. Some of these guys turned out to be worse gossips than most women, especially the tribal cop. At eight in the morning the talk concluded and the men went out to their jobs.

One morning I decided to make my move. I was careful not to tip my hand as to the true purpose of the question, "Has anyone seen any old cannons laying out in the hills?"

To my surprise an older Paiute guy who had been a wrangler and mustanger for many years said, "Yah, hell, I know where there's an old cannon out there in the hills. Damn thing's too heavy to carry out though."

I tried to hold down my building excitement, because this guy knew the hills like the back of his hand. So, in a casual and offhanded way I said, "Can you tell me where it is?"

"Sure, it's easy," said the Paiute. "Go out Highway 95 toward the Walker River Reservation. You know those hot springs out there? Well, at the next canyon you will find a road leading out across the flats to your left. You know the place I'm talking about?"

"Yah, I know that road," I answered.

He then continued, "Well, you take that dirt road out about ten miles and off to your right you'll see a saddle in the mountain range; be real careful here because there is a dim road that will disappear in the sand as you go higher. You get out of your pickup, and walk up and over that pass. Once you get through the pass you veer to the right along that slope and, in a rocky outcropping, you will find an old cannon."

All that day I had a hell of a time concentrating on my work. All I could think of was that at long last we might find that elusive cannon. I went over the directions in my mind, over and over, so that I committed them to memory.

When quitting time finally arrived, I rushed on home and excitedly told my son Adam, "Tomorrow we are going cannon hunting."

Early the next morning, a Saturday, Adam and I packed "Old Blue," our 3/4-ton pickup. The hood was all rusty and the paint was peeling or chipping off the chassis, but that rig could sure do the job. In went pick, shovel, come-along, and two-inch by twelve-inch planks, in case we got bogged down in the sand. Water! We need to take plenty of water. You never know about the high desert. We don't want to end up like those guys at Silver Peak. Bobbie packed a big lunch, and right after breakfast of bacon, eggs, toast, and coffee, we were ready for our big adventure.

It was a beautiful autumn day as we took the initial eight-mile trip to Fallon. In town we picked up Highway 95 and headed out toward the Walker River Reservation. My son Adam was my lookout. He said, "There's the hot springs." And a little later he said, "There's the road to the left leading out toward the flats."

Ho wah! Everything was just as the Paiute wrangler told me. About ten miles out in the flats, we spotted that little dim road leading up toward the pass and, just like the wrangler said, it petered out in the sand.

We parked Old Blue and grabbed our lunches and canteens. We'd go back for the heavy stuff after we located General Fremont's cannon. I chuckled to myself thinking of how easy it was for me to get the information about a historic cannon from that Paiute wrangler.

We hiked up toward the pass through the sage and scrub brush. My heart was beating harder now from the exertion of the climb and the excitement of being so close to our quarry. We finally reached the mountain pass.

"It can't be too far now," I hollered at Adam, who was walking along about thirty yards to the left of me. When we are hunting we usually spread out like this because it improves our chances of finding something.

Over the pass, we veered to the right as we were instructed. Something was different about this area though; some kind of powerful force had torn up some of the cedar trees and sagebrush. The further we walked along the slope, the greater the devastation we found.

"What the hell caused all this?" I shouted to Adam.

"Beats me!" he hollered back.

Before I could give it any more thought, I spotted the rocky outcropping.

"Look, there it is!" I happily shouted, for protruding through the rocks was a cannon barrel.

We scrambled up towards the rocky outcrop and the closer we got, the more our excitement cooled, for what looked like a cannon barrel was a four-inch by four-inch post lying down among the rocks. On the other end of the post was attached a sign, face down. We turned it over and the sign read "DANGER, U.S. NAVY BOMBING RANGE—KEEP OUT."

Ho wah! I was a victim of the Indian version of the white man's infamous snipe hunt. We could only be thankful the Navy wasn't using the Bravo 17 Bombing Range that day—and there's no way in hell I'm going to tell that Paiute wrangler that I got suckered in by his story.

How I Saved Patty Hearst's Father from the SLA

The Untold Story

As Oakland, California, School Superintendent Marcus Foster and Assistant Superintendent Robert Blackburn stepped out of their car, they were confronted by two armed men who opened fire, killing Marcus Foster and severely wounding Robert Blackburn, who escaped into the administration building. The gunmen fired four more bullets into Foster, just to make sure he was dead. Later, an American guerilla group calling themselves the "Symbionese Liberation Army" took credit for the killing as a declaration of war against the United States government.

Three months later, on February 4, 1974, an event occurred, garnering worldwide attention. At nine o'clock at night two armed men pushed their way into a Berkeley apartment and kidnapped Patty Hearst, a newspaper heiress, and disappeared into the night with their terrified captive.

It was not long until the senior editor of *The San Francisco Examiner* received a demand from the SLA to provide food for the needy in the Bay Area, including American Indians, at a cost of six million dollars. This modern-day version of Robin Hood by a band of criminals and killers did not sit too well with me and the United Bay Area Council on Indian Affairs, so I called on other Indian leaders, and we all agreed we could not accept any food under those circumstances. I called Mr. Randolph Apperson Hearst, owner of *The Examiner,* and told him of our decision and that we were going to call a press conference the following day to make that announcement. Mr. Hearst was very concerned about this new development, which he felt could jeopardize his daughter's life—she was at the mercy of those murderers. So, he assigned a reporter to meet me that night at midnight in the Montclair District in the Oakland hills.

This was turning into a cloak-and-dagger experience for me. We had no idea who the SLA was or where they were. And Mr. Hearst was taking no chances.

The reporter and I worked until two in the morning refining the press release to be given later that day, with the support of twelve other leaders of Bay Area Indian organizations. Surrounded by the media, we delivered our message, which in essence was: "We will not be coconspirators to extortion. Many Indian people are hungry today, but we will not accept any free food until Patty Hearst is released. She is our sister; let her be free." The media carried our message all over the country.

The following day I returned to *The Examiner* only to be greeted by several frantic editors who said, "Adam, you have to get yourself and your family the hell out of town!"

"Why?" I asked, because I was unaware of what was going on.

"This morning we got a message from the SLA that you are to be shot on sight!" said one agitated editor.

I had earlier offered my services to be a potential mediator between the Hearst family and the SLA due to my ten-year involvement with the American Indian Cultural Group of San Quentin Prison, but now all bets were off.

Instead of cutting and running, I went to an insurance company in San Leandro and took out a five hundred thousand dollar life insurance policy. In case something happened to me, my wife and family would be taken care of. Every time I made one of my numerous trips to San Francisco, I tucked a Colt .45 automatic into my belt. If there was going to be a shootout at Union Square, I was ready.

Mr. Hearst was grateful for our support and invited my wife, Bobbie, and me to visit him and his wife, Catherine, at their mansion in Hillsborough. It was everything we expected to see, and a lot more. Mr. Hearst had an extensive gun collection, one of the finest selections of antique firearms, which were engraved with gold and silver with ivory accessories. In one of their daughters' bedrooms were shelves displaying a beautiful Kachina doll collection. Under the ornate Persian rugs in the living room were wires that connected to a burglar alarm system.

In return for the Hearsts' hospitality, we invited them to our home in San Leandro for dinner, and they readily accepted. With our dinner appointment confirmed, I went to the San Leandro Police Department and said to the police chief, "Guess who's coming to dinner?"

"Sidney Poitier?" he asked.

"No, it's Randolph and Catherine Hearst," I replied.

"Oh damn! The people most wanted by the SLA will be right here in our town!" he cried.

After I left his office he summoned a police sergeant and told him, "If anything happens to the Hearsts while they are in San Leandro, I don't want any excuses. You can just throw your badge on my desk!"

The evening of the dinner a big black Mercedes pulled up to the corner of Manor Boulevard and Thoits Street, and before the question could be raised one of the little boys asked, "Are you looking for the Nordwall house? It's just down there on the right side." Mr. Hearst could only chuckle, as he was made aware that the neighborhood telegraph was working. My son had told his friend Bryan about the Hearst visit, and all the kids were aware of the plainclothes police that would patrol the neighborhood until the Hearsts left San Leandro safe and sound.

As Bobbie prepared the duck and wild rice dinner, Randolph played the role as bartender. Catherine Hearst served on the Board of Regents for the University of California and made a strange comment during her visit, "The horse was the worst thing that ever happened to the Indians because it gave them the mobility to attack other tribes!" In no way was I going to confront that form of logic. The evening progressed and Catherine became snockered—after all, she was distraught over the kidnapping of her daughter. All evening, we avoided discussing that terrible situation.

I happened to walk into the offices of *The San Francisco Examiner* the morning of April 3, 1974. They were listening to the audiotape announcing that Patty Hearst had joined the SLA and assumed a new name, "Tania." She declared herself a follower of Donald "Cinque" DeFreeze, an ex-convict of California's Vacaville and Soledad prisons. This announcement sent shockwaves throughout the Bay Area, adding further grief to the Hearst family. There's a photo of Patty standing in front of the SLA flag holding an automatic rifle. When I arrived at *The Examiner*, I parked in a multilevel parking garage across the street. For some odd reason, I decided to go to the top level, where I parked my car and then started to look around. I went to the abutment overlooking the street and *The*

Examiner building. I could see in through the huge plate-glass windows of Randolph Hearst's executive office. He sat there behind his large desk. If I were a sniper I could have easily picked him off, since he was less than fifty yards away. As I walked around the top level of the garage I noticed that someone had removed the steel door leading to the stairwell, making an easy escape route for any gunman.

After my greeting in Mr. Hearst's office, I asked him, "Mr. Hearst, could you go over to your window and tell me what you see?"

Mr. Hearst stood there and slowly looked around. "I only see other buildings and a parking garage."

I replied, "Mr. Hearst, if you can see the parking garage, they can see you behind your desk. You are an easy sitting target."

The following week I returned to *The Examiner* building for an update on the current events involving Patty. Once again I parked on the top level, and I found someone had replaced the steel door to the stairwell. Looking out across the street toward *The Examiner* building, I saw that all the plate-glass windows had been covered with film, like tinted windows in a car. They could see out, but I couldn't see in. In the lobby of the building I was confronted by a burly man with a walrus-like mustache who was sitting at a desk by the stairway and elevator. He looked up and saw an Indian with long braids. In a gruff voice he asked, "Why are you here?"

"I'm here to see Randy," I replied.

"So it's Randy you wish to see is it?" he continued.

"Yes sir, will you please call Mr. Hearst and tell him Adam Nordwall is here to see him."

He got on the telephone, and in just one minute he went from a grumpy security guard to a kiss-ass wimp. "I'm sorry if I offended you Mr. Nordwall. Mr. Hearst says to come right up."

The SLA crime wave continued unabated. In the robbery of the Hibernia Bank on Noriega Street in San Francisco, Patty is shown on the security camera brandishing an M1 carbine. Following that they robbed the Crocker Bank, where a customer, Myrna Opsahl, was murdered.

Then the robbery of Mel's Sporting Goods provided the SLA with more guns and ammunition.

The massive manhunt for Patty Hearst and the SLA intensified, and the dragnet was closing in. Patty and Wendy Yoshimura were tracked down by the FBI and the San Francisco police and arrested in a San Francisco apartment. Cinque and five other gang members fled to Los Angeles, and the Los Angeles Police Department surrounded the house where they were hiding out. Cinque refused to surrender during the standoff. Soon an all-out battle took place between the SLA and the Los Angeles police. A smoke grenade thrown in started the house on fire. The smoke and flames drove Cinque and his gang into the crawl space under the house. When the heat and flames became unbearable, Cinque put a gun to the right side of his head and blew his brains out. After the fire was extinguished, they found his body like burnt toast. It was barely recognized by his family.

After Catherine Hearst died, Randolph moved to New York, where we kept in contact until he, too, passed away.

Patty was convicted of bank robbery on March 20, 1976, and sentenced to thirty-five years imprisonment. After serving twenty-two months, her sentence was commuted by President Carter. Later she was granted a full pardon by President Clinton on January 20, 2002. She went on to marry her former bodyguard Bernard Shaw and they now have two children.

With the elimination of the SLA and Patty Hearst living happily ever after, I decided it was about time I put my .45 Colt automatic into the drawer of my nightstand.

Never Let a Good Deed Go Unpunished

As the drama of the Patty Hearst kidnapping was being played out, unbeknownst to me, another drama was starting to unfold. This time it was me and my career that were targeted, not by the SLA, but by the U.S. government itself. A secret document was distributed in 1973 to all FBI and CIA offices with the cover name COINTELPRO. FBI documents revealed tactics used by the FBI to destroy the effectiveness of militant groups, including blacks, Communists, and Indians. The memorandum directed FBI offices to "expose, disrupt, misdirect, discredit, and otherwise neutralize the groups, activities, and individual names of nationalist hate-type organizations and groupings, their leadership, spokesmen, membership, and supporters" in order to "prevent the rise of a 'messiah' who can unify and electrify the nationalist movement."

An FBI report called me the "principal organizer" of the nineteen-month-long occupation of Alcatraz Island. We used satire and humor as a weapon to win public support. However, the anal-retentive bureaucrats in Washington didn't see it that way, as I was destined to become dog meat because of their dirty tactics. Government officials declared me to be "an enemy of the state," despite the fact that I had violated no federal laws. Alcatraz Island was abandoned as a federal prison in 1963, and the island was declared surplus property in 1968. We occupied the island in 1969.

The covert actions of the government forced my wife and me to move to her reservation in Fallon, Nevada, where we started life all over again in 1976, two years before Patty Hearst was released from prison. On the reservation I built the Round House Gallery, where I sold my jewelry, pipes, sculptures, and leatherwork. I maintained my role as a traditional dancer and ceremony conductor.

Early one morning, I was laying in bed reading a book about Indian history. It is interesting to compare the stories of the past, and think about how circumstances have caused us to adapt to a new way of life. Many

Indians still strive to retain much of our cultural heritage through events like powwows, where living in a teepee can be a reflection of the past.

My reminiscing was interrupted by chattering outside my window. It grew louder and louder as if it was calling for my attention.

I put down the book and listened. It was not my imagination, it was a magpie talking!

I quietly moved to the window and on a fence post, hardly twelve feet away, sat the talking magpie, acting very proud in his black-and-white feathered outfit. He was gabbing away like a politician with a large audience. He paused every so often as if listening to some silent applause from an invisible audience. However, it became apparent that the magpie was trying to tell me something.

He made me think of Sitting Bull, who had been riding his horse out on the prairie when he heard someone call his name. Looking around, he spotted a meadowlark. Sitting Bull had a long connection to the wise old meadowlark. That meadowlark spoke to Sitting Bull, "The Lakotas will kill you! The Lakotas will kill you!"

Sitting Bull was saddened by the prophecy of the meadowlark that his own people would kill him. On December 15, 1890, forty-two Indian police, hired by the government, broke into his cabin and killed Sitting Bull and seven of his followers.

The meadowlark had spoken.

Now my little friend magpie stopped his monologue, took a long look at me, and flew off. What was he trying to tell me? Was he trying to warn me?

One day in 1982 I was approached by a heavyset Indian who identified himself as Keith Taylor of the Siletz Tribe in Oregon. He said he wanted to become a traditional dancer and needed eagle feathers, which I supplied to him, because I believe tribal dancing is a way of maintaining our cultural identity.

A few weeks later, I was surrounded by federal marshals and U.S. Fish and Wildlife officers and arrested for selling eagle feathers to another

Indian. I had been sold out by Keith Taylor, a bounty hunter for the U.S. Fish and Wildlife Department. I offered no resistance to the arrest and thus avoided the possibility of being shot and killed like Sitting Bull.

The magpie had spoken.

A federal jury, after seeing and hearing all the evidence could not convict me of a felony. In fact, it was eleven to one for acquittal, in spite of my admission to the charges. After dropping the felony charges, the government went after me with civil penalties. Without the shield of a jury, the federal judge found me guilty and assessed a fifteen thousand dollar fine plus interest, which I paid off in one-hundred-dollar monthly payments. The monthly billing stopped when I had paid approximately twenty-five thousand dollars. That didn't include my attorney's fees. After all those years of paying one hundred dollars a month to the government, I had finally paid off my debt to society.

As I look back, I can see what we inspired with the nineteen-month-long occupation under the Nixon administration, such as the return of the sacred Blue Lake to the Taos Pueblo, the return of Mt. Adams to the Yakima tribe and the return of thousands of acres to other tribes. And, perhaps more important, President Nixon ended the "Termination Policy" of 1953 and the relocation program of 1958. These were major policy changes that led up to the Indian Self-Determination and Education Assistance Act of 1975, which paved the way for a new future for all tribes. The government withdrew the surplus property status of Alcatraz Island and made it a part of the National Park Service in 1973. Alcatraz is now a major tourist attraction bringing in 1.3 million visitors each year.

To this day, the government refuses to admit the major changes the occupation of Alcatraz brought about, and the role I played as "principal organizer." All you have to do is go back and review the COINTELPRO policy to understand why.

The personal sacrifices I made were a small price to pay for the political advances we made during those turbulent times. Now I am eighty-four years old and I called a federal official and asked, "How long will I carry the title, 'enemy of the state'?"

He replied curtly, "Until you're dead!"

Ho wah! Now if only I could get a presidential pardon.

The Saga of the Lahontan Valley Long-Legged Turtles

Turtles have always played an important role in tribal mythology and lore. The Chippewa creation story tells of how the earth of North America was created on the turtle's back, and to this day we hear tribal references to Turtle Island.

Missed by all the tribal legends and mythology are the unknown, unheralded stories of the legendary turtles of the west.

This is a story of two different but related turtle species: *Owahenis marmorata* and their younger cousins, *Clemmys marmorata*, who took two different paths in evolutionary history. Each has their own story to tell, so I will start with the *Clemmys marmorata* whose story is told on the Fallon Indian Reservation in Nevada.

The fading sun sat down atop the Stillwater Mountains, pausing for a few moments before climbing down into the darkness. The light painted the neat white mobile home a light pink and lengthened the shadow cast by a tall cottonwood in the front yard.

The eager sounds of fighting, resembling loud claps and shouts, filtered through the sliding-glass door into the still air. I sat on the porch, listening to the muffled, slightly tinny noises, and smiled.

I rose from a creaking lawn chair. The white metal skeleton under the cracked vinyl floral cushion was rusted by too many winters outdoors.

"What are you boys watching?" I asked, as I slid the porch door open.

"*Teenage Mutant Ninja Turtles,* Grandpa," said one boy with deep brown eyes, dark skin and a head of jet black hair that was braided into an eight-inch tail. He answered without looking away from the television screen.

"It's this show about four big turtles who are ninja warriors," said the other boy with much shorter hair, who looked enough like the ponytailed boy to be his younger brother. "They fight against these evil guys

---

First published in *In Focus* 6, no. 1 (1992–93): 36–43, Churchill County Museum Association, Fallon, Nevada. Revised 2009 and 2013.

who look like rhinoceroses, rats, and other weird stuff. They're really awesome."

On the screen, one of the human-sized cartoon turtles leapt high into the air and kicked the head of a rat-faced creature dressed like a punk rock motorcyclist. In the same motion, he threw a fork-shaped knife at another creature that resembled a giant lizard.

"Did you know there used to be turtles in this area?" I asked.

"Yeah, right, Grandpa," said the boy with the ponytail. "It this another story like the one about the sea serpent that lives in Walker Lake?"

Smiling, I turned and walked back out onto the porch, closing the door behind me. Within seconds, the two boys opened the door and came out onto the porch.

"Do you boys want to hear about the turtles?" I asked.

"Only because I don't believe you," said the boy with the ponytail, who stood a few inches taller than his brother. "I know this is another of your made-up stories."

I shrugged and then said, "As you say," and began.

"During the heyday of the great dinosaur period, in what is now Nevada there existed a great inland sea. The water teemed with exotic prehistoric life forms ranging from the tiny trilobite to giant ichthyosaurs that were more than sixty-five feet long. And, of course, there was the turtle.

"Life was good in the prehistoric lake, which we now call Lake Lahontan. But one day there was a great upheaval of the earth's crust as the Pacific Plate collided with California and jammed its way into the Sierra Nevadas, crunching and grinding and forcing the mountains even higher.

"The great sea bed of Lake Lahontan was forced upward and the great waters poured onto the land to the south.

"It was as if someone had lifted up one end of a giant bowl of water and spilled it out. All the lake's waters rushed out, cutting a great canyon in the south, which we now call the Grand Canyon.

"Soon the tiny trilobite, the giant ichthyosaur, and all the other sea life disappeared, leaving only the turtle, who was fortunate enough to be able to live in the sea and on land.

"What remained is the land we now call the Great Basin, most of which is desert. In the summer months, the sun beat down on the land, drying out the once-wet ground and heating up the rocks and boulders strewn about the former lake bed.

"The turtle found he could survive the sun's rays but could not abide crawling over the hot rocks. The sunbaked stones blistered his tender underbelly.

"So the turtles began to walk about on their tiptoes to avoid the hot rocks. As each generation of tiptoeing turtles passed, the reptiles' legs gradually grew longer and longer.

"After several millions of years tiptoeing about, the Lahontan Valley turtles developed their unusually long legs, with most of them growing to be more than a foot tall. And the turtles were very proud of themselves for having outwitted the terrible hot rocks.

"Their smug pride was short lived, however, when the cunning coyote discovered the delicious taste of the turtles' long legs.

"So the Lahontan Valley turtle had to develop even longer legs in order to outrun the coyotes. In another million years or so, their legs had sprouted to more than two feet tall. These were turtles who could truly walk tall and proud.

"In time, however, that too was to change. About twenty thousand years ago, two legged ones, who were our ancestors, arrived in the Lahontan Valley. They came in small bands, hunting and gathering as they went. Some of the wanderers discovered the fertile marshes below the Stillwater Mountains.

"These ancient ones called themselves *Newa*, and their descendants are the Shoshone and Paiutes who still live in Nevada.

"The Newa of the marshes soon found out about the delicious taste of the long-legged turtles. But the turtles proved to be a difficult quarry as they outran even the fleetest of the Newa and the turtles' hard shells deflected the Newa arrows.

"To honor the long-legged turtles, the Newa decided to call them *hehwoosh*. The Newa found that the only way they could catch the swift creatures was right after they hatched and were emerging from their sandy nests.

"It also turned out the hehwoosh could be trained to be wonderful pets. The turtle could be taught tricks, just like a dog; they could learn to sit, roll over, and fetch. Additionally, the turtles were excellent babysitters, who could stand watch over an infant—their large shells served like umbrellas and protected a child from the hot sun.

"Soon the turtles were trained to be great watchdogs for the Newa villages. The turtle couldn't bark like a dog, but when a stranger approached, it would jump on top of the grass-thatched lodge in which the Newa lived and shake the hell out of the roof until someone came out to see what the commotion was all about.

"Changing times proved equally difficult for both the Newa and the hehwoosh. In the 1840s, the first of the ruthless and arrogant white men came into Newa territory. He chanced upon a beautiful blue lake in the Great Basin, a remnant of ancient Lake Lahontan.

"To the amazement of the Newa, the white man proclaimed himself the discoverer of the beautiful desert lake and proceeded to give it a new name, Pyramid Lake. The Newa could not believe the audacity of the newcomer, for they had called the lake *Anaho* for many generations.

"The white man who called himself Kit Carson also acquired a Newa name, Kwitup.

"When gold was discovered in California a few years later, the Newa way of life changed forever. Wagon train after wagon train crossed Newa territory carrying loads of gold-hungry white people, who were soon followed by thousands of emigrants and settlers.

"Conflicts developed over the possession of the land and waters of the Great Basin. The Newa found themselves being forced from the choicest of their ancestral lands.

"Not all of the white men were hostile to the Newa. Some accepted the Newa hospitality and camped among them, learning the ancient ways and joining in their feasts and celebrations. They were delighted to be served turtle meat, finding there was both dark and light meat.

"And the turtle could be cooked in many different ways; it could be baked, boiled, fried, roasted, and stewed. There was no need to make mock turtle soup when you had the real thing.

"The white guests were also amazed to see the Newa had trained the turtles to do many things. They could be couriers: the Newa drew messages on their shells (the white man later called these petroglyphs) and sent the hehwoosh running off to the next village.

"In this way, the Newa could invite nearby friends to a ceremony, feast, or other special event. The turtles were also used to send warning messages when hostile white men were approaching.

"And approach they did. Wave after wave of wagons came. The Forty Mile Desert became a mass of rutted trails that can still be seen almost a century and a half later. The white settlers wanted more and more Newa territory, until even the patience of the peaceful Newa was exhausted.

"It wasn't long before the Newa began protecting their lands, harassing the white settlers trying to make them leave.

"The settlers responded by appealing to the United States Army, which in turn summoned Kit 'Kwitup' Carson. Carson boasted, 'Give me eighty good men and I will conquer the entire Newa Nation.'

"Eighty men were selected from crack cavalry units and placed under Kit Carson's command. The arrogant frontiersman reasoned that the Newa were concentrating their attacks near the Forty Mile Desert, where weary and thirsty settlers were more easily assaulted.

"Riding with his unit along the sand dunes adjacent to the marshes in the Lahontan Valley, Carson spotted a dozen Newa men wading in the water, cutting *tule* reeds that could be used for mats or to cover their lodges.

"A Newa sentinel, a keen sighted hehwoosh, spotted the approaching cavalry and ran to the marshes and warned the Newa, who immediately ran to higher ground in the dunes. The cavalry sounded the charge and the eighty well-armed men rode toward the twelve Newa warriors, who were by now accompanied by a pack of turtles.

"The soldiers were supremely confident of a quick victory and they whooped and hollered as they charged the Newa. But their confidence quickly faded when they saw the dozens of long-legged turtles charge down the sand dunes at them.

"The hard shells of the turtles were like battering rams as they charged into the horses' knees and spilled the horrified riders into the sand. Then they faced the free-swinging clubs of the twelve Newa warriors.

"Kit Carson watched in amazement as his compliment of eighty men were rammed, battered, and beaten by the Newa and their turtle allies. He rounded up the remains of his troops, all bloodied and bruised, and headed for a safe haven.

"The place where this battle occurred is still noted on maps of Churchill County as 'the Battle Ground.'

"Soon after reaching Fort Churchill with his men, Carson wrote to the president of the United States, Franklin Pierce, to ask for additional aid. In his letter he explained the situation and noted, 'We cannot fight the Newa man to man. If we do, we will be defeated every time. If we are to subdue the Newa we must destroy his quartermaster, his messengers, and his battering rams, the accursed long-legged turtles.'

"President Pierce was no friend of the Native American and hated turtles even more. For one day, while he was a young man in New Hampshire, he dove into his favorite pond. Unfortunately for him, the pond was also the home of a nearsighted snapping turtle, who mistook Pierce's rather large big toe for a pond delicacy. Without warning, the turtle lunged for the protruding member as he would for a frog on a lily pad.

"Pierce's screams attracted neighbors to the pond, who dragged the young man from the water. They chopped off the turtle's head but were unable to detach it from the boy's toe.

"Now any man of the woods can tell you of the legendary tenacity of the snapping turtle and that even after cutting off its head, its jaws will not relax until the following day.

"Pierce spent a long night in agony and fear and swore eternal revenge on the entire turtle race.

"Needless to say, Carson's message provided him with an opportunity to gain, at long last, some measure of retribution against turtles. And, he realized, this also gave him a chance to remove some Indians that were blocking his dreams for western expansion.

"The president immediately wrote back that Carson had the full force and power of the United States government at his disposal to take care of both the Newa and the long-legged turtles.

"Now Kit Carson was not only mean and arrogant, but he was also extremely clever. His years in the Wild West had equipped him with the skills necessary to resolve almost any situation.

"Carson reasoned that his cavalry troops were no match for the turtles in the sand dunes. The horses foundered on the soft sand, while the turtles ran across the sand and hardly left a track.

"He needed to find an animal that was large and strong, could carry a rider, and was at home in desert sand. Suddenly, the idea was there: camels. He immediately sent for camels from Egypt.

"Once the gangly creatures arrived, however, Carson discovered they weren't the entire answer. For one thing, his soldiers couldn't shoot straight because of the camels' rolling gaits. And the soldiers could not maneuver the long barrels of their .54 caliber Springfields at such close range.

"Then he remembered a game he watched as a boy on the East Coast. The game was polo, performed by a visiting English team. He remembered marveling at the ability of the polo riders, who could, at full gallop, strike a small ball and send it sailing into a net.

"Carson decided to engage a handful of English polo players to teach his soldiers how to play polo from the back of a camel.

"After a few months, Carson had a thousand soldiers mounted on camels who could swing their polo mallets with great dexterity.

"On a cloudy fall morning before dawn, Carson led his men back to the Lahontan Valley. His plan was to surround a Newa village with his troop of 'camel jockeys,' as he called them.

"The faithful sentinel turtles spotted the approaching troops and began shaking the roofs of the tule-covered lodges to arouse the sleeping Newa. Upon seeing the large company of troops, the Newa quickly prepared to defend themselves and sent out the messenger turtles to alert the other villages.

"But Carson was ready. He sent a team of his crack polo soldiers after the messengers. A strange scene unfolded as the soldiers on camelback raced alongside the running turtles and began bashing their heads with the polo mallets.

"It wasn't long before the desert floor was littered with the pulverized remains of the long-legged turtles. Since the soldiers did not know the delicious taste of the turtles, they left them to rot in the sun, taking only their shells as trophies.

"Carson repeated his strategy in village after village until he wiped out every living long-legged turtle. His troops conducted turtle drives throughout the Great Basin to collect the wild turtles. His camel-riding soldiers, more than one thousand strong, formed circles around vast areas of the desert, then closed in on the hapless creatures.

"In less than five years, Carson and his camel jockeys effectively eliminated the long-legged turtle from the Great Basin. In fact, in their zeal, the troops even entered wetlands and marshes to kill off harmless pond turtles to ensure they wouldn't someday grow long legs.

"The Newa continued to fight courageously but without their ally and main food source, they too were powerless before Carson's forces. Eventually, the Newa were rounded up and placed on reservations throughout the Great Basin, such as Stillwater, Pyramid Lake, Schurz, Yomba, and McDermitt, where they live to this day.

"After Kit Carson's victory over the Newa and the long-legged turtles, he had no further use for the camels. History indicates he sold them to American and French entrepreneurs who used them as pack animals to haul supplies to Virginia City's mines.

"The victorious Carson departed Nevada for his next assignment, the conquering of the Navajo people. While the Navajos, who called themselves the Diné, did not have turtles, they did have cultivated gardens and orchards.

"Using a tactic similar to his Nevada campaign, Carson destroyed the Dinés' crops, which starved them into submission.

"An interesting side note is that following the campaign a couple of the soldiers returned to their homes in St. Joseph, Missouri, where they told friends of the incredible long-legged turtle messengers. While no one believed their story, it inspired a couple of local businessmen who copied the idea and organized the Pony Express, which linked St. Joseph with Sacramento, California."

"That's a ridiculous story," the ponytailed boy said. "There's no such thing as a long-legged turtle."

"Of course, you are right," I said. "You children today are so much smarter and more sophisticated than in my day."

The two boys jumped up from the porch floor where they had been sitting and headed back into the house and the flickering television set.

"Yes, these children today learn so much from the television and know so much more than I did when I was their age," I said to no one. Then I smiled again and nodded in the direction of a small, brown-green turtle that was laying in the flowers below the porch. The turtle solemnly winked his eye, stood to its full height of two feet, and trod softly off into the sagebrush.

Mark Your Territory

Have you ever wondered what makes a truly exceptional adventure become the source of legends and campfire stories? Of all the deer hunting expeditions I've experienced over the years, one stands out above the others because of its uniqueness and, perhaps, just a little bit of weirdness. Fifty years later, I can still get a laugh just thinking about it. So, before I take that final journey to the Spirit World, I feel compelled to share my story with you. Or, perhaps it might be a way of purging myself of any lingering guilt I may still carry over the events that occurred that cool autumn weekend.

It was the second week of October—the beginning of Nevada's deer season—when my Shoshone father-in-law, Bodie Graham, and I made our annual pilgrimage to the site of an old mining camp nestled in the foothills of the Desatoya Mountain Range. Our host was a Greek immigrant by the name of George Buzanis, short and stocky—a true western character. His hair was a wild salt-and-pepper gray and he sported a straggly beard that resembled a dandelion going to seed. George wore several layers of worn-out bib coveralls that looked as if they had never come into contact with soap and water. Because of his disconnection with the outside world, his thick Greek accent never seemed to improve. Rumor had it that he killed six men in Chicago in the 1930s. So to avoid the long arm of the law, he took it on the lam to the remote reaches of Nevada and a mining camp run by his Uncle George Makris. Makris later died, leaving George Buzanis the caretaker of a played-out deteriorating mining camp located five miles south of Highway 50, which is affectionately called "The Loneliest Road in America."

George had a small black-and-white longhaired spaniel that looked even worse than his master. What should have been long, silky hair was nothing more than a dirty tangle, locked together by sandburs. Hairballs coughed up by my cat looked better than Dawg. Yep, George was not a very creative fellow, he could not come up with a name for him, so he just called him Dawg. Dawg's only responsibility was camp watchdog, and he was good at it. He could hear an approaching vehicle more than a mile away. A telltale cloud of dust served as a warning to George that someone was approaching camp—was it friend or foe?

As we pulled up in our pickup, George recognized the brown weathered face of Bodie. George leaned his shotgun against a nearby tree, and approached us with a big, happy welcoming smile. "Hallo, my friends, welcome back." He vigorously shook Bodie's hand and then mine. His large powerful hands were like bear paws. As we had always done in past years, we offered George a handful of long, black cigars and a gallon of "Dago red" wine.

Among the groceries we brought were several large steaks we expected to enjoy for dinner. To our surprise, George took those beautiful steaks and cut them into small bits. He then chopped up some vegetables and threw all the fixings into a large pot on the stove. "Greek stew! We're gonna have my famous Greek stew!"

Common sense told me not to challenge George about those chopped up steaks, but I have to admit the stew as fantastic. Afterward the two old men lit up those awful black cigars to go along with the Dago red wine. While they swapped prospecting and mining stories, I turned in for the night.

The clatter of pans on the old wood-burning stove was our wakeup call in the early pre-dawn hours. George Buzanis was already preparing breakfast. The smell of hot coffee and frying bacon and eggs quickly filled the stone cabin. "You gotta eat good; you gotta long day ahead of you. Here, have some more coffee, good Greek coffee."

Ho wah! That coffee was hot, black, thick, and strong. I figure dried-up cow patties brewed in a pot could offer a valid challenge to George's coffee for true grossness and unique flavor. I was not about to criticize my host's prize coffee recipe. For all I knew, he could have killed those six men in Chicago for complaining—I wasn't ready to take that chance.

After loading up our hunting gear, Bodie and I headed out the cabin door. The air was cold and crisp. With no pollution to obscure them, the stars appeared more numerous and brighter than ever. Bodie decided to head out due west toward Buffalo and Skull Canyons, and I headed out toward the northwest, so I could end up north of Campbell Creek Ranch.

About two hundred yards from camp, I stopped to load my hunting rifle, which has a history of its own. It was a .31 caliber Japanese sniper's rifle from World War II, with a chrome bore to protect it from rusting in the humid jungles of the South Pacific. After "sporterizing" and the addition of a four-power telescopic sight, that rifle could blast five shots into a nickel-sized hole at one hundred yards.

Now, with the rifle loaded, I was ready for some serious deer hunting. I took about twenty slow and careful steps, stopped, looked, and listened for a few minutes, then repeated the process until I reached the ridge of the mountain. On the other side, I picked a comfortable spot with a good view of the canyon below me. I waited for half an hour but had no action, so I cautiously stood up and moved on.

The overhead sun told me it was lunchtime. My lunch was rather meager: beef jerky, an apple, and some Fig Newtons—that sweet juicy filling was like instant energy. Supplementing lunch were pine nuts, which lay in profusion around the bases of the piñon trees that dotted the mountainside. I had to be careful not to eat too many of those raw pine nuts, or they could give me a good case of the galloping trots—diarrhea. The pine nuts are much tastier and safer when they are roasted.

As I slowly made my way down the mountainside, I suddenly froze in my tracks as a movement on the mountain slope above me caught my eye. Carefully making its way down the slope toward the ravine below was a huge mule tail buck. He was coming from the direction of Skull Canyon, where I suspected Bodie had flushed him out. I carefully moved toward the ravine, where I hoped to intercept that huge buck. When I got there, the mule tail had disappeared. I stood on a small knoll just beyond the spot I thought I would have intercepted him. Seeing nothing up ahead, I turned around and followed my back trail to discover that wily buck sneaking away with his head and antlers held low. I figured he had laid down next to a sagebrush bush and let me walk by, no more than twenty feet away, and now he reversed course to make his getaway. One well-placed shot put an end to the game. He was magnificent! His horns had a twenty-eight-inch spread and were a classic four-pointer western count. He must have weighed over two hundred pounds. I field dressed him with a Mora knife made in Finland. Its laminated steel blade was as sharp as a razor, which made the job easier.

As I completed my messy task, I noticed the sun was dipping toward the western horizon. There was no way I could get that big buck out of the mountains before dark, and that left me with a real problem to deal with. I could leave the buck to become coyote bait, or I could stay with it all night and risk freezing my butt in the frigid high altitude of the mountains.

Out of desperation, I decided to try something different. Using the rope I carried coiled around my waist, I hoisted that buck as high as I could in a nearby piñon tree; even then it was within reach of the hungry coyotes. I put the liver and heart in a small cloth sack, which I tied high enough to be safe, and then dragged the guts and stuff thirty feet away.

Knowing that all carnivores mark their territory, I just had to take a chance it would work for humans as well. So, I whipped out my baby maker and peed the biggest circle my bladder could accommodate around the base of the tree that held my buck. Now, I wondered if the code of the wild would honor my marked territory. By tomorrow morning I would have the answer.

As the sun was setting, the "*yip, yip, yip*" of a nearby coyote let me know I was being watched. Hurriedly, I made my way down the canyon because darkness was settling in. Once I arrived at the mouth of the canyon at the valley floor, I tied a white cloth to a pine tree to mark the right canyon for the next morning. Heading south toward camp, I found it necessary to traverse several small foothills in the dark, not knowing exactly how far I was away from camp. Then, in the distance, I heard a horn honking. It had to be Bodie, knowing I might be lost in the darkness. On the crest of the next hill I spotted the welcoming glow of the headlights.

Bodie and Buzanis roared with laughter as I recited my day's adventure and how I marked my territory around my kill. Neither one believed my trick would work. It was a restless night of worry and concern for the safety of our winter supply of venison. Before dawn, Bodie and I were already in the pickup, the headlights picking out the dim dirt road, which skirted the edge of the mountains.

"There it is!" That white cloth marker had done its job. After a long hike up the canyon, I held my breath as we cautiously approached the tree that held my buck. To my relief, he was untouched and in perfect condition. The peace offering of the pile of guts had been completely eaten. Some coyotes tried kicking dirt over the invisible pee barrier to form a bridge, but my medicine worked.

"I wouldn't have believed it if I had not seen it with my own eyes," exclaimed Bodie in surprise.

After a struggle, we hauled that huge buck to the pickup and back to camp where Buzanis prepared a feast of fresh venison liver smothered in onions and a steaming side dish of boiled potatoes. It was so delicious. As my reward, I helped myself to seconds, after which I went for a walk to settle down the food.

An abandoned ore mill was only two hundred feet from the stone cabin. The massive wooden beams were showing the ravages of the elements, and what metal machinery was left was no more than rusty hulks. The fascination with the ruins turned to shock as I discovered a lone stick of dynamite sitting exposed on a remote shelf. A closer look revealed the dynamite was sweating from prolonged exposure. That sweat was pure nitroglycerine! I knew that liquid nitro was unstable, dangerous, and highly explosive. I remembered, too, that instructions on dynamite cases carry the warning to store in a cool, dry place. The coolest place I could think of that was nearby was the pit under the outhouse, which sat between the mill and the stone cabin. Ever so carefully, I picked up the stick of sweaty dynamite with the tips of my fingers. Slowly and gingerly I approached the outhouse with that lethal load in my trembling hands.

There was a small opening behind the outhouse that led to the pit below. Holding my breath, I slowly rolled the dynamite down that opening and took off running toward the stone house. A muffled boom made me stop in my tracks. Turning around, I saw the outhouse door blown off its hinges, followed by a loud "*Wahhh!*" and then a womp! George Buzanis laid in a cloud of dust, kicking and screaming in rage. I couldn't understand what he was hollering, so I figured he was cussing in Greek.

His three pairs of bib coveralls were tangled around his ankles and his big bare ass was exposed for all the world to see. When Bodie quickly ran to the scene and found that Buzanis was not really hurt, he couldn't suppress his laughter any longer, no matter how hard he tried. We both helped our stricken friend to his feet so he could pull himself together.

Buzanis gave me a look that reminded me of a little ditty, "Little man, little man, so spick-and-span, where were you when the shit hit the fan?"

"*Ho wah!* There must have been some pent-up methane gas that somehow ignited by spontaneous combustion," I alibied with the best excuse I could think of. George looked at me sideways. Those angry, beady eyes glared at me from under his bushy eyebrows and told me he wasn't buying my story.

George went to his grave never really knowing what blew his ass out of that outhouse, and I never told my father-in-law, Bodie, what really happened that day. Should anyone ever question the veracity of my story, I still have that outhouse door here on the Fallon Indian Reservation.

* * *

Every day Buzanis and Dawg walked two hundred feet along a dirt path to fetch water from a small spring snuggled into the hillside. That cold clear water provided for their daily use in the stone cabin. It was a simple daily chore, which turned tragic as Buzanis suffered a heart attack and fell dead on the dirt path. His loyal friend Dawg stood guard over his dead master.

Campbell Creek Ranch sits at the foot of a canyon in the Shoshone Mountain Range. At least once a week Buzanis and Dawg hiked from the mining camp to the ranch five miles away to pick up supplies, mail, and hopefully a check from George Scorros in Oakland, California, who was grubstaking Buzanis's mining operation.

One week Buzanis and Dawg did not show up for their weekly supply run. A few days later concerned ranch hands rode out to the mining camp to check on their old grizzled friend, only to find his bloated body lying on the dirt path, still being guarded by his faithful friend Dawg.

The ranch hands were shocked at the morbid sight of their dead friend, and their hearts reached out to poor Dawg, who had stood his post for more than a week without food or water. He was emaciated and near death, so a single shot from a .45 caliber Colt revolver put Dawg out of his misery.

Buzanis and his faithful companion, Dawg, were buried in a shallow grave on a bluff overlooking the beautiful Reese River Valley. A small pile of rocks marks the gravesite. There's a single eagle feather wedged among them.

Sonny Mosquito and the Chicken Dance

Starting out on the Powwow Trail is always a time of great anticipation and excitement, for we never know what type of adventures lie ahead. The preparation requires careful planning, especially for those trips that will last several weeks; for no one wants to find himself several hundred miles away from the reservation only to discover he forgot the Coleman lantern or its replacement mantels.

Over the many years of hitting the powwow circuit, I have found it interesting to note the changes in the equipment I take on the road and to experience how convenient and comfortable new developments make life on the trail.

At first, we took a steel grill to put over the campfire to cook on. We soon moved on to a secondhand, pump-up model camp stove that used kerosene. It was erratic and unpredictable, and, just like a woman, it would get too hot or too cold and it was stubborn! I'd fill the tank with fuel, pump it up, turn on the valve, and light it with a wooden match. If I was lucky it would burst into a beautiful bluish-red flame, and cooking breakfast on a chilly morning was an absolute delight. Or, I could pump the heck out of the tank, turn the valve, and light it, only to have the feeble flame quit after wheezing and chuffing along for a couple of minutes. I'd repeat the process several times, as I tried to keep my temper down. The worst situation occurred when I'd light it and the flame belched upward two to three feet like a huge blowtorch, sending everyone running for cover because they expected that fire-belching green dragon to blow up.

Finally, we could afford a beautiful propane-fueled cooking stove. The stove sits on its own little folding stand. On the ground sits the fat little gas cylinder with a little black hose connecting the two units together like an umbilical cord. No more pumping, no more trepidation at lighting

---

First published in *In Focus* 4, no. 1 (1990–91): 44–52, Churchill County Museum Association, Fallon, Nevada. Revised 2009 and 2013.

it—just open the valve on the tank, turn the valve on the stove, and light it. The only problem now is, where the heck do we find propane when the little tank runs out of gas? Some of the reservations are miles from the nearest town.

Camping equipment checked out, it's on to other tasks. Last minute repairs are made on our dance outfits; we check out our eagle feather bustles to see that everything is secure. If the strings are worn out, we replace them with new ones, as dropping a feather in a powwow can be a very bad experience. Our regular clothing is also checked, then packed. Over a period of time I have developed a system of packing the van—everything goes in its own place. Things we need most often are more accessible, while the camp gear is tucked into the most remote spaces.

Teepee poles are tied snugly together and then lifted up and onto the roof of the van. The teepee cloth cover acts like a cushion for the poles. Over that we tie down our camp chairs and grub box. After tying red warning flags to the front and rear ends of the long, overhanging teepee poles, we are ready. I jam a powwow tape into the cassette player to set the proper mood, and we head out our dirt driveway to the paved road. We are on the Powwow Trail!

Three days later, we are winding down the road from the Blackfoot Reservation at Browning, Montana, toward the grassy prairies of the southern Alberta province of Canada. It is a relief to get out of the Rocky Mountains, with its numerous wooden crosses marking the demise of the unfortunate travelers who failed to negotiate its treacherous curves.

Our destination is a small Kainai reservation at Stand Off, Alberta. As we approach the powwow area, all we can see is a thick stand of trees sitting out in the prairie. The encampment is well hidden in the shadowy depths of the grove. In no time, we too are swallowed up by its murky shadows—only it's like a journey into another time. Teepees and tents are everywhere and more are going up all the time, for this is camp day. The village is alive with people, and children are happily running around. The mood is definitely festive.

As is our custom when we arrive at camp, we circle it a time or two, searching for a nice place to set up our teepee and to gather the energy together. At a ceremonial gathering, we will circle the camp four times to bring good energy and feelings into the place. At the south side of the camp, a tall, gaunt man walks out to greet us. It's Sonny Mosquito! To a stranger, Sonny looks kind of strange: his deep-set eyes peer out through dark rims; his nose is long and angular, sticking out between hollow cheeks. His lips are a little pouty, and it seems like he has too many teeth—as his front ones are slightly protruding. His scrawny figure adds to Sonny's unsettling appearance, but those who know him see a very special and kind person.

Both his father and uncle are medicine men who seem to have a little competition going on between them. Maybe it's a sibling rivalry they never outgrew, but fortunately for all of us it is a friendly rivalry. In time, Sonny might become a medicine man, but in the meantime, he is very active in keeping the traditions and teachings alive. He is a renowned singer, knowing many powwow songs: Round Dance, Owl Dance, Honor Songs, and sacred songs—many of them handed down through his family. However, he did not come to the Stand Off Powwow as only a Grass Dancer. He has outfits for several different styles of dance, including the Traditional Dance.

Sonny gives me a big toothy smile, as he shakes my hand and makes us welcome. "Here's a good spot to pitch your teepee," he says, pointing to a smooth spot of ground below a large overhanging tree that would provide welcome shade during the hot part of the day. The spot is not too far from his group of family teepees, so later on it will be easy for him to visit.

It doesn't take my wife, Bobbie, and me long to set up our teepee. All seventeen poles have their places in the circle. After the canvas is stretched over the framework of poles, the lower edges are staked down and, finally, the poles holding open the smoke flaps are installed. Inside, a floor covering is laid on the ground and we haul in the bedding material and the rest of the items necessary to make our teepee a cozy home. While Bobbie is arranging the cooking area, we hear the powwow master of ceremonies announce that signups are open for the various categories of dance competition.

Sonny Mosquito stops by and says, "Come on, Adam. Let's go sign up."
Together we walk across the still-growing campground. A work crew
is stretching indoor-outdoor carpet over the dance arena. We stop in the
middle of it in wonder and stomp on it a few times to test it out.

"I've never danced on a carpet at an outdoor powwow," I comment.

"Me neither," answers Sonny. "This is what you call 'progress,' I guess."

We laugh as we continue our way to the sign-up table. Other dancers
are already there and, as they are signing up, we look at the bulletin board
listing the various categories—especially the men's categories—and the
prizes to be awarded. All the men's categories list first place winnings
at $800, second place at $500, and third place at $300. But something
is different! There, listed below the Senior Men's Traditional category is
"Prairie Chicken Dance." *Ho wah!* I've never seen this category listed in
competition at any powwows in the United States.

I ask the girl sitting at the table, "Who can get into this category?"

"Anyone who wants to give it a try," she says with a laugh.

"You mean a dancer can enter in more than one category?"

"That's right. If you are eligible, you can sign up in as many categories
as you want."

Sonny says, "Let's sign up and go for it. What have we got to lose?"
He also signs up for the Grass Dance category. I sign up for the Chicken
Dance, Men's Traditional, and, since I am over fifty years old, I sign up in
the Senior Men's Traditional category as well.

As Sonny and I walk back toward our teepee, he points to another guy
walking to the right of us. "See that guy over there?" Sonny asks. "He's
the champion Chicken Dancer around here. He's won the championship
three years in a row at this powwow. He's got some damn good moves.
Keep your eye on him during the powwow and you might be able to pick
up on them. Look at the proud way he walks. He even walks like a champion rooster."

When we arrive at my teepee, Sonny Mosquito turns into "Coach"
Mosquito. "Those Lakota Chicken Dancers down in South Dakota do
a lot more bending over at the waist during the dance. Sometimes they
look like nearsighted guys looking for dropped coins on the ground. Up

here, we don't bend so much and we shake our shoulders more." Sonny stands there assuming the posture of a Chicken Dancer, much to the amusement of my wife, Bobbie, who's watching the demonstration and coaching from the door of the teepee. I'm facing Sonny and feeling a little silly as I pose like a chicken too.

In the adult categories of the competition, three qualifiers are picked by the judges to go into the finals. So, at the end of three sessions, there will be nine finalists in each category. In the first session, all men who have signed up for the Chicken Dance are called out to the dance arena. The drum starts with a ruffled tempo. The dancers move out to the tempo of the drum, posturing and shaking their bustles like a covey of prairie chickens doing a mating ritual. The drum suddenly stops and the dancers have to stop right on the final beat. Then the tempo of the drum picks up into a solid War Dance beat. All the dancers change their dance steps to maintain the solid beat of the drumming, slightly bowing and shaking their shoulders as they go through the moves of a prairie chicken. All of us dancers stop right on the final beat of the drum, and the audience applauds the performance.

At the end of the first night's sessions, the emcee announces the qualifiers for the finals. The three-year champion is the first one called, followed by Sonny Mosquito and myself. On the way back to the teepee, Sonny and I congratulate each other for making it into the finals. It's then that I confide to Sonny that in all the dance competitions I have ever entered into during my many years of powwow dancing, this is the first time I've ever competed in the Chicken Dance.

Sonny laughs out loud in disbelief and says, "I've seen you dancing at powwows all over the United States for many years."

"But," I respond, "have you ever seen me Chicken Dance?"

Sonny stops and thinks about it a moment. "Come to think about it, I haven't." He starts laughing again. "Damn, Adam, you're all right!"

The next morning, Bobbie fixes us breakfast over our new propane gas stove. The smell of fresh-brewed coffee in the outdoors takes on a special fragrance along with the sizzling sound of bacon and eggs. The coolness of the morning only serves to stimulate our appetites. We chow down breakfast, sitting on folding camp chairs at a folding table with one gimpy leg that requires a little wire wrapping to make sure it doesn't fold up on us while we are eating.

Mid-morning at many powwows is a great time for visiting. It doesn't take long for the sun to take the chill out of the air, and life in the camp picks up in quiet intensity as the women tend to their tasks around the teepees and dress up the children so they can go out and play. Sonny Mosquito stops by to visit. We invite him to sit down and then pour him a cup of coffee. Our little coffeepot sure gets a workout at the powwows. We always serve coffee to our drop-in guests. It seems to relax them as they sip the steaming hot coffee and we talk.

"You know there's a buffalo jump a few miles over there." Sonny sweeps his arm in the southeast direction. "There's still a lot of old bleached buffalo bones at the bottom of the cliff. One of these days I'd like to take you guys over to see it."

Anyone who's read books about the early Indian days in the prairie knows about the buffalo jumps. Waving blankets and pounding their hand drums, the Indians stampeded the buffaloes over a cliff. It was a time of great celebration and feasting. Delicacies like tongue, liver, and heart were eaten while they were fresh. The meat was sliced thin by the women and hung up to dry, and then stored away for the winter months. Sometimes several tons of buffalo jerky could be prepared in this way. When the cavalry attacked the Cheyenne camp of Morning Star in October 1876, they gathered up all the possessions of the tribe: buffalo robes, teepees (some were beautifully decorated with sacred designs and quillwork), and all the cooking utensils and tools. The troops threw everything into a huge pile. The troopers also found tons of buffalo jerky and threw that onto the pile, and then they set fire to it. The surviving Cheyennes were reduced to hunger and starvation and were more easily rounded up and put on a reservation at Lame Deer, Montana. Afterward, the cavalry realized they had made a stupid mistake. They were short on rations and a brutal winter was rapidly approaching, and they had just burned tons of meat.

It's conversations like this that are part of the oral traditions of our people. Legends and the ceremonial ways are also discussed, so there can be a beautiful understanding of our heritage. It's powwows like this that draw together people of many tribes in a social way, so that this knowledge can be shared and passed on. Young urban Indians find these types of gatherings very educational in the traditional ways of our people, since such experiences could never be obtained from a book.

I pour Sonny another cup of coffee and we switch our conversation to powwow talk. He laughs as he tells Bobbie about us qualifying in the first round for the finals of the Chicken Dance. That means we can sit and watch the next two qualifying rounds. Sonny also qualifies for the finals in the Grass Dance competition, and I still have enough stuff in me to qualify in both the Men's Traditional and Senior Men's Traditional categories. Now we can both kick back and watch the other dancers do their thing. When you are over fifty years old, you have to take every advantage to save your energy and strength.

As in any athletic or dancing competition, I psych myself up before the actual event and get the adrenalin pumping in my sometimes-protesting veins. When the drumbeat starts, I move out into the arena, stomping in rhythm to the beat of the drum. Sometimes the dancing produces a euphoria and exhilaration found nowhere else, because the solid drumbeat is like the beat of my heart. The chiming of the bells strapped around my ankles are like a chorus of small spirits singing to my delight—twisting, turning, and bowing—all in time with that lovely drum and the singers with their high falsetto voices that climb to the heavens. All around is a swirling mass of other dancers: men bedecked in eagle feather bustles that gently brush against me as they dance by, and women Traditional Dancers in their hand-tanned buckskin dresses that are decorated with a profusion of beads and dentalia shells. Or, occasionally, I've seen a classic elk tooth dress. The younger women have colorful shawls draped over their shoulders, with various traditional decorations on them. The shawls are trimmed with long fringes that add to the movement of their graceful, active footwork. The Shawl Dancer is the women's version of the men's Fancy Dancer.

"When you dance, dance proud," my Crow brother once told me, "for you are dancing before the Great Spirit who made a dancer of you. Show your pride!"

There is no question about it. Everyone in that circling mass of dancers is both proud and happy.

The three-day powwow passes all too quickly. Before we know it, the final night of the powwow has arrived and the final competitions for all the adult categories are to be held. The master of ceremonies calls out the finalists in each group—Women's Fancy Shawl, Women's Traditional, Men's Fancy, Men's Traditional, Grass Dance, and Men's Senior Traditional. Each group goes through a series of songs appropriate for that category. Sonny and I both go through our categories and, in between sessions, we stand together, happily talking about the competition.

"Adam, those shoulder moves you do look good. Those ermine skins attached to your shirt swing and move real good as you shake your shoulders!" Sonny "The Coach" Mosquito is at it again, offering his knowledge of the dance and type of moves that looked best in that dance.

The time of the Chicken Dance competition finally arrives. The emcee calls out the nine men finalists into the arena. The champion strides out with a look of confidence on his face, for he's been in this situation many times before. Sonny and I shake hands and wish each other good luck, and we both go out into the arena to assume our positions.

Waiting in that cool evening for our category to start causes me to cool off and my muscles to stiffen a bit, so I start a mild form of calisthenics to loosen up my aging bones. All the time I'm thinking, "I've gotta loosen up, 'cause when the dance starts I'm going to dance like I've got no bones in my body. I'm going to shake and bow and make those moves in the most fluid way possible. Remember, this Prairie Chicken Dance is a reenactment of the mating ritual of the prairie chicken. I've got to dance like a horny little rooster putting the make on those cute chicks out there. Yah! That's it! Dance like a horny chicken and go all out in the contest 'cause this is the last category."

I take several breaths of air, deep, real deep, filling in all the little pockets in my lungs with air almost to the point of hyperventilating.

"Dance like a horny chicken," I mutter again to myself as the drum starts the ruffle part of the dance, in which the little rooster goes through a series of moves, shuffling his feet rapidly as he struts and preens his extended feathers. I try to think of myself as that little rooster trying to stir the libido of the admiring hens.

"Shake those shoulders; shake those shoulders!" It seems as though I can hear Sonny's instructions in my ears as I shake my shoulders, bowing and turning in graceful circles as I shuffle along. *Ho wah,* this feels good!

The drum suddenly stops. I stop right on the beat, bowing and shaking my shoulders as I do. Then the drum starts a solid War Dance beat. We stomp that indoor-outdoor carpet until the dust flies out. All nine dancers really turn on the moves. The champion whoops and hollers as he raises his coup stick and makes a beautiful turn, and he stomps the trembling ground in time with the great drum. I wear an eagle feather back bustle with the feathers spread out, similar to that of the rooster prairie chicken. When I shake my hips, the eagle feather bustle exaggerates the moves, making it appear as though I'm moving more than I really am. I sneak a quick look at the audience and spot several young women looking at me with admiring eyes.

I think, "*Ho wah!* This aging rooster can still turn the heads of chicks!"

The powerful beat of the drum, the high-pitched singing, the loud tinkling of ankle bells, and the rhythmic stomping of our moccasined feet create a mood that makes me forget I'm over fifty, and I'm out here dancing with guys young enough to be my sons. We are dancing a dance that takes us back in space and time to a more peaceful time when the Indian lived as one with all life around him—emulating the forces of nature, of procreation, of life itself! The mighty drum suddenly stops. All nine dancers stop right on the final beat. We let out war whoops to express our joy. We line up by the announcer's stand, enjoying the applause and shouts of approval from the audience. The judges have their jobs cut out for them as they mark their scorecards, double-checking the numbers pinned to the dancers. Their faces are stoic and give no hint of who they are voting for. When they are through marking their scorecards, the head judge waves us off. Sonny and I almost stumble out of the arena as the exertion of the dance starts to show itself. I am puffing and wheezing, still trying to catch my breath, as we find a space under the arbor to await the announcement of the winners. At the other side of the arena, the champion is surrounded by a circle of friends who had been cheering for him during the contest.

"And now, for the winners of the Chicken Dance competition," the announcer booms out over the PA system.

Sonny looks at me with a big smile on his sweaty face. "It's time," he shouts over the din of the crowd.

"The third place winner in the Chicken Dance contest is Charlie Fast Bull from Hobbema, Canada!"

"Hey, that's the champ!" yells Sonny. "Somebody has just knocked off the three-year champion!"

Charlie, the dethroned champ, walks slowly across the arena to receive his $300 prize.

"For second place in the Chicken Dance contest, we call out Sonny Mosquito."

"Way to go, Sonny!" I shout, slapping him on the back. "You've beaten the champ!"

Sonny runs in a slow gait over to the head judge to collect his $500 prize.

"Who's the new champ?" I think to myself as I look around the arena at the other competitors. "They all danced great."

Before I can make my guess, the announcer breaks into my thoughts. "And now, ladies and gentlemen, I'm proud to announce the new Chicken Dance champion, from Fallon Indian Reservation in Nevada; a member of the Chippewa tribe, the new champion is Adam Fortunate Eagle!" The emcee milked that announcement for all it was worth, but who cares? I am the surprised winner!

The audience lets out a roar of applause and shouting as I bound across the indoor-outdoor carpet–covered arena.

Sonny rushes out to greet me. "You did it, Adam. You did it! You pulled it off! You've beaten the three-year champion!" He pumps my hand and pounds me on the back at the same time as we walk over to the head judge to collect my $800 cash prize and a small trophy which reads: KAINAI INDIAN DAYS—1982—CHICKEN DANCE.

That little trophy may look a little funky for a tribal event, for standing on top is a figure representing a Roman athlete holding aloft a laurel wreath as a symbol for victory. That little Roman athlete represents a winner, a champion from another culture, and he appears to be saying to me, "You, too, are a winner, a champion. In fact you, Fortunate Eagle, are an international Chicken Dance champion!"

Come to think of it, have you ever met a Chicken Dancer?

Ho wah!

White Man Sweats Him

It was the fall of 1982 when I had the great honor of presenting a special pipe to Elwood Cashuway. He is an elder of a tribe in Oklahoma, and he is a roadman in the Native American Church. I wanted to dedicate the pipe and present it to Elwood at a particular ceremony. And so I called on friends. I called on two Sun Dancers who were to conduct the ceremony. One was Delmar Blind Man, a Lakota. The other was Lee Palonca, who also ran sweats. He is a Chicano guy, but his heart is really Indian. Actually, Delmar was to lead the ceremony and Palonca was to back him up and act as his helper, his assistant.

We planned the ceremony, and along with those two were my niece Cathy, my son Adam, and two of Cashuway's sons. And as we prepared the day of the ceremony itself, we had to wait for Palonca to show up from Carson City. He had no car of his own so he had to hitchhike from Carson City. Well, as it turned out, this white guy, Bob, was driving along the highway and he saw this little Chicano standing there beside the road with his suitcase. First he passed him and went on to do what he had to do, and then he circled back. And when he drove past that spot, there was Palonca, still standing out there waiting for a ride. So Bob thought, "Well, why not give him a ride?"

Bob turned around and stopped and asked Palonca where he was headed. Palonca told him Fallon, and as it happened, that's where Bob was also headed. Well, they got to talking, and when Bob asked him where in Fallon he was going, Palonca said, "The reservation to perform a ceremony."

That piqued Bob's interest, and when they pulled into Fallon, instead of just dropping Palonca in town, Bob asked where the reservation was located. And when Palonca told him it was only eight miles out of town, Bob said, "Oh, I'll take you out to the reservation."

So, Bob drove Palonca out to the reservation, and in the meantime, we were wondering where Palonca was, because he was late and all the preparations had been made. The rocks had been heating for the sweat and everything was ready. And we kept looking down the road hoping to see Palonca. Finally, there came this car, and we saw Palonca with a white guy. We thought maybe Palonca was bringing a friend. Palonca introduced us to Bob and told us how he'd been so nice to pick him up and drive him all the way from Carson City, and how he had this great interest in the Indian way. So, being hospitable, I asked Bob if he had ever seen a Sweat Lodge Ceremony, and if he would like to participate. He said, "Oh, yes. I'd love that."

I asked if he had swimming trunks with him. He said, "Yes." I told him to get his trunks and grab a towel and he could join us. And, that's how a white man came to be in our sweat lodge. Well, the rest of us were all primed. Some of us had swimming trunks on, and some didn't have anything—just a towel wrapped around. So, we all squatted down inside the lodge. Elwood and I were on the west side of the lodge in the place of honor, because the honor was for him—the Ceremony of the Pipe—while Delmar and Palonca were to run the sweat ceremony. So, we had a ceremony within a ceremony—that is a Dedication of the Pipe within the Sweat Lodge Ceremony.

We closed the door, and went through the first round of prayers. And it was hot. Delmar is a Sun Dancer, and he likes his sweats hot. And Bob, well this was the first sweat for that white man. He was rather heavyset, big and somewhat overweight. From where we sat we could see everyone inside, and we could see Bob was kind of squirming around. The water was just pouring off his body, and he seemed to be having trouble with his legs being held so long in one position. So he moved them about, and because his legs were so wet, he kept picking up dirt from the floor. But he said he wanted to continue.

So we went into the second round—this, by the way, was an herbal sweat—we had prepared various types of herbs and put them in the water. And so when the water with the herbs was poured over the hot rocks, it made a beautiful aroma. And some of those herbs were sacred—tobacco, sweetgrass, and sage—and their combined strong aroma added to the spirituality of the sweat.

And when it got to the end of the second round and the flap was opened, and the water was passed around, Delmar drank it with the herbs and commented on how good it was, "Hey, this tastes good." Palonca sucked the herb water through his teeth to strain them out, so he ingested the water flavored with the herbs, but not the herbs so he didn't have the aftertaste. Then he gave water to the Stone People, drank some, and blessed the water. It is a renewal when we take the water. The next dipper of water went to the younger Cashuway, Bob Cashuway, and then to his brother. And they did it like Palonca, sipping from the dipper and straining out the herbs with their teeth.

Now Bob, the white man sitting next to them, did not know what was going on. And when Delmar Blind Man dipped into the bucket and handed the full dipper with the herbal water to the white guy, the water had all these branches and twigs in it. So Bob gulped the water down as if it was ordinary water. He started coughing and choking and gagging on all the leaves and little sticks. And, of course by this time, the end of the second sweat, he was pretty well caked with mud. He was in real agony and made all these horrible animal noises trying to get that material out of his mouth and throat. We all watched. There was really nothing any of us could do in that situation, because Bob had to work it out himself. He made retching sounds, and kept coughing, and spit out that mixture of phlegm and herbs in his hand, and he said plaintively, "What do I do with this?" because obviously he doesn't want to do the wrong thing and maybe offend us Indians.

"Well," Delmar said quietly, "rub it on the ground." And Bob looked relieved and rubbed it on the ground. The water ritual continued, going around the circle until everyone had taken water and blessed the Stone People.

By this time Bob was obviously very uncomfortable. He was kind of sulking and he explained to us that this was his first sweat and that he just wasn't used to that kind of heat. His body was very grimy and he was very sweaty, and to us he really looked to be in pretty bad shape. So, I suggested that perhaps this was enough for him, seeing as it was his first sweat. But he said that he would like to go through at least one more round, and that he would like to be involved in the Pipe Ceremony. So I said it was okay. If he felt he could take it, all right, so long as he wasn't going to come to any harm.

So, new water was brought in. We closed the sweat lodge and the prayers were called. And then I noticed that Bob was praying in Japanese! He got so involved he stopped speaking English and started praying in a different language—in Japanese. To my ears it was an unusual thing to be hearing in the sweat lodge.

We completed the third round and opened the door. And Bob said he hoped that now we would have the Pipe Ceremony, because he could not take any more. We purified the pipe and blessed it. The pipe was outside on the mound that is the altar of our Earth Mother. And we blessed the pipe again, brought it inside the lodge, and prayed over it. This was a very emotional time, because this was the coming out of a very special pipe, and it was going to a special person. So we again blessed the pipe and all the people that would be using the pipe, so that no harm would come to any of the people who would be smoking it. I handed the pipe to Elwood, and he prayed over the pipe and, as I said, this was a very emotional moment, and while Elwood was praying he was also crying. Elwood was the oldest among us, and there was this beautiful elder sitting among us, praying and crying at the same time over that pipe. That was good medicine. Elwood returned the pipe to me, and I lit it, made the offerings to the Four Directions, to the Great Spirit in the center above and the Earth Mother in the center below, and I passed the pipe around the circle until everyone had smoked. Then I smoked out of the pipe and then had the pipe replaced on the altar outside the lodge.

Then I told Bob, "I think maybe you better leave, because we are starting the fourth round and you need to take care of your body. It's the only body you got, and you got to take care not to hurt it."

So Bob took his leave at that time from the sweat lodge. He crawled out of the lodge, and we commenced with the fourth and final round.

Now, we didn't know what was going on outside, but what happened was this. Bob headed for the house and he went inside. And there was Bobbie, and she had never seen him before. And there was this strange white man in bathing trunks, wet with sweat and covered from head to foot with mud. Then she realized that this was the man who had brought Palonca and, being who she is, said, "Would you like a shower?"

And he said, "Oh, yes. Yes."

And she showed him where to go. He went into the bathroom, washed down, and came out dressed. And Bobbie said, "Well, that's better. Would you like to stay and eat with us?"

He thanked her, but declined. He was exhausted, he explained, and a bit upset. He had some medical problems, and he had better head on home.

Well, she thought that was odd and not right, that he had been in the sweat and now he had showered, and he should have stayed and eaten and he should not just leave Palonca there. But that is what he did. He got in his car and drove off.

Well, as I said, we didn't know any of this because we were back inside the lodge, commencing the fourth round. And in that, when the water was poured on the red-hot stones, I suddenly noticed something very strange. Coming out of the pit where the rocks were, was a purplish material mound of fluid, just sort of bubbling up, and I kept watching that purplish material come higher and higher, and then subside again and disappear under the rock. I shook my head, and sang along with the singing. And then I saw that purple material coming right up again from the pit. I just couldn't believe this thing, and I reached over and shook Elwood.

"Elwood. Hey, look at that," and then I stopped. I thought this is what I was seeing, and he may not be seeing the same thing at all. So I shut up. But that purple stuff bubbled up and then went away again. And, so we completed the ceremony and the door was opened. And we talked about what a beautiful sweat it was, that what had occurred was one of the most profound and heavy ceremonies. We compared the emotions that took place when the pipes were brought in—different people had different emotions, different feelings.

We left the lodge and went into the house, where Bobbie had prepared a feast. We took offerings of the foods, a little bit of each of the foods, out to the fire that had heated the stones. We made the food offerings to the Sacred Fire and all the spirits. And after the Offering Prayers were said over the food we sat down to eat. And when I started to eat, some of the others started to tell their versions of what had happened. And it became more and more hilarious, because each of us perceived what had happened with Bob in a different way. Because when the first and second doors were opened, the Indian guys were watching Bob, who was looking straight across at an Indian woman—looking at her legs. And one of those guys, Bob Cashuway, had this thought running through his mind, "Look at that white man, admiring that beautiful Indian girl here. He shouldn't be doing that kind of thing."

We were all chuckling over that, and then somebody said, "Well, he paid for it—choking on that water with the herbs, all that choking."

And Delmar Blind Man said, "Yes. When he started choking on those herbs, I moved a little away from him. I watched him and I kept thinking, this guy is going to barf and I just hope he doesn't barf on our rocks, because if this white man barfs on our rocks, that would be just terrible—that would drive us right out of the lodge."

That caused great amusement. So, as each of us told something else, there was more and more hilarity, and everybody agreed that that whole episode was going to go right into our store of sweat lodge stories.

So, somebody said to Lee Palonca, "Your friend Bob."

And Lee Palonca said, "What do you mean, my friend? I never met the guy before today. He just gave me a ride." And he explained what had happened with Bob—how Bob had seen him with his suitcase hoping to get a ride, and how Bob had picked him up, and gotten interested, and volunteered to drive him all the way to the reservation. "I never met the guy before."

I said, "But he had his swimming trunks with him!"

"Well, sure," said Lee, "but that was just a coincidence. He didn't know anything about any Sweat Lodge Ceremony."

And, of course, that started us all laughing even harder. Because there I was, inviting a total stranger to participate in a sweat, because I thought he was a friend of Lee's, whom Lee had invited to the ceremony.

And we practically choked over what we imagined that white guy was going to tell his friends: "Hey, there I was, driving down the road, minding my own business, and I gave this Chicano a ride. And before I knew it, I was on the reservation and I was stripped and boiled half to death, and they tried to choke me to death with some water full of vegetable matter. They almost killed me, almost cooked me to death. And I was covered with mud." And he went home to his wife. Can you imagine the kind of stories he told his woman? "Honey, you'll never believe what happened to me. I picked up this hitchhiker, this Chicano, and we went out to this reservation, and they asked me if I wanted to be in this sweat and I didn't even know what they were talking about. They asked me if I had a bathing suit, and then we all got stuffed into this little round thing, covered with blankets, and they made this hot steam. Then they gave me water to drink with all these vegetables in it, and I almost choked half to death."

And we laughed and laughed and started making up more and more stories, more and more wild tales that the white guy was spreading to his family and friends—his interpretations of what he had gone through.

And then, oddly enough, a week later Bob showed up at our house. We never thought we'd see that man again, and here he showed up. Bobbie invited him into the house and prepared coffee, and we were sitting there drinking coffee when he started telling us about his experiences. He told us that he had traveled all over the world and he had lived among different peoples, and he had always tried to learn as much as he could about those different people, including even learning their languages. So he had learned four different languages in addition to English, and that explained why he had been praying inside the sweat lodge in different languages, including Japanese.

And he said, "You know, inside that sweat lodge I felt so spiritual. I was so involved with what was taking place that I felt myself transported outside myself. And those different languages came to me and I just prayed in those languages, because it was the most spiritual thing that I had ever experienced." And not once did he mention choking on the herbs.

Tell Me Another Damn Indian Story, Grandpa

It was late August when our firstborn daughter informed us she was splitting the blanket with husband number two, an Assiniboine from the Fort Peck Indian Reservation in northeastern Montana.

Before starting the rescue mission, we first attended the famous Crow Fair in south-central Montana, where we enjoyed a family reunion with my adopted Crow family, the Old Elks. We took along two of our granddaughters, Benayshe Ba Equay and Mahnee Shawandenoke. My wife, Bobbie, and I have always believed it is important to immerse our children and grandchildren in the Indian ways and traditions. Perhaps they can pass that knowledge down to future generations.

Virtually everyone has experienced moving days. Many may look forward to a new chapter in life, and for some, it is a new beginning. As for me, I hate moving days, because it represents a week's worth of work condensed into one day. My lifestyle doesn't lend itself to working my ass off, when I consider the prospect of having to do it all over again unloading. Our children seem to take turns at this new style of migration. Statistics tell us that, on average, Americans move every seven years. My wife and I have lived at the same address on the reservation for thirty years, becoming the exception to the rule. Not so for our three children. At times, when they plan to move again, I strongly suspect they have Gypsy blood coursing through their veins.

Arriving at Ft. Peck, the entire family pitched in and loaded the large U-Haul van with all our daughter's possessions.

With three adults, three vehicles, and five children, we divided the children. Our granddaughter Mahnee drew the short straw to be my copilot on the long return trip to Nevada.

I consider myself to be somewhat like a barn horse. After a long ride away from the ranch, I turn around, heading for home and all the creature comforts. The barn horse knows that feeling and instinctively wants to make the return trip as short and as fast as possible. With this in mind, I avoided the longer, roundabout, four-lane interstate in favor of the smaller, two-lane roads cutting through the heartland of Montana.

Truly, the road was less traveled, as we went miles without seeing another vehicle.

From Wolf Point to Brockway I entertained Mahnee with Indian stories and legends. She was a plump nine year old with an infectious giggle, who demonstrated a genuine interest in her tribal past.

As we left Brockway, we spotted a small Indian man with long braids standing alongside the road with his thumb out. He looked so pitiful, standing in the middle of nowhere pleading for a ride.

I pulled over, in a cloud of dust and grinding gravel, alongside the road. Swinging open the door, I welcomed our weary traveler.

As we pulled back onto the pavement, I made a surprising discovery. Under that brown weather-beaten face was a white woman! When she smiled, her yellow-brown teeth told me she had never made friends with a toothbrush. If I were to make a weak attempt at political correctness, I could describe her as intellectually challenged, lacking in hygiene and cleanliness, which left her in a perpetual state of high odors. Now, I simply call them as I see them. She could not put two coherent sentences together, leaving me to conclude she was retarded, and to the total dismay of Mahnee and me, she smelled to high heaven, like a person who had been skunked a couple of times.

Of all the warnings about picking up hitchhikers, none of them warned us about picking up a little, crazy, stinky woman, who soon drove me to distraction with her persistent incoherent babbling.

Ho wah! How could I ditch this stinky, mentally challenged woman and at the same time act like a gentleman? This was not a concern to little Mahnee, who beat a hasty retreat into the sleeping compartment behind the front seat and left Grandpa to cope with this diplomatic dilemma.

The opportunity was not far away as we approached a stop sign at an intersection near Jordan, Montana.

I told my now unwelcome passenger this was where she gets off, as we are going toward Jordan. Reluctantly, she got off at the intersection, and we headed for the hamlet of Jordan.

With the smell of fresh air, Mahnee crawled out of her compartment like a prairie dog. She was all smiles again at the prospect of fresh air. We enjoyed lunch at an old-time restaurant, which was a throwback to the 1890s. Mounted heads of buffalo, elk, deer, and bear lined the walls surrounding the huge stone fireplace. It was likely we were chomping on the meat of one of those critters.

As we drove back to the intersection, there stood little Stinky Woman with her thumb out.

"Don't look! Don't look!"

We pretended not to see her as we turned the corner and headed west, leaving Stinky Woman in the clouds of exhaust fumes from our U-Haul truck.

With that odd experience behind us, Mahnee and I were left deep in our own thoughts.

Finally Mahnee broke the silence. "Grandpa, can you tell me another damn Indian story?"

I sighed and said, "You just experienced one, my dear."

Alcatraz Is Not an Island

Gary W. Mull, the San Francisco Bay Area yacht builder and racer published "The Infamous Floating Alcatraz" in 1990. After reading his account, I became painfully aware of how newcomers to our land perceive things with their own bias and how they arrive at conclusions on the basis of superficial or incomplete evidence.

I will admit that Gary was on the right track and his historic navigational charts prove that Alcatraz is indeed a floating island. As I read his article, I literally held my breath to find out whether Gary had actually stumbled upon a long-held secret of the American Indians. However, after finishing the story it was obvious to me that he had not. Everything he did reveal in his story is true, to the extent that he understood the phenomena of a moving island.

It is my feeling that someone will eventually come along who is challenged by the facts Gary revealed and will investigate the matter even further. Perhaps he or she will find the real truth of the matter.

Feeling that this may actually occur and, again, to avoid any further misinterpretation of the events of time, I have decided, instead, to come forward and give you the real story.

The origins of this story actually go back millions of years to the Pleistocene epoch, which was the age of dinosaurs. There existed, in what is now the state of Nevada, a huge inland sea called Lake Lahontan. Among its various inhabitants were the humble turtles (*Owahenis marmorata*) happily coexisting with the huge sixty-five-foot-long ichthyosaurs.

Unfortunately for them, the Pacific Tectonic Plate moved inland, crushing and grinding up the landscape as it went. The Sierra Nevada Mountains were pushed up to greater heights and lifted the sea bottom of Lake Lohontan. This caused the enormous waters of the lake to rush to the south, cutting out a giant canyon in the process. This canyon is what we now call the Grand Canyon. Most of the aquatic life inhabiting Lake Lahontan was destroyed in the process, but not the turtles, who were forced to adapt to a land environment. However, the elements of change were not yet complete, as the uplifting of the Sierra Mountain Range also triggered violent volcanic activity along the entire range. Unfortunately for some of the turtles, the volcanic activity along the northern rift cut through a radioactive strata. The resultant volcanic ash, or pumice, settled all over the landscape and it also piled high on the backs of several turtles. This form of ancient radioactivity did not create the problems it does today. Instead, it caused a glandular imbalance in the turtles that was to result in uncontrolled growth. Over a period of several thousand years, the turtles became giant size. The largest dinosaurs that ever walked the earth looked puny in comparison.

Nevada had been reduced to nothing more than a huge basin with only a few potholes of water, none of which could support the likes of the giant turtles. Separated by vast expanses of sand and sage, the ever-growing turtles took to these ponds and did their best to cope with the hostile environment. The ongoing volcanic activity continued to dump pumice and stone on the backs of the huge turtles. More water and a bountiful food source was what the turtles needed.

"Enough is enough!" the turtle chief Iktomi declared. "We've got to get out of this place."

Iktomi's sixth sense indicated to him that there was lots of water to the west of the big mountains. Rounding up his fellow giants, Iktomi led a bizarre caravan of two columns across the sands to the mountains. The weight and size of those huge turtles created a couple of deep furrows that became the river channels of the present-day Carson and Truckee Rivers.

The ordeal of the journey took a terrible toll on the lumbering behemoths, who carried tons of volcanic ash and rubble on their backs. Some of the round mounds found in the Sierras all the way down to the Sacramento River are the remains of these giant turtles. Some giant turtles got as far as San Pablo Bay before they expired, creating several islands, called Brothers and Sisters, or Red Rock.

Iktomi, their leader, was the largest and strongest of the bunch and made it into the middle of San Francisco Bay. There he took advantage of the tidal flow between the bay and the Pacific Ocean to bring him food.

Iktomi was in turtle heaven for food was in great abundance. Sardines, mussels, clams, oysters, salmon, squid—you name it, Iktomi had it. He positioned himself in various parts of the bay or near the outlet, and when the rip or flood tides occurred, seafood of all types were washed into his gaping maw.

Iktomi, like all turtles, moved slowly and, like all turtles, hibernated. Normal small turtles hibernate only in the winter months. Due to Iktomi's great size, he hibernated for fifty years at a time because he had a different internal biological clock. This accounts for the long time lag between his movements in the bay.

For many more thousands of years, Iktomi lived a happy and contented life in San Francisco Bay. When the Indian people came to that area thirty-five thousand years later, there was a peaceful coexistence between them, for Iktomi was a gentle giant, who often helped the Indians secure food from the bay. The Indians made offerings to Iktomi as a sign of appreciation.

Then the Spaniards came to the bay in the early 1700s.

It is from that time to the present that Gary Mull's research documented the movements of Iktomi (Alcatraz) from the first navigational charts made by the Spaniards. If you read his original account, you can see how and why his original hypothesis was incomplete. As Gary so astutely reported, the Spanish navigational charts showed the island of Alcatraz had moved several times, much to the consternation of ships' captains, who needed a more accurate fix on the island's whereabouts.

The helmsman on a sailing ship that ran into the island had a lame excuse for the captain, "The damn thing wasn't there yesterday."

As a result of these problems, the Spaniards took several heavy ship anchor chains and secured Alcatraz at its present location in the bay. They also installed a small lighthouse to prevent any other ships from ramming the island.

In spite of all these precautions, Iktomi stirred from time to time. He drug those cumbersome anchor chains like a macabre ghostly figure looming out of the fog. He made grotesque moaning sounds, and the anchor chains clanked and rumbled along the bottom of the bay.

The Indians told the terrified Spaniards, "It's only Iktomi. He is our friend."

The Spaniards believed that the Indians had made a pact with a great supernatural power they could not understand, and from then on they treated the Indians with more respect. They thought Iktomi was a water spirit or monster, and superstitious sailors didn't want to offend him.

When the American government took over California in 1847, they further compounded Iktomi's problems. American ship captains noted the island shifting. Iktomi's Indian friends loosened one of the three anchor chains the Spaniards had attached to him, and that gave Iktomi somewhat greater latitude in his foraging for food.

The Army Corps of Engineers was summoned and they discovered what the Spaniards had attempted to do to stabilize Alcatraz. Gary Mull was correct when he discovered that the government had spent 182 million dollars in casting four stainless steel anchors, each weighing twenty-six tons. Those, in turn, were connected to the island with stainless steel cables and a water-cylinder damping system. These acted like aquatic shock absorbers against the struggles of Iktomi.

The Indians were greatly disturbed by the series of events that hampered their friend and ally, Iktomi, but were helpless to do anything about it. In 1934, shortly after the Army Corps of Engineers performed their dastardly deed further restraining Iktomi, the United States government decided to build a federal prison on him to house America's most desperate criminals. The guard towers surrounding the island kept the inmate population in its confines, while at the same time it discouraged Iktomi's Indian allies from attempting to undo those terribly restrictive bonds the Corps of Engineers had so elaborately installed.

It was during the time that Iktomi was a federal prison that one of the most bizarre events in the annals of prison history took place. In 1946 the federal authorities claimed there was a massive attempt at a prison break. Troops were called in to quell the disturbance.

Neither the federal government nor the American public ever knew the real reason for that alleged outbreak. Every one thousand years or so, the small number of giant turtle females undergo estrus. Their bodily change sends powerful messages to all male turtles of their intentions. Poor Iktomi was aware of this female stimulus, but was unable to do anything about it, bound down as he was. On the night of May 1, 1946, Iktomi became overwhelmed by estrus emissions. His body shuddered and his amorous moans created a panic among the island's inhabitants. The entire island was caught up in convulsions like an incredible earthquake, and Iktomi's moaning echoed throughout the corridors and cellblocks on the island.

Most of the inmates knew that the main cellblock was constructed over the old Spanish tunnels and dungeons. Rumors were that the dungeons were inhabited by the tortured spirits of the many men who died there. It was said that if those spirits ever got out of the dungeons, every man on the island would die a horribly violent death. Now, with the violent shaking of the island and the loud moaning of Iktomi, the terrified convicts believed they were doomed and that the world was coming to an end. (Instead, it was the end of the coming for Iktomi.) The guards could not quell the efforts of the inmates to "get the hell off this island" and called for outside help.

Clarence Carnes, The Choctaw Kid, knew of Iktomi and tried to calm the panic-stricken inmates, but to no avail. They grabbed anything that might be used as weapons. They were no match against the fully-armed guards and, later, the military reinforcements that were called out.

Blind and unreasoning terror can readily overcome rational behavior in any instance. Several of the guards, unnerved by Iktomi's apparent cataclysmic antics, fell easy prey to the hardened criminals who saw an opportunity to escape what they felt was sure death on the island. "Better to die trying to get off this cursed island, than to die a horrible death right here in the cold, dark cells."

It took the prison authorities, with the help of military support, three days to quell the uprising. Two guards and three inmates died in the violence and many more were injured. Twenty-two thousand pages of testimony, detailing the tragic events, were all duly recorded by the United States district court. These documents were declared "secret" and were stored in the San Francisco Federal Records archives, under file 30316-S.

The federal authorities knew something was terribly wrong with Alcatraz, and under no circumstances did they want the public to know about it. The authorities believed that if the public was made aware that Alcatraz was inhabited by forces no one could comprehend, it could easily result in panic. The authorities also suspected that Clarence Carnes, The Choctaw Kid, knew much more than he was willing to divulge about the mysterious forces on the island. Carnes simply dummied up, he became the stereotypical silent, stoic Indian.

The federal authorities may have succeeded in keeping this information from the public, but they couldn't suppress the fears and anxieties of the people on the island. The prison authorities found it increasingly difficult to keep experienced guards and staff members on Alcatraz. Morale among the staff was at an all-time low. The turnover of personnel was so rapid, that inexperienced people were hired for the very dangerous job of guarding this country's most desperate criminals.

The inmates felt their situation was even worse than their guards. At least the guards could get off that damned island—the inmates couldn't. Fear and anxiety gripped the island with relentless power.

Prior to this time, poor Iktomi had been sulking alone and lonely on the bottom of the bay. The San Francisco Bay had long been turtle heaven for Iktomi, providing everything he needed in great abundance. Since the white man's arrival, however, everything underwent a sad change for him. The once-plentiful sardines totally and mysteriously disappeared. All the other seafood delicacies Iktomi so enjoyed were also diminishing in numbers. He brooded over the indignities the white people had heaped upon him. First, he was frustrated at being chained and anchored to the bottom of the bay by the Spaniards. After they installed a lighthouse on Iktomi's back, he felt strange, for night had been changed into day. And, later, they added that dreadful foghorn. The constant *ooogh— ooogh* caused Iktomi fitful times during his fifty-year hibernations. Soon the Americans added gun emplacements and fortifications onto his back.

Iktomi was saddened to find his Indian friends held captive on the island for resisting the white man's aggression on Indian lands. Warriors of the Apache and of the Modoc were held in shackles and chains. It has been told that one of Captain Jack's Modoc warriors was chained to the wall in the Spanish dungeon for an unbelievable sixteen years! Iktomi felt a great kinship to those poor Indians. His stainless steel bonds were a constant reminder of how confining civilization can become.

Then, on the night of June 11, 1962, three prisoners, all serving time for bank robbery, fashioned dummies out of old blankets, which they placed in their bunks to make it appear they were sleeping. Then they climbed to the roof of the main cellblock. They lowered themselves to the ground with some stolen electric cord and cautiously made their way down to the water's edge, confident that they could make good their escape.

That night Iktomi had been agonizing over his ignoble fate and worked up a quiet anger about it. He was still frustrated over missing out on an amorous adventure in 1946. When, all of a sudden, three escaping bank robbers slipped into the cold waters of the bay, right over Iktomi's head. Iktomi's anger and hunger were both satisfied at once. *Chomp! Chomp! Chomp!* The three escapees disappeared into oblivion.

The cycloptic lighthouse atop the island makes a full circular sweep of the bay every thirty seconds. From their vantage point on the second tier of the cellblock, The Choctaw Kid and Robert Stroud, the Birdman of Alcatraz, saw the three escapees slip into the water in the temporary glow of the lighthouse beam. Darkness then enveloped them and when the beam once again played over the area, all that could be seen was water turbulence—but no convicts! The Birdman went into a panic and was quickly put into restraints by the guards. "The old man must really be stir-crazy," a guard said, as they hauled the babbling, terrified Stroud to a padded cell. The Choctaw Kid laid back on his cell cot, coolly lit a cigarette, and smiled. His friend Iktomi had struck again.

The discovery of the escape resulted in a massive manhunt of Alcatraz and around the Bay Area. Only small pieces of debris were found from the materials the authorities believed the convicts had used to escape. No one has ever seen or heard of them since.

When this new wave of terror gripped the island, the federal prison authorities threw up their hands in despair. "That's it!" exclaimed the prison director. "We've got to close down this hellhole of a prison!"

On May 15, 1963, Alcatraz was officially closed. The entire inmate population was transferred to other federal prisons. Another phase in the history of Alcatraz had come to a close.

Nothing in life can exist in a vacuum. The changes in the seasons create change within, and Alcatraz was no different, for in 1964 a new chapter in the long life of Iktomi began. A group of Lakota Indians, accompanied by friends of other tribes, rented a launch and went out to the island. Five of the Lakota men drove small stakes in the ground affixing their names and tribal roll numbers and then filed a legal claim to the island pursuant to the Fort Laramie Treaty of 1858. They stated that their understanding of the treaty was that all abandoned federal land can revert back to the Indians. The federal government, however, turned a deaf ear to the claim.

The news media focused their attention on the Lakotas during their initial staking of their claim on Alcatraz. What they failed to notice were the other Indians, offering tobacco ties and prayers to Iktomi!

Before the Indians left the island, they did a Victory Dance in front of the main cellblock.

Iktomi heard the heavy beat of the big drum and the singing of the men, and it made him very happy to know that his Indian brothers had not forgotten him. As the launch pulled away from the dock, Iktomi could hear the Indians say, "We'll be back, Our Brother, we'll be back."

And, come back we did. This time, in far greater number.

Onward Christian Soldiers

On a recent trip from Nevada to California, we made a pit stop at the Donner Summit rest area. As I emerged from the building I was confronted by a pretty young lady who offered me a religious flyer.

Waving her off, I said, "I don't believe in your fairy tales."

She quickly snapped, "What do you believe in?"

My response was just as fast, "I believe in my own fairy tales."

Good Medicine

For several months I had been bothered by a nagging cough; or was it a persistent cough, a hacking cough, or a chronic cough? It certainly was a rasping cough.

My knowledge of medicine could not come up with any answers, so I went to the Fallon Tribal Health Center for a checkup by the Indian health care doctor.

After a brief examination the doctor asked me to go back to the waiting room, because he wanted to talk to my wife in private.

The doctor told her if she wanted to keep me around a few more years, she would have to prepare me three square meals and day and give me sex anytime I wanted it.

When she returned to the waiting room I was anxious to hear the results.

"What happened? What did the doctor tell you?"

My wife coolly replied, "The doctor says you're going to die."

Then the doctor entered the room and said, "By the way, the EKG and X-rays indicate you have an enlarged, slow-beating heart. Several alcoholic drinks a day should keep that old heart pumping."

I just love those Indian health care doctors.

I do have some important role models in the drinking department. Just look at some of the men of history:

Franklin D. Roosevelt drank eight to ten martinis a day.

Winston Churchill drank a quart of whiskey each day.

A man who never smoked, was a vegetarian, and only had an occasional beer went by the name of Adolph Hitler.

I think I will stay with my martinis 'cuz I don't want to kill anybody.

Brokeback Boulder

Perhaps one of the most prestigious conferences dedicated to the broadening of national and global understanding is the annual Conference on World Affairs at Boulder, Colorado.

After several months of drum beating and hyping the event, Tim Findley, a graduate of the University of Colorado's School of Journalism, got me to consider being a participant at this special event, which does not require academic credentials. Nor does it tend to define a problem, or even clearly define what the world's problems are.

Not long after, I received a letter of invitation from Professor Howard Higman, founder of the conference. When one gets such an invitation from Professor Higman, it is more like a demand for a command performance, which many renowned world leaders, scholars, authors, and, more often than not, free-thinking movers and shakers feel compelled to attend. There is no financial reward associated with the conference, only the distinctive honor of being an invited delegate. Everyone pays their own expenses to participate in this circus of freewheeling intellectuals and corporate leaders.

So, why in hell was I invited to attend? I am an academic "fish out of water" character. Professor Higman, with his sense of comedic drama, included me on his list of plenary speakers. That professor had the academic guts to put an American Indian activist on the roster with such luminaries as Donald McHenry, ambassador to the United Nations; Roger Ebert, Pulitzer Prize–winning critic; and Ted Turner, president of Turner Broadcasting. I could only assume my role of plenary speaker was to provide a little comic relief to the often serious debates.

The first two days of the conference established me as a straight talker and a loose cannon, with a sense of humor, in the various workshops and panel discussions I served on. The planning committee expected about two hundred people at my plenary session. The advance buzz resulted in over eight hundred in attendance. One lone Indian surrounded by mostly white people. If I wasn't careful, I could become dog meat.

Vine Deloria, noted Native American author and university professor, had the dubious honor of introducing me. He set the tone for what was to follow by telling the audience, "When electricity came to his reservation in Minnesota, his grandpa installed a light bulb in the outhouse, thus becoming the first Indian to wire a head for a reservation." Vine was a tough act to follow.

I proceeded to tell the story of scalping Columbus and my subsequent discovery of Italy on behalf of the American Indians. One woman in the audience picked up on a statement I made describing my scalping of Columbus: "When Columbus came forward, I did not give him my annual hug." During the question-and-answer session after my presentation, the woman shouted out, "You didn't hug him? Does that mean you're homophobic?"

I was shocked and stunned by the question, as I didn't know the meaning of homophobic. I thought it might be some kind of religious order, so I responded, "I am not homophobic. I am an Episcopalian."

Another woman took exception to my reference to an "ugly woman" in one of my stories. I patiently explained to her that I was a member of the "Teasing Clan" of the Crow tribe. "If we tease someone and they get angry with us, their anger offends us. And if they are to make things right between us, they must give us a gift."

The next morning, a dozen red roses were delivered to me with a note of apology. Now, if I had just known who that woman was, I would have given her a hug, hopefully, without being called a sexist.

At ten o'clock A.M., I attended what turned out to be my final panel discussion. Tim Findley sat next to me at the head table, along with author Peter Tauber, who was doing his own version of shit stirring, when he made reference the day before to militant lesbians as "angry and obnoxious." When people become too analytical about humor, they miss the entire purpose of humor. The two of us were like lightning rods, just waiting for lightning to strike. *Ho wah!* That didn't take long. Our room was packed to the rafters—standing room only. People were standing in the doorways when the distant roar of thunder distracted them, and they immediately gave way to four half-naked women, who burst into the room holding placards protesting the conference.

Now, I'm just going to call 'em as I see 'em. Our seminar was titled "Multiculturalism: Boon or Bane." Well, those four militant lesbians represented the "bane" of society through their outrageous appearance and conduct. All four of them were naked from the waist up. Their bodies were painted in colorful designs. Their tits looked like dried figs, the kind you see in the "before and after" photos of breast enhancement ads. All four of the women were in the "before" category. Three of them topped off their weird ensembles by attaching long, flexible rubber penises to their noses. They looked like cartoon characters of freaky elephants. As they talked, they hyperventilated, causing those rubber penises to throb up and down. *Eeeuuuwweeee!*

Trying to maintain my cool, I told the protesters they were not only interrupting the continuity of the program, but also violating a cultural taboo. "In our cultural society, people show a great respect for their elders. Besides, I am the only American Indian in this conference."

"You are nothing but a 'token' Indian."

"If you don't leave, I will," I said.

"Well," came the stubborn response, "we're not leaving."

After that exchange, I got up and walked out, leaving those three throbbing rubber penises behind me.

Grandpa Amabese always said, "Never get into a piss fight with a skunk."

Filipino Gold

For most Indians, life on a reservation can be a very trying thing. Our statistics, which even the U.S. government hates to reveal, of unemployment, lack of income or poverty, alcoholism, and a host of other socioeconomic problems show that the social experiment of total dependency for services has not worked.

When you are wracked up in the system, it's easy to sit back and moan or cry about your predicament. But that solves nothing. It only worsens your self-esteem and shoves you deeper into depression. It is important to think about the joys of life, even in the most trying conditions. Laughter and humor are of vital importance in maintaining one's sense of balance in coping with the vagaries of life. I am a Chippewa pipe carrier and ceremonial leader. I very proudly carry the robe of the four sacred colors given to me by my people. We call ourselves *Annishinabeg*, and the robe acknowledges my acceptance by my people in the ceremonial long house, sweat lodge, and Pipe Ceremony.

In these days of enlightenment or New Age religions, Indian medicine men, shamans, teachers, and traditional pipe carriers find themselves in greater demand by members of society outside the reservation. Many of the medicine people simply refuse to leave their sacred circle. Some venture out and try running ceremonies or seminars, only to retreat back to the reservation because of criticism from both on and off the reservation. Some are disillusioned in what they see as a passing fancy, fad, or entertainment for people looking for diversions from their everyday lives. Other medicine people respond to basic human needs wherever they find them, for their teachings tell them that all people of the sacred colors are our brothers. If someone approaches with a good heart and a good mind to ask for health and help, the shaman will willingly respond.

The word of one's ceremonial activities extends beyond the reservation, as many of us have non-Indian friends who like to sing the praises of their spiritual friends and teachers. This can sometimes be embarrassing.

Last fall I received an excited call from Eddie, a friend of mine who works at Lake Tahoe. He said he met a Filipino man who very much wanted to meet with me, and he hoped I wouldn't be upset over the fact that he gave the man my telephone number. Eddie then continued, "He has an incredible story to share with you and he's looking for your help. He may even call you this evening."

Eddie was right about that phone call, for at six-thirty that evening, the telephone rang and it was a Filipino man on the other end of the line. After cursory introductions, he immediately started to talk about the purpose of his call. He said he had something very important to discuss with me. I responded that if it was so important, he ought to come down to the reservation and talk to me in person. He readily agreed to the invitation and asked if the next morning would be soon enough. There was no question—this man was anxious and eager to relate something to me.

The next day was a beautiful day in the high desert country, where our reservation is located. About ten in the morning, a blue Toyota came wheeling into our gravel driveway. I walked out to greet a charming young Filipino couple. After introductions and greetings, they were welcomed into our house. My wife, Bobbie, served hot coffee to all of us.

The young man, I'll call "Ramon," started telling a fascinating story of buried treasure on his family's property fifty to eighty miles south of Manila, near the coast. For many centuries pirates and even governments buried loot throughout the Philippine Islands. This went on right up to World War II, when Admiral Yamamoto of the Japanese Navy buried much of the treasures he looted throughout the South Pacific. The loot included a gold Buddha, which was found by a Filipino, and then stolen from him by President Marcos. The whereabouts of the Buddha is a mystery since Marcos's death.

Ramon said about a hundred and fifty years ago some Spanish pirate ships pulled into the harbor adjacent to their village. They recruited a group of Filipinos to help them carry about forty barrels of loot out into the jungle. They then dug a huge deep pit, lined it to keep out the moisture, and then set in the forty barrels. Some of the barrels were filled with beautiful ornate guns, the kinds that only the wealthy or nobility could afford. Silverware and other expensive items for elegant palaces were in other barrels. And then there was the gold, both in solid ingots or bars and coins. There were so many coins that some accidentally dropped on the ground and were found years later by Ramon's family.

To the shock and horror of the Filipino work crew, the Spaniards rounded them up and murdered them. Then they threw their bodies alongside the barrels. For good measure, the pirates kidnapped a missionary priest, murdered him, and threw him in with the rest of the bodies. Then the huge pit was covered up. Shrubs and plants were replaced to hide the spot. The purpose of the brutal murders was to play on the superstitions of the natives. No one dared to go to a place inhabited by so many spirits that were still in agony over the loss of their host bodies.

Ramon said, "If anyone dares touch the earth in the area of the buried treasure, they will go down." As he said this, he gestured downward with his hand. "They will go down!" he added again for emphasis. He was very serious about this as he narrated the story. This area was on his family's property and even though they all knew about the treasure, no one dared touch it, and it had been this way for one hundred and fifty years.

He continued, "Several months ago I had a dream, and in this dream I saw an Indian performing ceremonies in which he was communicating to the Spirit World. When I woke up, I was very excited. I thought, that's the answer—the way we can get to the treasure. We've got to get an Indian to perform a ceremony."

Ramon immediately set about finding such a person, and after several false leads, he finally met my friend Eddie at Lake Tahoe. Eddie had been wearing some Indian jewelry, which prompted Ramon to ask, "Do you know any Indians?"

Eddie responded he did.

"Do you know any of them who know how to perform ceremonies?"

"Yes, I do," responded Eddie. "His name is Fortunate Eagle and he lives on the reservation down by Fallon, Nevada.

Ramon got very agitated and said to Eddie, "I have something very important to ask him."

Eddie told me later, "That's when I gave him your phone number."

Now, here he was, Ramon and his attractive young wife, sitting at our kitchen table. He became more animated as he talked. Now that he had given me the historical background to the story of the buried treasure, he started to ask me questions.

"Do you do ceremonies?" he asked.

"Yes, I do," I answered.

"What kind have you done?"

I told him that I was not a medicine man who can doctor people for their illnesses. My role is more in the ceremonial area, like weddings, namings, adoptions, sweat lodges, pipe ceremonies, and funerals.

"Do you do ceremonies for the spirits?"

"Yes," I responded. "There have been a few occasions when I have been called to do such ceremonies as renewal to placate the spirits."

Ramon was really warming up to the issue now. "Do you think you can do a ceremony to placate the spirits guarding the treasure?"

"Yes, I think I can, but it would take at least four days and everyone involved would have to follow the instructions very carefully, because if they don't, the whole thing could go bad."

"Fortunate Eagle, if you can do this, you will become a very rich man. We need the ceremony for our own place, but we also have friends, further down the coast, who have treasure hidden in the caves down at the water's edge. And they don't dare touch their land for the same reasons we can't touch ours." Ramon was really getting into his pitch to me. "If you do this, word will travel all over the Philippines, where other people have buried treasure. Man, you could become a millionaire!"

"Really?" I asked, "How could that happen?"

"Well, for starters, Fortunate Eagle, if you come over to the Philippines, we will pay all your expenses—round-trip on the airlines, accommodations, and we will give you one hundred thousand dollars cash for your ceremony! Then we can dig up the treasure."

"Ramon, before I give you an answer, I would like to tell you a story. To the east of the reservation, there is a mountain range called the Stillwater Mountains. The highest peak in those mountains is called Job's Peak. Every summer a wise man sits on a large boulder on the very top. People seeking his knowledge and wisdom climb that steep mountain and seek him out. One day a young man with a special need climbed the mountain of Job's Peak and sure enough, at the very top, he saw an old Indian sitting on a large boulder.

"The young man sat awhile to recover his breath after such a long and arduous climb. Taking an offering of tobacco, he handed it to the old one.

"The wise one accepted the tobacco then said, 'What can I do for you?'

"The young man replied, 'Oh, wise one, tell me what is the secret of success?'

"The old Indian very slowly looked out over the expanse of the Lahontan Valley below them, and then looked down at the young man sitting below him. 'The secret of success,' he said, holding out his hand toward the young man, 'is always get the money up front!'"

Ramon's mouth dropped open at the conclusion of the story. He and his wife bid us goodbye and we have never seen him again!

Good Medicine II

A lone crow was flying over the prairie and was struck by a bolt of lightning. After a few minutes, he woke up from unconsciousness. He didn't know what hit him. His wing and leg were broken. He was missing most of his shiny black feathers and his head had no feathers at all. He had the appearance of a scuzzy buzzard.

Checking himself out, Crow came to the conclusion he was dying.

"Oh, woe is me," he croaked over and over. "Oh, woe is me. I'm dying. I'm dying." When, suddenly, he noticed a slight movement in the tall buffalo grass. It was his old friend Coyote, rolling over as he was taking an afternoon nap.

"Coyote, Coyote," Crow called out.

Coyote rubbed the sleep out of his eyes and became wide awake at this pitiful apparition lying on the ground.

"Coyote, my friend, I am dying, and I just wanted to say goodbye before I go on my journey to the Spirit World."

Coyote looked over the stricken crow.

"Man! You look worse than a buffalo bladder shriveling up under the hot prairie sun. However, I don't think you're quite ready to die."

Nearby, a huge buffalo bull was taking a crap.

"You see that buffalo taking a dump?"

"Yah, I see him."

"Well, you know the buffalo is big medicine, and so is his poop." Coyote continued, "You drag your pitiful scrawny carcass over to that pile of hot crap and eat all your little belly can hold."

Crow protested, "I've eaten all kinds of things in my life, but I've never resorted to eating buffalo crap."

"You want to get well. You don't want to die, and now I'm telling you that shit is good medicine."

Coyote was right, and so Crow dragged his mangled body over to the large steaming pile of buffalo dung. And, as instructed, he started to scarf up all his little belly could handle, and to his surprise and delight he actually began to feel better.

"See, I told you so," bragged Coyote. "Now, you just follow that big buffalo everywhere he goes and every time he takes a dump, you go over and load up on that good medicine."

Following the instructions of Coyote, the little crow never let the buffalo bull get out of his sight and he was getting stronger and better each day. His leg and wing were healing and his beautiful black feathers grew back.

A large granite boulder stood tall in the buffalo grass, just ahead of Crow. He stood there for a moment, sizing it up. "I think I can. I think I can. I've got to try it."

With that, he took a mighty hop and landed victoriously on top of the boulder. From that vantage point he saw the big bull taking another dump. "I gotta go get some more of that prairie pie."

Two days later Crow was happily hopping across the buffalo grass, when he came to the largest cottonwood tree on the endless prairie. Looking way, way up, to its lofty heights, Crow mustered up his courage and bravely launched himself up toward the great arbor of the cottonwood tree. Landing on its uppermost branches, Crow realized he had overcome the adversities of life, and he started singing out his Victory Song.

Blam! A shot rang out, feathers flew, and Crow crashed to the ground, deader than a doornail.

The moral of this story is, "Bullshit may get you to the top, but it may not keep you there."

Italian Mill House

The year 1982 was a very important year for me, for that was when I took up sculpture in stone. It happened when I was doing a gallery show with my catlinite ceremonial pipes at Phil Navasye's gallery in Santa Fe, New Mexico. The exhibit was to hang for an entire month. Typically, artists make an appearance on the opening night of the show, then they go back to their homes or studios and pick up their work when the show is over. This time was to be different. Bobbie and I were going to stay in Santa Fe the entire duration of the show, because I had a feeling I was going to learn something in that beautiful, cultural, and artistic city.

During the trip, I had the great opportunity to meet Gordon Van Wert and Pressley LaFontain, both Chippewa sculptors. In their shared studio, Gordon pointed to a large three hundred pound alabaster boulder. Gordon said, "See what you can do with that, Adam."

That first full-bore sculpture launched a new career for me, for out of that rugged boulder emerged a beautiful traditional dancer. While it was being exhibited at the Los Angeles County Museum of Natural History, it sold for five thousand dollars. *Ho wah!* I didn't have an amateur career. Right out of the chute, I became a professional sculptor.

The summer of 1987 found me doing a six-week tour of Italy as a teacher and a conductor of ceremonies. In between weekend seminars, I caught the train to Pietrasanta, a fabulous village on the Mediterranean Coast of Italy. That village has more professional stone sculptors for its size than any other city in the world. Henry Moore, the famous English sculptor, had a home and studio there. Historic giants of the art world, like Michelangelo and Donatello, worked there. The famous Carrara marble comes from the mountains only twenty miles north of Pietrasanta.

It was on my visits to Pietrasanta that I met several contemporary "maestros of the marble." It was easy for me to get acquainted, for I wore my hair in long braids, and when going to the ancient village, I often wore a ribbon shirt. Many of the professional studios are closed to the public, since people sometimes disturb the sculptors at their work. The studio directors often found me peering through the wrought iron gates, staring in amazement at the way the artisans were working the marble. The big smile on my face was often the ticket that got me an invitation to enter the premises. The Italian artisans were extremely cordial and friendly and took the time to show me in sign language what they were doing. They frequently let me sit on a block of marble or a wooden stool and watch them work.

A great place to meet the sculptors was in the two sidewalk cafes in the village. You could always tell the sculptors on their lunch breaks by the marble dust on them. In short time I had the good fortune to meet other Americans, Englishmen, Puerto Ricans, Spaniards, Germans, Japanese, Africans, and many other nationalities, who were plying their trade in the numerous studios situated throughout the village. This ancient, little stone-walled village also housed several sculpting schools, where I found more Americans, including Clifford Fragua of the Jemez Pueblo in New Mexico. Clifford was delighted to see another Indian in that little village, so far away from home. Sometimes after school, we would have dinner in the Donatello Hotel, where he and the other American students stayed. We talked about the importance of Indian artists and sculptors going to Europe to expand their awareness and understanding of art on a global basis. While learning European technology, they are also able to draw on the rich cultural heritage of the American Indian.

The courtesy and hospitality of the international group of sculptors was a wonderful experience. It was a great honor to be invited to have a sumptuous dinner at the home of the renowned Gigi Guadagnucci and his wife, Inez. All sculptors vied for Gigi's attention in hope of getting an invitation. Some got their hopes up, only to find the limited space for twelve at the planked table in his villa kept the number of guests down. Somehow, Gigi always found room for me. After a veritable feast and a delicate desert, all accompanied by the appropriate wines, Gigi, the silver-haired patriarch of the villa, entertained his guests with his guitar and singing. He delighted in calling on me to sing Indian songs to provide his guests with a Native American flavor. That, in turn, opened other doors for me to be invited to other dinners, for I could always be counted on to provide another cultural dimension to the event.

It was in this way that I met another American couple, a Texan I'll call "George Nelson," and his New York woman, called "Katchi." George and Katchi were a fascinating couple. George had a home and studio in Texas, and Katchi had a condo and studio in New York City. Together they bought a four-hundred-year-old mill on a mountainous slope, fifteen miles inland from Pietrasanta. Katchi had a great sense of interior design. She incorporated the heavy, round millstones in their bins with homey interior design, which blended the old and the new with a sensible harmony. The outside grounds of the old millhouse were laced with water channels to the various areas of the mill, or the water could be directed around the structure by strategically placed head gates. George delighted in creating little waterfalls and fountains along the run of the small canals. The whole yard area became an aquatic landscape with George's ingenuity. George and Katchi's studio was a small, two-story structure, on the upslope behind the millhouse. Her painting studio occupied the upper story, and George's sculpture studio was on the ground floor, where he fashioned delicate, curving, intertwining sculptures of marble.

At dinner Katchi brought out steaming bowls of Mediterranean seafood stew and placed them in front of George and me. Long loaves of delicious Italian bread were cut up and served. Katchi saw to it that the wine glasses remained well-filled. As we enjoyed the delicious food, George told me of his and Katchi's careers, of their early struggles for recognition and financial stability. Now, in their late fifties or early sixties, they were finally able to afford the kind of life they had always dreamed of and worked for. Six months of the year they worked and enjoyed the laidback social life in Pietrasanta, and the other six months they returned to the states, where he did exhibits and shows around Austin, Texas, and Katchi had shows and exhibits of her impressionistic paintings in the New York City area.

George was unhappy with the ways of many of the American sculptors who came to Italy to work in the studios of Pietrasanta. They socialized only with other Americans and interactions between them and their Italian hosts were kept to a minimum. "But you, Adam, are different. You come over here and you seem to enjoy everyone you meet and everyone here is happy to see you. I think that is good."

On a Thursday, it was time for me to leave Pietrasanta to attend another weekend seminar at Pesaro, located on the east side of Italy, on the Adriatic Coast. My train took me to Florence, over there they call it "Firenze." Roberto was there at the station to meet me. We then went to his place, where other friends were waiting with their camping equipment, ready to drive the final leg of the journey to Pesaro. The countryside of northern Italy is a special treat to see. We passed ancient walled villages, reminders of early days when invaders crisscrossed their country; those formidable-looking walls would hardly keep the villagers safe from modern warfare. At the summit of a high mountain range, we stopped to stretch our legs and enjoy Italian ice cream. At Pesaro, Roberto drove me around the village, and to my surprise, I saw billboards proclaiming the upcoming seminar I was to conduct.

The hosts of the seminar were excited about our arrival. Preparations had already been made for a civic reception in the walled-in village plaza, but first they had to feed the weary travelers. We were escorted north of the village to a restaurant constructed of hand-cut stone. The interior had a warm, Old World charm. A long table was set for our party and we dined. We admired the beautiful, sparkling blue Adriatic Sea. Like they say, things just couldn't get any better than this.

That evening people gathered in the village square. So many turned out, they couldn't fit inside. Many of them stood outside the gates, peering in to get a glimpse of the festivities. The mayor and I were led in a Grand Entry to the stage. The local scouts serenaded their Indian guest and the mayor read a proclamation of welcome, and then presented me with a gift of carved marble, representing friendship and hospitality. To the delight of the crowd, the chairman of the organization then introduced me. With the help of my host, Roberto, as an interpreter, I presented the mayor with an eagle feather, representing peace and goodwill from the American Indian people to the people of Italy. I then added, "In my country, you must have a permit to possess the eagle feather, and the feather must be registered with the U.S. government. If you don't do this," I continued, "the government could consider you to be a criminal."

The next day, the headline in the local paper proclaimed, "Mayor of Pesaro is a Criminal."

The seminar itself went over very well, and at the end of the three-day event, as the participants were packing up and leaving, we saw a small procession of children accompanied by several mothers. They had hiked two miles up the curving mountain road to "see the Indian." I was very honored and flattered by the kind and special attention of the little ones. I took my hand drum and sang them an Indian song. They listened in rapt attention, their eyes wide in the wonderment of it all. Here, serenading them was an American Indian. The children were delighted and many came up to shake my hand, or to hug me. Older ones kissed me on both cheeks, before they turned around and headed back down the mountainside. The hopping and skipping was a joyous way of saying the long walk had been worth it. I left Pesaro with a special fondness for its hospitable people and its quaint village.

Upon our return to Florence, we found that traffic problems in Italy are just like any large city in the United States. In some cases it's a lot worse, for it seems that pedestrians do not have the right of way when crossing the streets or boulevards. They take their lives in their own hands as they dodge their way through the traffic to get to the other side of the street. And, it seems as though speed limits are only for the timid tourists to obey. The Italian drivers tear down the streets with reckless abandon, shouting obscenities at anyone who dares to block their way. Roberto, however, came from a kinder, gentler lineage of Italians. He found his way to one of several city parking lots in Florence, and we started walking toward our destination, dragging my suitcase by its leash, just like a little dog.

The wheels of my suitcase made a happy clickety-click sound as I pulled it over the cobblestone sidewalk. After several blocks, we approached two soldiers and a jeep parked next to the curb. One soldier sat behind the wheel of the jeep, an automatic weapon laid on the seat beside him. The other stood outside the jeep, holding his weapon at port arms. Both soldiers looked almost grim as we approached. As we came alongside the armed duo, I stopped dragging my suitcase and looked at the standing soldier for just a moment. And, suddenly, I reached up and pinched his cheek in a friendly way, smiling a big smile as I did so.

"Smile!" I said. "Smile, be happy!"

The startled soldier looked at his companion behind the wheel, confused about this unexpected occurrence. His partner broke out in a big grin at the ludicrous situation. My victim then broke out into a smile of his own and, in a spontaneous way, we all broke out laughing.

"You men are doing a good job in protecting your country and your families," I said. "Keep up the good work." And off Roberto and I went, clickety-clicking our way down the sidewalk.

A short distance away from the soldiers, Roberto turned to me. "Adam, you're crazy. Those guys could have blown your head off for that," he admonished me, while all the time laughing. "Those guys are guarding the French Consulate there. We're going to have to keep an eye on you to keep you out of trouble."

We arrived at our destination, where a local goldsmith, his tall slender American wife, and two little girls offered me a room in their apartment that overlooked the historic River Arno. Florence was noted to be a noisy city, traffic seemed to run all night long, and I heard the honking cars and revving motorcycles below my shuttered bedroom window. In the morning I had a chance to check out the numerous pictures hung on the walls of the room, and it was then that I realized the tall slender American woman was a top fashion model in Italy. Her face and figure were promoting all types of products, including western-type jeans and boots.

When I opened the shuttered windows, after I mentally blocked out the motor vehicles, a sight right out of medieval times greeted my eyes.

The River Arno slowly drifted along, a rower in a one-man scull was plying his oars down the center of the river. To my right was a classic arched stone bridge and to my left was the fabled Ponte Vecchio, the most famous bridge in Florence. This is the kind of scene Degas or Monet loved to paint.

There was so much to see and do in Florence. However, it was important to me to return to Pietrasanta and continue my education in working with the beautiful marble of Italy. My driver, Fillipo, and I set out early Monday.

In Pietrasanta, my hostess was to be Paula Raffo, whose family owned one of the largest marble factories in Pietrasanta. She lived in an ancient converted monastery, far up a steep canyon road. A narrow, steep hairpin-curve driveway led me to a small parking area, located below the high stone wall on the lower side of the villa. I entered a passageway in the wall, and a cavernous underground chamber was barely visible in the gloom. In the Second World War it was a sanctuary for the local people when the Allied Forces were fighting to reclaim Italy from the German occupiers. Now, it was a damp and foreboding cavern that was slowly silting in. The thought of all those people who sought shelter there was like a ghostly memory of the past. To the left of the chamber was a set of stone stairs leading upward through an opening above. As I ascended the stairs, I got the feeling of being like the ancestors of the present-day Pueblo people, for they ascended from the four levels of the Lower Worlds to the Upper World we inhabit today. Emerging into the space above was a beautiful experience, once my eyes became adjusted to the bright sunlight. Two large, friendly, police dogs greeted me. After checking me out, they retreated to the shade of a plum tree and laid down. Then I took in the beauty of the green lawn and the stone terraced gardens that climb the mountainside like giant steps. On each level was a variety of fruit trees. In the center of that beauty sat a former monastery, more than five hundred years old. Its stone construction gave it the appearance of an old medieval fortress. We walked up two more flights of stone steps and arrived at the heavy oak front door of the villa.

Greeting Fillipo and me at the door was Paula Raffo, the lady of the manor. She impressed me as a person of Italian aristocracy—full eyelids of the kind in a Michelangelo painting, aquiline nose, and rather narrow lips. Her hair had several fashionable gray streaks, and she had the manner of a person who grew up in wealth and power. Along with her charm and grace was a sense of great confidence in who and what she was. Since this was my second visit to her villa (my wife, Bobbie, and granddaughter Shaunte had been there with me a year earlier), she dispensed with her customary tour of the villa, which is composed of three levels. The first level is dominated by a private chapel. Adjoining that is the wine cellar. The second level is Paula's rambling quarters. And the uppermost she rented out at the urging of her older brother, who didn't want her living alone in that huge place.

Paula took Fillipo and me out to dinner in one of her restaurants. This one was located off one of the very narrow streets near the cathedral, in the center of Pietrasanta. Fillipo and I were delighted at the range of hors d'oeuvres, appetizers, entrees, and wines Paula ordered for our table. The burning candles set on every table in this small cozy restaurant added their warm glow to a festive evening. After dinner, Fillipo excused himself, as he had to drive back to Florence. Paula gave me the keys to the small stone guesthouse located below the lower wall of the villa. This was to be my home for the next two weeks.

Every morning I hiked down the narrow canyon road leading to the village. People smiled and nodded to me and said "*Buon giorno.*" My breakfast was usually at one of those quaint sidewalk cafes the sculptors liked to hang out in. I'd order a steamy, strong cup of cappuccino with sugar and cream and a piece of Italian pastry.

Guadagnucci was working on a huge marble piece he had been commissioned to do for a sculpture garden. For this he rented space in the exclusive Giorgio Angeli Studio. He invited me to share that space with him. This was a great honor for me, and as it turned out, the studio was the envy of all the American sculptors in Pietrasanta.

Later at a birthday party held for one of Giorgio's sons, the entire Angeli clan turned out. Giorgio invited me and asked if I could do a ceremony for his son. Through an interpreter, I told him he honored me with such a request, and that I would be happy to do a Blessing Ceremony. Afterwards, the celebrants were enjoying the beautiful buffet and fine Italian wine, when I was approached by the only other American there.

She said, "You don't know how lucky you are to be invited here. It took me three years before I was accepted by them."

After she left to mingle with the others, Fonsecca, an unknown Italian sculptor, leaned over from his chair and whispered, "She only thinks she's been accepted. Not yet. Not just yet." Then he chuckled as he raised his wine glass toward mine and said, "*Salute.*"

A journalist from Carrara heard I was in town and tracked me down. Over lunch at the Michelangelo Cafe, he shared a story of tragedy and sadness. It seemed that every month, for two whole years, a worker at the Carrara marble quarries got killed in an accident of one type or another. Trucks loaded with tons of marble slipped off the tiny steep roads, plunging into the rocky canyons and killing the unfortunate driver. Or, there were those who were electrocuted. The marble is quarried using a diamond-studded cable that is driven by huge electric motors. Water is used to cool the diamond cable and pools of water build up, touching the high power lines strewn on the ground. A worker touching the charged water would be instantly killed.

The journalist told me, "A young worker in a small restaurant, perched on the mountain slope where the quarries are located, told me the last one to die was the second of his closest friends to go. He was on the bottom of a five-hundred-foot shaft when a crane lifting a forty-ton block of marble broke loose, just as it was reaching the top. There wasn't much left they could find of his body for the funeral. The young restaurant worker said he quit his job in the quarries after that tragedy."

The journalist then asked, "Fortunate Eagle, can you do a ceremony for the workers of the quarries?"

I said I could and that it was an honor for me to do so.

He smiled and shook my hand. "I'll make the arrangements and we will be ready for you in two days."

The word quickly spread around the village, with notices being posted in the restaurants. The sculptors were also invited to participate.

On the appointed day, Paula Raffo and Gigi Guadagnucci picked me up and drove to Carrara. This would be the first time in history an American Indian was to conduct a ceremony at the Carrara quarries. The workers had cleaned off a flat plateau of solid marble where the ceremony was to take place. The years of taking out marble had left a manmade cliff hundreds of feet high and created an amphitheater of marble.

The sculptors and workers, some accompanied by their families, started arriving, hiking their way up the slope to the plateau. They were instructed to form a large circle. Paula was my interpreter. I explained to the people the Indian way of always giving something back to our Earth Mother when we take something from Her.

Several bowls of tobacco had been placed at the base of the sheer wall of marble. I asked all the workers and sculptors to make a Prayer of Thanksgiving to the Mother Mountain and then give a gift of tobacco. It was surprising how quickly the people of this Catholic-ruled nation responded to this Native ceremony. We had a heartfelt ceremony of Thanksgiving for the Mother Mountain of Carrara, which had provided generations of their people with a livelihood. Now the people were showing their appreciation.

Afterward, a group of us went to Paula's small restaurant for a feast. It was evident that Paula and Gigi were very proud of their Indian guest, as there were many "salutes" during the feast. The journalist gave a talk expressing appreciation and told me that the next time I came to Carrara, other quarries wanted me to perform ceremonies for them. This was flattering, heady stuff. But more importantly, it was a positive image that was created for the American Indians, the result of activities and ceremonies like this, that have reached out to many in the Italian communities of Carrara, Pesaro, Pietrasanta, Florence, and Bologna.

Back in Pietrasanta, I heard the news that George Nelson, the American sculptor, had been working among the little canals of the Italian millhouse, when he slipped and hit his head against a stone wall. Unconscious, he rolled into a small canal and drowned. The dreams he worked all his life to fulfill had drowned with him. It was a sad tragedy, but then I looked at it another way—we are all going to die sometime. And George died doing the things he loved most in life. It's the best way to go. Goodbye, George. Your ancestors will greet you in a good way in the Spirit World.

Peace and Friendship

Stillwater Reservation
Fallon, Nevada

February 29, 1985

Dear Peter:

On my way to the plane at Kennedy Airport, I picked up a *New York Times* to see what they did with our ceremony the day before yesterday at the United Nations. I finally found it, way inside—a little story titled, "Peace Pipe at the U.N.," with a picture of Allan Houser's monumental bronze *Offering of the Sacred Pipe* in the foreground, and three of us in the background during the Honoring Ceremony. The picture looked real good—the photographer made the sculpture in this new permanent home at the UN the important thing, not us, which was right and proper.

But you'd never know from those few paragraphs how moving it was, or what a historic moment it was for Indian people, to have our Apache brother's monument, the work of a great modern Indian sculptor, installed in the United Nations courtyard in front of the U.S. Mission, as a gift to the people of the world and a permanent prayer for peace.

So, let me tell you about it the way it happened after the four of us Indians, Delmar Boni, who is also an Apache artist, Doc Tate Nevaquaya, who is a Comanche and an artist from Oklahoma, and his wife, Charlotte, and I, arrived to honor Allan Houser and the presentation of his sculpture to Ambassador Jeanne Kirkpatrick and the UN with a traditional Pipe Ceremony and the Ceremony of the Sacred Circle.

We formally opened the gift giving with a procession to the plaza, the courtyard of the U.S. Mission, where Allan's sculpture was standing. All the guests were assembled there in a circle. We were wearing different sorts of Indian attire, reflecting our different cultures and the modern world in which we found ourselves. Delmar had long hair, Indian style, and his Indian clothing; Doc Tate wore his eagle feather warbonnet with a western-style light suit, his wife wore buckskins; I wore my beaded Chippewa outfit and roach headdress. I was there as another Indian artist, but more because I am also a Pipe Holder. Allan Houser and his friend Representative Glen Green decided that the giving of the gift should be acknowledged in a traditional way, to please the spirits and invoke their blessing in return. It did me honor. The beautiful bronze statue is of an Indian of the Plains holding his sacred pipe mouthpiece-first toward the spirits—it has such elegant lines; it's seven feet tall, soaring like the wings of an eagle! It brings the Indian message to where it should, and must, be heard and seen and heeded: the Indian message of peace, of respect for the land, for Indian culture, and religious freedom. Allan Houser did me honor, and so I honored him.

Doc Tate played a traditional melody on his old-style flute, a tribal serenade in honor of all those present. As master of ceremonies I motioned to Delmar to sing an Apache song, a song of his and Allan Houser's Chiricahua Apache people. And with that, the ambassador to the United Nations, Jeanne J. Kirkpatrick, followed by former UN Ambassador John Scali, Allan Houser, Glen Green, and other dignitaries, made their formal entrance.

Ambassador Kirkpatrick gave a welcoming speech, followed by John Scali, who explained how the idea of bringing the statue as a gift to the UN came to be. Ambassador Kirkpatrick spoke again, stressing the significance of the event, and introduced Allan Houser, whose words were brief and spoken with his characteristic humility, to the effect that the honors and recognition were not for him but for all American people, in whose name this monument was being dedicated. Ambassador Kirkpatrick's politics are surely not mine, and right at that moment some people in her administration were probably thinking up new ways to deprive Indian people of the economic and social help they need on the reservations and to continue making war on the Indian people by other means. But she was there representing the American people as ambassador to the UN, and with all its shortcomings the UN is, as has been said, the last best hope for mankind. And she was gracious in her acceptance of the gift, paying tribute to the Indians and expressing respect for our customs. She told us that the presentation and the ceremony we were conducting to bless and consecrate Allan's work of art was a moment she would always treasure. "In my last days," she said, "as I count my achievements, this will be among the most lasting." And she told the audience that, as a native Oklahoman, she had grown up with "an abiding respect for the traditions and views of American Indians." It did us honor to be so recognized in such a forum.

Then, Ambassador Kirkpatrick signaled to me, as master of ceremonies, which I was sort of by default, to begin the Indian Ceremony of the Sacred Circle and the Pipe. First I blew four times on an eagle bone whistle, once in each direction. The eagle, *Mi'gi'zi*, is our messenger to *Gitche Manitou*, which is what Chippewas call the Great Spirit, who is also called Grandfather. The four whistle calls were to notify Grandfather, the spirits of the Four Winds, and our Earth Mother, that a sacred ceremony was about to take place.

Tobacco offerings, *ah-say-ma*, were then given to the spirit of the sculpture, to our Earth Mother, from whose body the materials were taken to create the sculpture, to Allan Houser, and to the special guests. This was a ceremonial way of making peace with our space and our place.

There was a ground altar at our feet and all the ceremonial objects on it were purified by the smoke of four sacred herbs, which were burned in an abalone shell. After Delmar Boni was purified by smudging with the smoke, he took the shell with the smoking herbs and an eagle wing fan and went in a clockwise circle around the assembled guests, and then to Houser, Kirkpatrick, Scali, and other dignitaries, wafting the purifying smoke on them. All this time, Doc Tate accompanied the Purification and Blessing Ceremony with the music of his flute. That way the harmony of human beings with the earth and the universe was celebrated.

Next, I brought out the pipe from its beaded buckskin pouch to make it ready by cleansing and purifying it with the sacred smoke. Six sacred offerings were given to the pipe. (You know this pipe, I was working on it when you visited with me last summer. It has a flat wooden stem decorated with four turtles carved from the red pipestone, and another turtle that is part of the bowl. It represents Turtle Island, which is our name for this earth of ours.) The first offering was to Grandfather, the Great Spirit Gitche Manitou, the originator of all life and keeper of our spirits. The second was to the spirits of the East, the source of light and wisdom, represented by the color yellow. Next was the South, the spirit home of our ancestors, represented by the color red. The fourth offering was to the spirits of the West, the source of our medicine and home of the Thunder Beings, represented by the color black. Then I offered to the spirits of the North, represented by the white swan, who acknowledges the four seasons and who is represented by the color white. The sixth and final offering to the pipe was dedicated to our Earth Mother, Keeper of the Sacred Circle of Life, the protector of all living things that share life with her. Then the sacred pipe was filled in the proper way and placed on the altar, and after that I handed Delmar the eagle feathers, the sacred feathers.

Delmar prayed over the feathers, to all living things that share our Earth Mother, for the water that nourishes life—the two-leggeds, the four-leggeds, the winged ones, the creatures that inhabit the water, and the creepy-crawly things—to all the green things that nurture all of us. Delmar then took the feathers and started them in the clockwise circle, the path of the sun, among all the assembled guests. Some just stroked the feathers as a symbol of respect, and others spoke words of praise and honor, the special purpose of this event, and a plea for world peace and harmony. When the Talking Circle was complete and the feathers were handed back to me, it was time to continue the Pipe Ceremony.

I picked up the sacred pipe and prayed to Grandfather, to the spirits of the four directions, and to our Earth Mother. I prayed to the four sacred colors, the four colors of human beings, so that one day we can truly come together as equals, showing respect and understanding for each other; so that we can all walk in balance and harmony with all living things that share our Earth Mother and her bounty. Then Delmar lit my pipe and I again offered it to the six directions . . . to Grandfather, the four cardinal points, and then to our Earth Mother. Then I handed the pipe to Delmar and Doc Tate. They carried it around the circle. Those who did not smoke were touched with it on both shoulders, the right, then the left. Allan Houser, Ambassador Kirkpatrick, former Ambassador John Scali, and the other officials all smoked the pipe.

Delmar and Doc Tate smoked the pipe and handed it to me at the altar. I smoked the pipe out to its finish. Then I "broke the pipe," which means separating the bowl from the stem, in the name of all our relations. For the pipe has power only when it is joined—when the male part, the stem, and the female part, the bowl, have become one. By joining the two halves the pipe is "charged," and when they are separated the power is withdrawn.

This officially ended the Pipe Ceremony. The ashes were taken from the pipe bowl and put in a small box, which, along with an eagle feather, I presented to Allan Houser. "The ashes commemorate this sacred ceremony," I said to him. "Place it in a special place in your house, in a sacred area in the mountains, or give it to a small plant or tree in your yard so that it will be given renewed strength." And I said to him: "The eagle feathers are for your special gift that you have given to the people of the world in the name of peace, and for the honors that are bestowed upon you today." I then presented eagle feathers to Delmar Boni and Doc Tate Nevaquaya, "for the special sharing and honors which have occurred today."

There was one more formal thing to be done. I picked up the empty pipe, joined bowl and stem together once more, and handed it to Allan Houser. We approached Ambassador Kirkpatrick together: "We present this sacred pipe to you in the name of world peace and because you represent the keepers of the peace for our nation. This is the Turtle Island Pipe, it represents this land we live on, which our people, and Annishinaabeg, call Turtle Island. The four turtles on the stem represent the four sacred colors and the colors of man. The bowl represents our symbol for peace. When you take the pipe, always take it with a good heart and of good mind." Allan Houser then handed the Turtle Island Pipe to Ambassador Kirkpatrick, who acknowledged it, with words expressing the great honor and pride that she felt in accepting the pipe on behalf of the United States Mission to the United Nations. And she said that a plaque will be attached to its display case commemorating the event.

That is how it went at the UN. On the way home, on the plane, I tried to read but couldn't concentrate on the printed page, my mind was so full. So I thought about everything I have been telling you since we met, everything you have on tape, all those milestones on the road I chose for myself, this Indian Road, when I could so easily have gone on a different path. . . . Early childhood on the Red Lake Reservation, back in Minnesota . . . the old-style powwows. . . . Indian boarding schools, where they surely did not have the abiding respect for Indian ways of which Ambassador Kirkpatrick spoke. Trying as hard as they could to educate the Indian out of us, make us into good little brown white kids. . . . Learning from the old-time Indian pipe carvers at the Pipestone Quarry, the old legends, the way the stone is carved. . . . Meeting that beautiful Shoshone girl, Bobbie, at boarding school. Bobbie, who has now been my wife of thirty-five years . . . marrying, moving with her to the Bay Area. . . . My wars with the termites . . .

Termination, relocation during the Eisenhower years. . . . First steps on the Red Road, the Indian path, picking up traditional knowledge I never had a chance to learn as a kid . . . Chippewa ways, Plains Indian ways, picking up from books, from traditional Indian people, what had been held back from me. . . . Bay Area Indian politics, the United Bay Area Council of American Indian Affairs becoming a real force. . . . Working with Indian people displaced in an alien urban world. . . . The heady days of the Indian occupation of Alcatraz. . . . Getting prison authorities to recognize the religious rights of Indian convicts. . . . Scalping Columbus. . . . Discovering Italy and claiming it for Indian people to bring home something important—how silly and insulting it is to talk of the "Discovery of America" when Indian people were here for tens of thousands of years. . . . Traveling the powwow circuit with Bobbie, winning prizes as a ceremonial dancer—first prize at age fifty-three—and seeing my son Adam do the same, starting as the littlest kid and winning his fame. . . . Testifying, demonstrating, writing, speaking, and teaching for Indian education, Indian religious rights, Indian economics. . . . Adoption by my Crow family, being given my Indian name, not "also known as" but a proper name conferred in an Indian way. . . . Carving pipes for Indian people . . . for white collectors who honor Indian culture, Indian art. . . . Going on to become a Pipe Holder, learning to conduct sweats and pipe ceremonies in the proper way . . .

And then goodbye to the First American Termite Company, goodbye to Indian small business, to Bay Area Indian politics . . . back to the "quiet life" on a reservation. . . . Being set up, arrested, hauled off in handcuffs to Reno like some violent desperado, jailed, tried. But the government failed to get a conviction for a charge I admitted to, selling eagle feathers to an Indian, which I maintain is my right though the government says is not. . . . The government not letting go, because it can't stand being defeated. . . . Adventures with the "wannabes," the "seekers." . . . Slowly moving from craft to art, from pipe carving to sculpture . . . becoming a full-time artist, a sculptor, still only a junior member of the august company of modern Indian sculptors, of which Allan Houser and Doug Hyde are the leaders we honor, all America honors, but trying . . .

And all the while I was searching for meaning in my life, finding it in my sixth decade in the practice of my religion and my art at the same time. Not "reinventing" but reclaiming my identity as an Indian person. This strange thing, which I do not quite understand yet: my growth as an artist going hand in glove with my becoming more and more an Indian spiritual person. Putting the pieces together, learning to fit the pieces of my life into the larger whole of a pan-Indian consciousness that is itself the consequence of the government's long effort to deculturate and alienate us from our own tribal traditions. Being arrested had something to do with that, surely, jerking me back from a too light-hearted, perhaps even too commercialized path, and turning me in a different direction,toward being a serious sculptor who tries to find meaning through his work and his being in the Indian past and the Indian present.

So the government really did me a favor. A lot of what the government does and says to us Indians is ironic and, in a sad way, even funny. Look how concerned they are with the rights of the Miskitos in Nicaragua! I'd be embarrassed, making noises like that, with the kind of record our government has piled up with respect to Indian people in this country. And that it still piles up to this day. It may be low humor, unconscious, but it's still funny. Just think of the irony of me at the United Nations ceremony as an Indian artist and religious person, blessing Ambassador Kirkpatrick with eagle feathers while another part of the government she represents denies me my religious rights and seizes my eagle feathers as "contraband" because they are not registered with the government. It was not Indians who brought the eagle close to extinction, but whites. And whites are still doing it with their deadly poisons, their rifles, and their invasions of the eagle's habitats. Yet it is Indians who, due to restrictions on their customs and their religions (not to mention the possibility of being set up), must bear the brunt of good and useful laws designed to protect this bird that has been sacred to us and whose feathers we have used for thousands of years without ever threatening its survival. And, anyway, why do Indians have to register their sacred objects when white Christians do not? Is all that not ironic and laughable?

I must tell you, it took me a few days to come down from that emotional high of the United Nations Plaza. Now it is back to business as usual. I am working on the largest sculpture I have ever attempted— seven hundred pounds of beautiful stone I must get ready for an exhibition at the Museum of the American Indian. And, meanwhile, I wonder how much more of my time and the government's time, how much more of the taxpayer's money, and the money I work hard for as an artist to use to support my family but instead have to spend on legal fees, is the government willing to spend going after this one fifty-five-year-old Indian? And I wonder, how much of its interest in me, this whole three-year-long business with the eagle feathers, can be traced to the Alcatraz affair, to my once having been that heinous thing, an "Indian activist," even if that "activism" has always been peaceful?

You tell me.

Your friend,
Adam

The Goose Hunter

Below our reservation here at Stillwater exists a huge wetlands, remnants of an enormous inland sea called Lake Lahontan. Thousands of ducks, geese, and swans use the wetlands as a stopover during their annual migration along the Pacific Flyway, making the wetlands a hunter's paradise.

On the only main road out of the wetlands, the United States Fish and Wildlife Service set up a check station, to assure that all hunters comply with the law.

One particular weekend the check station was manned by the most racist redneck wildlife agent in the west. More than anybody, he hated Indians. Manning the checkout station to nail one of those game-stealing redskins gave him the opportunity he was waiting for.

After the morning hunt, vehicle after vehicle went through the checkout. Finally a beat-up old Ford pulled in and, lo and behold, behind the steering wheel sat an old Indian.

As the game warden approached the car, the Indian rolled down the window.

"Been doing a little hunting today, Chief?"

"Yup."

"Had any luck?"

"Yup."

"May I check them out, Chief?"

With that, the Indian opened the trunk, revealing six dead ducks.

The warden licked his chops thinking, "Now I'm going to cook this Indian's goose."

Picking up a mallard drake, the warden put the duck's butt up to his nose and took a long, slow sniff.

"Say! This here's an Idaho duck. You got an Idaho duck stamp, Chief?"

Whipping out his billfold, the Indian produced the Idaho duck stamp.

The warden threw the duck back into the trunk of the car and pretended to study the others. Picking another one up, he repeated his procedure for the first duck. After sniffing the duck's butt he announced,

"This here's an Oregon duck. You got an Oregon duck stamp, Chief?"

"Yes sir, right here," replied the Indian.

The warden slammed the duck down. Determined to nail this Indian, he picked up a third duck. Again he stuck the duck's butt up to his nose, and slowly smelled it. "This time I got you, Chief. This here's a Montana duck. You got a Montana duck stamp?"

To his amazement, the Indian produced a Montana duck stamp.

The warden realized the game was over.

"You're one damn smart Indian. Where you from, Chief?"

The Indian dropped his pants and bent over and said, "You're the expert. You tell me."

Going Back

We had returned to the Red Lake Indian Reservation in Minnesota for the annual Fourth of July Powwow and celebration. With my Shoshone wife, Bobbie, and me was our firstborn granddaughter, Benayshe Ba Equay (Bird of the Water Woman). She was born on the fifth anniversary of the Indian occupation of Alcatraz Island, November 9, 1975. She was now a beautiful, bright-eyed teenager, and I wanted to show her the place of my birth, way back in time—1929, to be exact.

We started at the site of the old tribal blacksmith shop, where my grandfather used to work. I could literally smell the smoking coal from the forge, as Grandpa cranked the bellows and a hail of sparks danced around the red-hot coals like fireflies on a cool summer evening. Grabbing a set of tongs, he fished out a hunk of red-hot metal from the coals and commenced to beat it on an anvil with a four-pound hammer. That red-hot glob of metal took new shape under the skillful hands of my grandpa. Yes, he could give that metal a new shape, a new life, a new purpose.

Benayshe interrupted my reverie. "But, Grandpa, there is no black-smith shop here," she protested.

She was right, for I was seeing and talking about something of the past, which sat on this very spot that is now occupied by the tribal police station.

Undaunted, I led her down the small path we used to walk when we went from our cabin to the tribal agency. A small gravel pit was on the downslope. We stopped as I examined the pebbles.

"What are you looking for Grandpa?"

"Little stones of hardened clay. When my mother was pregnant with one of my little sisters, she used to stop here and gather little stones of hardened clay and eat them."

"Oh, yuck!" responded Benayshe, but she joined in the hunt. With feminine instinct, she picked up a small rounded stone. "Is this one?"

Yes, it was. And I found another. "*Wesinin*, let's eat," I told her, as I popped the small clod into my mouth and started chewing, setting an example for my reluctant granddaughter. Obediently, she put her stone into her mouth and slowly started chewing. Benayshe now joined the long line of women going back into the mists of time, who hunted and ate those little clay stones. There was no way I could tell the nutritional value of those stones for pregnant women, but it certainly could not be any worse than eating pickles.

As we continued down the path, the low brush and trees seemed to close in on us. The beautiful songs of birds hidden in the deep shadows of the woods called out to welcome us into their world, in spite of the fact we could not see our feathered hosts.

We stopped in the middle of a small footbridge, which spanned the little creek below. It sparkled with a clarity I found hard to believe, because strewn along its banks were old automobile tires and other debris. It was more than sixty years ago that my older brothers and I used to come down to the little creek and fill our three-gallon buckets with its cool, clear water. We often stood on the two-by-twelve-inch planks peering into the pristine waters looking for the huge trout lurking below.

Benayshe and I continued our stroll through family history, up the opposite slope to the place where eight children were raised in a log cabin so many decades ago. Where little boys once carried buckets of water up the path and then crossed the grassy area to our log cabin, we now crossed the grassy area to a HUD home occupied by total strangers.

The vortex of childhood memories collided with modern reality in a gut-wrenching way. That modern HUD house seemed somehow to rob me of my past, depriving me of my childhood memories of family and friends long gone. It's a story repeated over and over, as other elders recount their past that can no longer be reclaimed.

"Oh, it's you, Adam," said the tribal police officer as he drove up to us in a squad car. "We just got a call complaining about prowlers in the area."

Welcome home, Adam. Welcome home.

Two years later we visited the great Pipestone Quarries in southern Minnesota, now a national monument. Bobbie and I enjoy bringing along our grandchildren to experience culture and history. This year it's

Tsosie's turn. His name means Tall Slender One in Navajo. His mother came from Window Rock, Arizona. Tsosie is a champion Northern Traditional Dancer. His passion is to follow the Powwow Trail in summer. He was feeling real good, as he had just taken second place and eight hundred dollars at the Red Lake Powwow the weekend before. Not to be outdone, I had taken second place in the Men's Senior category, so I was feeling pretty good myself.

Tsosie brought me down to earth. "You were just lucky there weren't more than two old men in your category, Grandpa."

We stood at the base of Winnewissa Falls. The peculiar smell of the mist took me back to my childhood, when that earthy odor was a frequent experience for all the little Indian kids who played there. Palma Wilson, the superintendent of the Pipestone National Monument was with us. I again started to reminisce about the past. As I talked, more and more tourists stopped their wanderings and joined the circle of curious people. They expressed a genuine interest in how little Indian kids lived in the federal boarding school. Palma suggested I sign on with the National Park Service as an interpretative guide. There was no question about it, I was flattered by the request.

And if there was an audience for such a story, I felt it necessary to write a book about my childhood experience before all memories of such times are lost forever. So, I wrote *Pipestone: My Life in an Indian Boarding School,* and the University of Oklahoma Press published it in 2010.

The Nickel Hunter

Fallon, Nevada

A little bit of local folklore is mysteriously occurring on the nearby reservation at Fortunate Eagle's Round House Gallery. Rumors are rapidly being circulated around the area that if anyone wants to have good luck, they toss a nickel on the pavement between the Round House sign and the corner mailboxes.

It is believed that if Fortunate Eagle finds the nickel and blesses it, good things will happen to the person who dropped it there. In the past three weeks, Fortunate Eagle has picked up and blessed a total of fifty-three nickels.

"I don't know if anybody is getting good luck as a result of this," said Fortunate Eagle with a smile. "But I believe my luck will change when the people start dropping quarters."

Medicine Gift

Survival on any Indian reservation today depends on making use of what gifts you have, or what gifts you can produce, to meet the economic struggle. For my wife, Bobbie, and me, it has required a way of life of developing all the creativity we could manage, over these last twenty-three of our sixty-three years on earth together, into marketable skills.

August of 1996 found me in the sculpture studio I had built for myself on the reservation, preparing for the annual Santa Fe Indian Market. The event at Santa Fe is the mother of all Indian art shows in the country, with the very best artists from Native America, and the very best prices to be commanded from the trend-driven interest in Indian art. The proceeds from our sales there would, hopefully, carry us through the long winter months ahead.

I was bending over, bowed in the back, as I moved one of the large alabaster boulders in which I would find the shape and spirit of a new creation, when I felt a sickening stretch of flesh in my lower stomach, like something pulling apart. Walking slowly in a half-hunchback to the house, I braved myself into reaching down to my left groin, where I could feel the bulge of intestines pushing through the muscle wall of my stomach.

It had been my way to push the limits of my skills and my strength to the boundaries of my own pride, but the pride and arrogance of my youth could not carry me far this time. I had to acknowledge that I was a gray-haired old man with a busted gut.

The surgery that followed was one of the most painful torments I have experienced. And, never had I felt so pathetically helpless as when my wife drove me home from the hospital in Reno back to the reservation east of Fallon, where the long, slow road to recovery was just beginning.

I laid in bed, unable even to begin the daily routines that had been my life, and I tried to take stock of what had happened. The surgeons and the medical staff had performed their jobs in a most professional manner. I was sewn back into myself, however sorely. The rest of the healing process was left to me alone.

In the past, I had conducted many ceremonies for the health and spirit sense of others. One of these was comparable to shamanic spirit journeys performed in conjunction with the Cleansing and Purification Ceremonies of the sweat lodge. I wondered if it would be possible now for the physician, so to speak, to heal himself. "And, why not?" my spiritual side asked my physical side. "Why not?"

It was not to be a Vision Quest—looking for new answers to life. Rather, it was meant as a journey into time that was there, in my mind. I closed my eyes and found myself talking and interacting with people I know, both living and dead, as if they were there with me, sharing in conversation about pain and existence. It was so real that I wanted to loll in it, lay back and ease along with the talk. But when I opened my eyes, *poof*, they were all gone. And when I closed my eyelids again and began searching, there was a black-and-white landscape, like one from an old movie, that slowly bled into full color, the way it happened in *The Wizard of Oz*. I just watched as the colors seemed to grow in intensity. They seemed to be glowing, and I was feeling better and more comfortable and even started enjoying it all.

Then the phone at my bedside rang. The colors of Oz were wiped away as I took the call from my friend Tom.

"Adam, we have a problem in our family, and I'd like to ask your advice on a couple of questions my mother has."

"Okay," I said, still uncertain of where the line had been crossed from dreams to reality. "Go ahead, ask."

"About a year ago my father passed away and, well, he left behind a car. My mother thinks the spirit of my father is still in that car. And what she wants to know is whether she can burn this car, maybe, and then bury it out in the desert someplace."

In terms no less real than my other recent conversations, I told him, "Well, Tom, I think you have a problem there. First, I don't think the Environmental Protection Agency will appreciate your polluting the atmosphere with a burning car. And, second, I doubt the Bureau of Land Management will allow you to bury the hulk of it out in the desert."

It could have been my imagination, or just my instinct, that kept my thoughts racing.

"Tom, how long ago was it that your father died?"

"A year ago. December twenty-fourth last year."

"Tom, are you aware of a ceremony performed a year after a period of mourning called Wash-Away-the-Tears?"

"No, but it sounds right. It, it sounds interesting."

"Why don't you tell your mother I would be honored to conduct the ceremony for the entire family to wash away their tears, and then, at the end of the ceremony, she can give the car to me as a medicine gift."

He hardly thought about it at all. "Adam! Hey, that sounds pretty good. Pretty good. I'll tell my mother about it, and then I'll get back to you. About a week, I'll get back to you."

My eyelids went back in search of the long talks and the glowing magic colors, but instead I went to a slow fade into sleep.

Moving about my house was not only a pain, but it was a challenge. By the end of that first week out of the hospital, I was able to negotiate myself at last into a recliner chair in the living room. I was sitting there when a friend of mine paid a visit to check on my condition. I told him the story of reaching into a Spirit Journey to heal myself and of the conversations and the colors and the phone call. I wasn't really certain if any of it had actually happened. So, searching for where the line between reality and dream had been, I called Tom later that evening.

"Adam, not only was that call for real, my mother loves the idea and wants you to start making the arrangements as soon as you can."

At least now I had something besides alabaster boulders in which to direct my energy. The ceremony would take my focus off my own problems and occupy my time with fulfilling the needs of others, even if I still wasn't sure about how much was memory, and how much was a dream.

Calling together my family, I outlined the Wash-Away-the-Tears Ceremony and delegated duties among them, giving each a task, including my grandchildren. By December twenty-fourth, all the initial preparations in my home had been completed. The ceremonial altar was a buffalo robe, on which there was a buffalo skull, an eagle fan, and my medicine bundle. Pendleton blankets were spread out on the floor for the family to sit on, and a lone chair was provided for Tom's mother.

A caravan of cars entered our gravel driveway that afternoon at the appointed time. Tom led the group in his Blazer, followed by car after car of his extended family.

It went well, a beautiful and emotional experience in which members of the family said their final goodbyes to Tom Senior embraced by the Sacred Pipe. At its end, each of the family took a sip of water to symbolically wash away their tears, and at the same time renew their own spirits.

The feast that followed was held with celebration and joy, marking not the end, but the continuation of life. When one of Tom's brothers said it was time for him to leave in order to catch his flight from Reno to New York, it signaled the reluctant end to the ceremony and celebration.

In turn, each of the family came to Bobbie and me with their thanks for what they had shared and experienced. The last to grasp us in a hug before leaving was Tom's mother. She looked warmly into my eyes and then drew a manila envelope from her purse. It was heavy with papers and keys as she led us out to the row of cars in our driveway.

"Here is the medicine gift we promised," she said quietly. "This is yours."

It was a gleaming, metallic pewter Mark VI Lincoln Continental in mint condition.

Newt

Red Lake Indian Reservation is what is called a "closed reservation," meaning it was never opened to white settlement through the Dawes Act of 1887. The land is still held "in common" by the tribe. Hunting and fishing on the reservation is controlled by the tribe and is for tribal members only.

Newt Gingrich, Republican Speaker of the House, was on a national tour in an attempt to recruit Indians into the Republican Party and to latch on to more of our casino money. Despite the fact that he had never hunted in his life, he wanted to prove he was just one of the boys, and decided he would like to go deer hunting. Not wanting to offend the congressman by stating it was a closed reservation, Tribal Chairman Duke Red Moccasin gave his official blessing on the condition Newt hire an Indian guide. "No problem there, Chief," Newt replied, and then impatiently listened to the chairman instruct him on the fine art of deer hunting.

Early the next morning, Newt was suited up in the finest deer hunting outfit Bemidji Woolen Mills could provide. On his belt was a beautiful Buck knife with an eight-inch blade. He carried a Winchester Model 70 .30-06 rifle, which fired a 180-grain bullet that traveled 2,800 feet per second, capable of knocking down a bull moose with a single shot.

Newt could just picture himself as a Teddy Roosevelt out on an African safari, hunting the biggest, baddest beasts of the Kalahari. As they approached the narrows on the west side of the lake, Newt's guide, Orville Moose Nose, tried to calm down the nervous congressman: "When we get out of the SUV, don't slam the door or make any noise. We will space ourselves one hundred feet apart and start a deer drive."

Loading their rifles, they quietly slipped into the deep woods—took five steps, then stopped and listened. Newt was really nervous. They took another quiet five steps, stopped and listened. Five more steps. Newt hadn't traveled one hundred feet into the deep woods when he heard a noise. He whirled, shot, and heard a scream. He shot his Indian guide, Orville Moose Nose, who was flat on the ground. "Oh my God!" Newt babbled over and over, as he drug the stricken Orville back to the SUV.

At the Indian health hospital, Newt was pacing back and forth in the waiting room.

Finally the doctor emerged.

"Will he live doctor? Will he live?"

The doctor replied, "Well, congressman, I believe he would have had a better chance if you hadn't gutted him before bringing him in.

Come to think of it, Newt, as Speaker of the House, used to gut favorable legislation for the tribes before sending it on to the Senate. Way to go, Newt!

Art Imitates Life—Or Does Life Imitate Art?

I first wrote the story about Newt twenty years ago and stashed it away in my growing pile of short stories. Now that I am in the process of putting them all into book form, I am shocked and amazed that the vice president of these United States, Dick Cheney, had the audacity to upstage my story, by shooting his hunting companion and lawyer, Harry Whittington.

Harry survived the shooting, and if he were an old time Indian, he would have earned the name, "Shot in the Face."

It is a hot day in the desert southwest. Dust devils whip up the sand and sage like miniature tornadoes. A lone figure is seen on top of a mountain doing a rubbing on a huge boulder covered with Native American petroglyphs. His excitement is obvious, as he finishes the rubbing. Rolling up the paper, like a sacred scroll, he is seen leaping, jumping, and running down the mountain to his small camp, which is quickly packed and loaded into his SUV. He roars off to the south, where he connects with Highway 15, and heads toward Los Angeles.

A month later, the same desert floor is covered by what looks like a Gypsy caravan, only this is an independent film company.

The executive producer/director/writer is a short, squat, arrogant Jew named Bernie. He has the unique distinction of producing the worst movies in Hollywood. His movies are so bad, he makes Ed Wood look like a theatrical genius.

His budget is so small Bernie is lucky if he can rub two nickels together. With so many Hollywood wannabes, he is still able to assemble a motley crew of performers, such as over-the-hill Las Vegas showgirls, including many who have gone to pot. Native Americans want to break into the Hollywood scene, following the success of *Dances with Wolves*. Young, toothy men want to be the next Brad Pitt. The entire film crew sets up camp on the California-Nevada state line. Bernie cannot afford the license fees of either state. He reasons that if a California official is seen approaching from the west, he will simply move his camp a few feet to the east, into Nevada. In order to find the exact state line, Bernie has his computer nerd, Alphie, use his GPS to make an accurate determination.

Let's flash back to 1856, when California became a state. Surveyors then laid out the state boundaries. No problem there. Eight years later, Nevada became a state despite the fact it did not have the required population. What it did have was plenty of gold and silver to help finance the Civil War for the North. To survey the state lines, Nevada hired a German named Allexey W. Von Schmidt, who was nothing more than a pickled-brain alcoholic. Look this up in your atlas. There is a straight line extending from Lake Tahoe, four hundred miles south to Arizona. Von Schmidt used the wrong California survey takeoff points and mapped a parallel line, leaving a strip of land two hundred feet wide, and four hundred miles long. It's a literal no-man's-land. When you do the math, this figures out to be more than fifteen square miles, an area larger than both the Vatican and Monaco combined.

Using this information, Bernie has Alphie and his crew drive stakes into the ground one hundred yards apart, on both the California and Nevada sides. Bernie now believes he is beyond the jurisdiction of either state.

Walking Eagle, an aspiring actor/activist/historian, sees this as a great opportunity. He takes a mud flap, depicting a shapely chrome-plated nude, off a supply truck, and attaches it to a pole. He makes a makeshift flag.

Surrounded by a group of Native American actors, Walking Eagle seriously intones, "In the name of the American Indians and pursuant to the Doctrine of Discovery, I hereby lay claim to this land to be known as "Walking Eagle Nation." It's obvious Walking Eagle is no slouch when it comes to self-promotion. Bernie is quick to seize upon this new opportunity and instructs his attorney to file papers seeking sovereign status for Walking Eagle Nation with the United Nations and the World Court at The Hague.

The lone man who did the petroglyph rubbings returns to Los Angeles with exciting news of his discovery. He emails the "Original Man Club" members: "Slow Deer has a very important announcement to make at our next meeting." Fifty members show up at their spiritual center, not knowing what to expect. At the front of the room, Slow Deer takes his place in front of a large flag on the wall, which shows a man-like figure in the center of a circle and four turtles facing outward, to the four directions. They're painted red, white, yellow, and black.

Slow Deer is beaming with delight when he announces, "I have discovered the center of our spiritual universe, and now I show you proof." Slow Deer then unfurls a large sheet of paper on the conference table, displaying the rubbings of the ancient petroglyphs that are estimated to be ten thousand years old. There is an audible gasp from the members, followed by shrieks of joy and laughter. The entire group goes into a spontaneous hug fest. Some reverently touch the sacred rubbings, which include the identical design as the Original Man flag. It is symbolic of the Shroud of Turin, depicting the likeness of Jesus.

"Pilgrimage! Pilgrimage!" shout the members, as plans are made to visit their sacred site. It is impossible to tell there is a mass exodus out of Los Angeles when the traffic is bumper to bumper anyway. All their vehicles have small Original Man flags attached to their radio antennas.

Arriving at the state line, they are confronted by the bizarre sight of an encampment of teepees stretched out between parallel lines of wooden stakes. Those stakes run for miles and miles, including the very top of the mountain containing the sacred petroglyphs.

Slow Deer signals the caravan to pull off the road a half-mile from the strange camp, not knowing what to make of it. The members form a circle to discuss what to do next.

In keeping with ancient tradition, it is decided to send two emissaries, bearing sacred gifts of tobacco and white sage to the leaders of the strange camp. Slow Deer and Tamara are selected. After dressing in beautiful tribal outfits, the two set out to walk to the camp.

Walking Eagle and the rest of the Indian actors see them coming and prepare a welcome by forming a circle of their own.

Walking Eagle and Bernie are the welcoming committee. They acknowledge the gifts of tobacco and sage, and then introduce themselves as Walking Eagle and Bernie.

Slow Deer says, "But Bernie doesn't look Indian."

Walking Eagle counters, "He is one of the lost tribe of Israel. Neither of you or any of that group back in your camp looks Indian."

Slow Deer proudly says, "That's because all of us were Indian in our former lifetimes."

"Oh shit!" exclaims Walking Eagle.

Slow Deer lays out the rubbings of the sacred petroglyphs and explains that the mountain to the north of them represents the center of their sacred universe. While Slow Deer is talking, Walking Eagle is slyly checking out Tamara and says, "Man, she's a hottie!" Then he says, "Tell you what, folks. You and your group can go to the mountain for four days in order to do a proper series of ceremonies."

Slow Deer, recognizing a challenge to real Indians would be a stretch for his group, accepts the invitation.

Bernie and the film crew continue filming a cheesy version of history, where painted women of the East are paid to marry the nouveau riche men of the gold mining fields, only to find their wagon train surrounded by a tribe of angry Indians. Bernie hires the retired Tonto, who now weighs 350 pounds. As he mounts his pony, the poor beast slowly sinks to the ground accompanied by loud farts.

Tonto says, "We need a larger horse, Kemo Sabe."

"No, we need a smaller Indian," replies Bernie.

The teepees Bernie rented do double duty. Not only do they serve as props for the Indian village scenes, they also provide lodging for the actors and crew.

All the teepees have electric lights installed high in the center. The light in the showgirls' teepee is deliberately placed waist-high. So, after the evening shoot, while the women take off their cumbersome frontier clothes and change into something more comfortable, the men sit around the outside of the teepee and are entertained by a beautiful light show. The shadows of the women changing clothes are silhouetted on the white canvas cover, much to the delight of the men.

The large mess tent is where meals are served every day. In the evening, it becomes a disco or a nightclub, where the entire camp comes to party. Bernie doesn't care about the wild parties, because he figures booze is a lot cheaper than high salaries for the actors.

While all the partying is going on, Walking Eagle is working on plans to consolidate his holdings of the new nation. After several meetings with the Indian actors, they decide to form a new tribe: the Fugawi. Walking Eagle tells Bernie, "Hey, Bernie. We named our new tribe in recognition of your people, the Jews."

Bernie is stymied, "How do you figure?"

Walking Eagle replies, "Remember the story of Moses and his followers wandering for forty years in the desert? Each morning at sunrise, he looked around him and muttered, "Where the fuck are we?""

To become a member of the Fugawi Tribe, everyone is expected to give flesh offerings—Indians and non-Indians alike. Bernie knows of the Jewish tradition of a flesh offering called a "bris," where the foreskin of the penis is cut off in a ritualistic manner. Giving a small piece of flesh from his arm is no big deal, as his bris was ten times that size.

The motto of the Walking Eagle Nation is, "Always do good, do no one harm." They don't need ten commandments when two will do.

Bernie is well aware the prolonged stay in the desert is costing him money he doesn't have, and all fifty of his credit cards are maxed out. He approaches Walking Eagle and says, "Chief! We need 'em wampum!"

"What?" asks Walking Eagle.

"We need 'em wampum!" repeats Bernie.

Walking Eagle replies, "I don't understand your Jewish mumbo jumbo. Can't you just say it in plain English?

Bernie snaps, "We need shekels, I mean money. If we don't get something soon, we'll just have to give up on this film project."

Walking Eagle gets a map of California and Nevada and shows it to Bernie. "Check this out Bernie. There are five major roads and highways crossing Walking Eagle Nation. We can put up tollbooths at every crossing and charge a toll of two dollars for every car. We will have a money pump! I just wish my ancestors had been so smart. We'd all be rich redskins today."

Bernie is thrilled by the concept, and soon tollbooths manned by skimpily dressed showgirls are on all five crossings.

"Two dollars to go two hundred feet? You've got to be crazy," is the usual response from motorists.

"Well, you can always go around," is the polite response the showgirls give.

The first day's take comes to twenty-five thousand dollars. Bernie almost craps in his pants when the total is announced. "We're all going to be friggen' rich!" He is jumping up and down, flapping his chubby little arms like a dodo bird in heat.

This incident is not lost on the governors of California and Nevada.

Pounding his desk in a rage, Governor Schwarzenegger yells, "Ve got the California tribes to pay up to twenty-five percent of their revenue to the state in order to secure a state compact. They gotta pay!" I'm not making this up, there really was an Austrian-born governor running the state of California.

"Governor," says a state aide, "Walking Eagle Nation is not in California."

"Ve will soon find out. Call out the state militia. Ve are going to have a showdown with those insurgents!"

"Yes, Herr Governor. But do you think a blitzkrieg tactic will intimidate those Indians?"

Soon state militia units from California and Nevada are converging on the main camp of Walking Eagle Nation—armored personnel carriers, half-tracks armed with rocket launchers, and Humvees, two of which were donated by Governor Schwarzenegger from his personal collection. Both state militias stop four hundred yards from their respective state lines. Their weapons trained on the camp.

"Not to worry, not to worry!" shouts Walking Eagle to his people. "They cannot afford another Wounded Knee Massacre."

"Turn up the music, bring out the beer and drinks, and smile girls, smile!" yells Bernie.

The temperature in the desert soon reaches 110 degrees. The interiors of all those armored vehicles soon reach 150 degrees. Their sweat-drenched occupants bail out and seek what little shade their hot vehicles provide. And, just a few hundred yards away, they observe beautiful dancing girls holding up cold beers and drinks. What the hell kind of war is this anyway?

By nightfall all the armored units are turned the other way. Their former occupants are now in the huge mess tent enjoying a great party.

"Governor Schwarzenegger, they beat our sweaty asses off without firing a shot. Our troops are now under the control of enemy forces."

The governor of Nevada orders the water trucks from Las Vegas to stop their deliveries. "Nobody can live in the desert very long without water."

Walking Eagle calls in a drilling rig and with a dowsing stick, he paces out his territory. "Dig here," he orders, not knowing he has found the fault line between the Pacific Plate and the inland tectonic plate. Instead of water, they strike light crude oil.

"Oh shit! No water?" cries Bernie.

Instead of a water aquifer, they have struck the largest pool of oil in North America. The oil gusher gives another reason for a major celebration by the oil-drenched celebrants.

Returning from the sacred mountain, Tamara and two other members of Original Man request membership in Walking Eagle Nation.

"What sources or talent can you bring to us?" asks Walking Eagle.

Tamara replies, "Well, for starters, my father is a professor of international law at UCLA."

The second person says, "I call myself Stone Man, a geologist."

The third claims, "I am called Craps. I serve as a consultant for the Indian gaming tribes of California."

"Welcome! Welcome! Welcome!" proclaims Walking Eagle to the three new members.

Soon Tamara's father, Professor Dumbtreaty, files an amicus curiae brief to the United Nations and the World Court at The Hague.

The ACLU and the Native American Rights Fund now throw their legal support behind the claims filed by the Walking Eagle Nation. They claim the historic precedent established by the Doctrine of Discovery, used by Columbus and all other nations. Their claim to the New World has never been repudiated by law.

Francisco de Vitoria is considered the father of international law. He issues a legal opinion stating that the act of having discovered an inhabited land still gives them the right to take it into possession. The Indians have just as much right as others to extend their sovereignty over unclaimed lands.

The United Nations and the World Court of The Hague side with the

Indian claim and officially recognize Walking Eagle Nation among the brotherhood of world nations.

The celebration at Walking Eagle Nation's capital goes on for four days and four nights. Everyone wants to give flesh offerings to become members of the Walking Eagle brotherhood.

"Just imagine. We now officially have the longest, skinniest nation on earth. It's four hundred miles long and only two hundred feet wide," proclaims Walking Eagle.

With the technical expertise of Craps, Walking Eagle soon has a consortium of casino, restaurant, and hotel investors.

In a matter of months, visitors coming from the east or west are confronted by what appears to be the Great Wall of China, standing on eighteen-foot columns providing a roadway and parking facilities beneath what was to be the longest, skinniest, destination resort on earth.

Tamara says to Walking Eagle, "Let's go to the sacred mountain to give thanks to the spirits for our success."

Once they arrive at the sacred rock, Tamara gently reaches up and pinches Walking Eagle's earlobe. The sensation is so erotic, Walking Eagle almost comes in his breechclouts.

"How did you know I would react that way?" asks a turned-on Walking Eagle.

Tamara replies, "It's because we were married in a former lifetime. You were a great chief, even then." She continues, "By the way, how did you get the name Walking Eagle?"

"It's an earned name."

"What does it mean?" asks Tamara sweetly, as she gently rubs his earlobe.

Walking Eagle replies, "It means, er, ah . . . that I am too full of shit to fly."

Jewish Indian

One of the greatest, legendary Jewish comedians who ever lived honed his comedic skills over several decades in the Catskills, known as the Borscht Belt. He went on to enormous success in Hollywood, and always nurtured a secret desire to be an American Indian. His library of historic books, including works by Will Rogers and Vine Deloria, gave him a sense of balance between the historic injustices against the Indian and contemporary Indian humor.

In order to protect his true identity, I will simply call him "Mendel." As he approached death at the ripe old age of ninety-five, Mendel told his beloved wife of six months, Roxie, "I have always lived as a Jew, but I would like to die as an Indian."

As it turned out, Mendel died as a result of an overdose of Viagra, leaving his overwrought widow, with forty-four-inch knockers, to carry out his final wishes.

I was contacted to conduct an Indian ceremony at the temple of the recently deceased Jews at Forest Lawn Cemetery in Los Angeles.

Mendel was laid out in a resplendent casket at the front of the temple. With my hand drum, I sang a Memorial Song to the spirit of Mendel. Then I lit a braid of sweetgrass and with the beautiful aromatic smoke, I smudged the remains of Mendel, and in a clockwise fashion smudged the bereaved widow, family members, and members of the vast congregation. I continued by blessing an eagle feather, which I reverently placed on Mendel's chest. I snuffed out the burning sweetgrass and placed it next to Mendel's body. My assistants then closed the lid to the casket.

Standing between the casket and the assembled congregation, I sang a Going Away Song, accompanied by my hand drum. As I sang, thin wisps of smoke started coming out of the casket, followed by thicker and thicker smoke. It appeared as though we were going to have a barbequed Jew. One alarmed woman in the audience cried out, "We came to bury Mendel, not to cremate him!"

I turned around and saw the casket engulfed in smoke. I immediately opened the casket and it released a greater cloud of smoke, which triggered the smoke alarm and the fire-control water system. The raucous noise of the smoke alarm and the drenching effects of the fire suppressant system soon had the congregation reduced to a soggy element of humanity. One elderly Jew remarked, "Well, this sure beats the hell out of being gassed at Buchenwald."

A man of the synagogue grabbed a nearby fire extinguisher and sprayed the smoking remains of Mendel, as he lay peacefully unaware of the turmoil around him.

As peace and tranquility finally took control in the synagogue, Roxie slowly and reverently approached the smoking remains of her dearly departed husband, who was now under four inches of fire suppressant foam, and uttered a famous quote: "Mendel would have loved that."

Don't Take Chances

As a child in the Indian boarding school at Pipestone, I found books to be a constant source of information about the outside world. I hung out in our small school library and entered the worlds of literature and of events I could only dream about. However, one book about geography and statistics had a profound effect on me.

Years later, when I married my Shoshone wife, Bobbie, we had three children, and then stopped.

When we raised our three children to young adults and they got married, I passed on the knowledge of statistics to them. Each of our children then had three children of their own, and then stopped.

The statistic I learned as a little boy in the boarding school was, every fourth child born in the world is Chinese.

The Four B.C.s

When you think about it, being an Indian is a lot more difficult than being a white man.

Basically, the white man has to remember only one B.C., that is, "Before Christ." The Indian, on the other hand, has to remember four B.C.s. We, too, remember "Before Christ." We also remember "Before Columbus." We remember "Before Custer." And now we remember "Before Costner."

Twelve Disciples

If I had a following of twelve disciples singing my praise songs, I too could become a messiah.

Two Tents

An old Indian who appears to be rather stressed-out goes to visit the Indian health doctor.

He tells the doctor of his recurring dreams: "First I am a teepee, and then I am a wigwam. First a teepee, then a wigwam."

The doctor thinks about it for a few minutes. Then he says, "Ah ha! I know your problem, Chief. You are two tents."

This Is a Mini-Joke, So You Give Me a Mini-Ha-Ha

I felt weak, rundown, and suffered from frequent bouts of vertigo.

My wife looked at her pitiful husband. "You're going to be dead in less than five months," was her somber prediction.

That was over five years ago.

Boy, is she pissed.

Spiritual Leader, Shaman, Almost a Messiah

There can be no doubt that mankind has always reached out to higher beings to give relevance to their lives. We have sacrificed both animals and humans to propitiate the Gods, seeking their favors of rain, good harvest, and the procreation of man.

Over the centuries the gods have taken on many shapes and identities from Isis the Sun Goddess of the ancient Egyptians to the rain gods of the Mayans, on to the present-day Christians, Moslems, Buddhists, and to the Native Americans from Gitche Manitou, Wakan Tanka, *Wah'kon-tah*, and many, many others according to tribal traditions.

In the 1960s, '70s, and '80s there appeared a great outpouring of non-Indians we called "seekers" or "New Agers." The Beatles traveled to India to seek spiritual enlightenment from a famous guru, Maharishi Mahesh Yogi. Others flocked to build a new spiritual center in Oregon, dedicated to Bhagwan Shree Rajneesh, and showered him with expensive gifts, including seventeen Rolls-Royces. They somehow felt those extravagant gifts would pay their way to spiritual enlightenment. *Ho wah!* Their lives must have been totally screwed up for them to believe their generosity could buy them the way out of their spiritual dilemma and send them enlightenment.

In truth, that practice is no different than the organized religions of the world, led by Christianity, who impress on their followers that they can buy their way out of purgatory through lavish and expensive gifts to the church. That is a form of religious shakedown. Other Christian sects impress upon their followers that they must tithe ten percent of their income to the church if they are to achieve salvation. What a bunch of insecure dorks! Imagine those religious zealots in their TV evangelical sermons who pontificate, "Put your hand on the TV and send us money and you will be saved!" Those who follow these instructions are weak-kneed individuals, afraid of their own destiny. They've been taken in by spiritual hucksters. Most of those people have children to feed, bills to pay, debts to settle, and yet, like a flock of sheep, they are compelled to give their hard-earned money to a TV evangelist. What a crock! What we really need is another belief system which doesn't require demands for money.

Mankind, like the dinosaurs, is subject to the whims of nature. Tsunamis, hurricanes, floods, and pestilence will rapidly give way to two other global catastrophes: another giant meteor from outer space or a huge volcanic eruption. Yellowstone Plateau is ready to burst and send those God-fearing Christians all to Hell. Like my guru, George Carlin, would say, "I can hardly wait."

I must now admit I, too, had what some people would call a higher calling. Ever since the early 1960s I have been involved in tribal ceremonies. As an acknowledged Pipe Carrier and ceremonial leader in our Native American community, I was invited to conduct blessing and purification ceremonies and sweat lodge ceremonies among non-Indians from California to New York. I have to admit, the reverence and respect those participants showed toward me was heady stuff. It was as though I was one step short of walking on water. The cult leaders Sun Bear, Swift Deer, and Michael Harmer—the bottom-feeders of spirituality— exploited this spiritual quest for their own gain, small titties compared to the financial largesse of organized religions.

However, we must acknowledge survival is survival, no matter what format it takes. If it means we cannot earn a living for ourselves and must rely on the generosity of others, we become parasites of spiritual humanity.

If it weren't for the generosity and sharing of their followers, almost every organized religion on earth would shrivel up and die.

The question remains, is it Christian idolatry or do financial or political rewards drive the system? I can never know the answer to this global spiritual question, as I am a simple reservation Indian who questions the unanswerable.

One of the greatest items of spiritual bullshit is the Ten Commandments. If Moses had actually carried those marble tablets of sacred inscriptions, where are they today? We have the Rosetta Stone from Egypt one thousand years before Christ. It translates ancient languages. If the Ten Commandments were so important to those ancient

Jews, why couldn't they take the time and effort to preserve them? Or, are they just a ploy to enslave the masses to Christian dogma?

"Thou shall not covet." "Thou shall not steal." "Thou shall not kill." It appears that none of the commandments applied to how Europeans treated Native Americans, as those good, God-fearing hypocrites found a way to circumvent those alleged sacred commandments. Native Americans were considered savages, barbarians, and heathens, and thus were beyond papal protection. So much for all people being considered equal, huh?

I realize I am getting on my high horse of righteousness; however, all I am doing is asking you, the reader, to question the hypocrisy of our system of religious rights and freedoms in America.

Indian Health (You're Gonna Die!)

Adam Fortunate Eagle
Fallon Indian Reservation

January 6, 2013

Dear Editor:

It's a cold January morning here on the reservation, and I am sicker than a dog. According to clinic policy, I checked in fifteen minutes before my eleven A.M. appointment with the doctor. The receptionist directed me to the records department, where I was told they could not pull my medical records, as the computers were down.

I then proceeded down the hall to the medical department for my appointment with the doctor. The nurse informed me that the doctor had quit and walked out of the clinic, leaving no other doctor on duty.

Undaunted, I walked to the pharmacy to pick up my medications, which I have been taking for five years, only to be informed by the pharmacist they could not provide them without a doctor's approval.

In effect, I was told to, "Come back when you're feeling better."

I should live so long.

* * *

President Obama's Reply

THE WHITE HOUSE

WASHINGTON

June 5, 2013

Mr. Adam Fortunate Eagle
Fallon Indian Reservation
7133 Stillwater Road
Fallon, Nevada 89406

Dear Adam:

Thank you for writing. I have been moved by the stories of Americans struggling with health care, and I appreciate your perspective. It is because of the many men and women facing frustration, hardship, and financial burden in addition to significant health problems that we worked so hard to get health care reform done.

I am working diligently every day to address the hardships people like you continue to face. Across our Nation, families are grappling with many difficult issues, including family illness, job losses, difficulty in paying the mortgage or rent, and staggering medical bills. It took many years to create our Nation's current challenges, and it will take time to bring about the changes our families need—but I will continue to do everything in my power to help all Americans live out their dreams.

For more information on resources that may be available to you, please visit www.HealthFinder.gov/FindServices. For help with insurance or finding free or low-cost care, please visit www.HealthCare.gov. To learn about help available through the Center for Medicare and Medicaid Services, visit www.CMS.gov. Information about affordable insurance for children can be found at www.InsureKidsNow.gov. Those seeking assistance with health care can also call the department of Health and Human Services at 1-877-696-6775.

As we work together to improve the lives of all our citizens, please know the trials and triumphs of Americans like you motivate my

Administration to work even harder to overcome the challenges before us. I am confident we will emerge from these tough times stronger than before with a renewed promise of a better future for all.

Again, thank you for contacting me. I wish you all the best.

Sincerely,

The Nine Lives of Fortunate Eagle

What is the best way to live to a ripe old age? The simple answer is to stay alive, and that means overcoming many obstacles, which could be life-threatening. The following is a list of the major challenges I was forced to contend with in order to reach the tribal elder category of eighty-four years of age:

ONE

At nine years of age I suffered a ruptured appendix which resulted in peritonitis. The Pipestone Indian Boarding School doctor telegraphed my mother saying, "Come to the boarding school, your son is dying." The doctor was right, because 98 percent of people with that horrific illness died within hours. This was at a time before penicillin came into wide use.

TWO

For one summer break I was sent to the Ponemah Indian Health Camp on my reservation of Red Lake. Not knowing what it was, I made the mistake of kicking a hornets' nest, which caused all hell to break loose. I ran, panic-stricken, through the deep woods with angry hornets stinging all over me. Blinded by the stings and the pain, I ran into a barbed wire fence, which entangled my left forearm, slashing my wrist. My quick-thinking counselor put a tourniquet on my arm and carried me piggyback to our camp clinic. Either one—hornet stings or loss of blood—could have killed me. However, a week later at ten in the morning I was standing in line with the other children waiting for our daily dose of cod liver oil and then our reward of a juicy sweet, sweet orange.

THREE

Not once in my ten years at the Pipestone Indian Boarding School was the medical staff at the hospital aware that I had contracted primary tuberculosis in both lungs. It wasn't until years later that X-rays and tests showed proof of that dangerous disease. My lungs carry the scars of a critical, untreated medical condition to this very day.

FOUR

My Shoshone father-in-law, Bodie Graham, and I were hoping to discover a vein of pitchblende, from which uranium can be produced. It was a hot day in the high desert mountains of Nevada. While prospecting in a small mountain pass, I came across a seep—water just pushing its way out of the ground. By that time I was sweaty and thirsty and, like a dunderhead, I drank some of that water. I didn't know then that it was polluted, poisonous, or both. That night I became violently ill, and at daybreak we hastily broke camp and headed across the desert playa to Highway 50. We drove to the emergency room at the Fallon hospital where I arrived in a semiconscious state. I have no idea what treatment I received; however, I was up and around in short order. Years later my wife, Bobbie, and I moved back to the Fallon Indian Reservation and we were notified that our tribal drinking water has high amounts of selenium and arsenic. Just to be on the safe side, I took up drinking vodka—after all it's distilled from wheat or potatoes.

FIVE

Many things occur in our lives that we cannot see coming—just like the old phrase, "shit happens." A few years ago, all of a sudden it seems, I came down with double pneumonia. Again modern medicine intervened and saved me from the Grim Reaper.

SIX

I was driving into Fallon one day, and while I was waiting to make a left turn a school bus lost its brakes and slammed into the back of my truck. That little accident put me in the hospital with back and neck injuries. To this day, when my back goes out, I have to crawl on the floor to get around.

SEVEN

I was busy at my table saw, cutting a four-inch by four-inch timber for a sculpture stand I was making. The table saw kicked back and slammed that six-pound hunk of wood into my head like a sledgehammer. The force of the blow spun me around to a bent-over position. As I opened my eyes, I saw blood dripping on the floor. I reached up to feel my head, and my palm was covered in blood. I did have the presence of mind to turn off the table saw. The next stop was the emergency room at Banner Hospital, where the doctor removed a piece of wood imbedded in the brow line of my skull. As he was stitching me up, he observed, "If that timber had hit you a half-inch higher or a half-inch lower, you would be a dead man." It took a full year to recover from that blunt force trauma.

EIGHT

With my lungs bearing the scars of TB and being weakened by two bouts of pneumonia, I knew when I felt something wrong was going on in my chest. Dr. Mabundi of the tribal clinic broke the news, "You have a lung infection called pleurisy. We can stop that infection by treating it with antibiotics." *Ho wah!* It worked! It left me very weak and tired, but I'm still alive.

NINE

My crowning survival achievement is my sixty-four-year marriage to my Shoshone wife, Bobbie. That's a record of survival few people can ever achieve. *Ho Wah!*

Glossary

ah-say-ma. *Tobacco offerings*

Anaho. *Pyramid Lake*

Annishinabeg. *Chippewa people*

boogit. *Fart*

dawsa. *Herb for blood purification and chest congestion*

gebic. *A small buckskin pouch that hangs by a leather thong either around a man's neck or across his chest*

Gitche Manitou. *Great Spirit*

hecetu. *So be it*

hehwoosh. *Long-legged turtles*

heyokas. *Contraries*

ho wah! *Man alive! Hot Damn! Wow! My goodness! Damn! Shit!*

kwitup. *Shit*

manoomin. *Wild rice*

Mi'gi'zi. *Eagle messenger to Gitche Manitou*

mii gwitch. *Thank you*

Mitakuye Oyasin. *All my relations*

naboob. *Soup*

ogichida. *Warrior*

tule. *Reed used for mats and thatching*

waboose. *Rabbit*

Weendigo. *A horrible cannibal spirit*

weh-eh. *Namesake*

Wesinin. *Let's eat*

Appendix

Percentage of Bullshit per Story

Foreword   90% BS—10% true

Moose on the Loose   100% BS

Three Hole Outhouse   100% BS

TP   100% BS

Grandpa's *Gebic* Bag   100% BS

How Poor Were You?   100% BS

Ancient Ojibwe Recipes   50% BS—50% true

Amos Gets a New House   0% BS—all true

Damn Hippies   0% BS—all true

Hurling With Lucy   0% BS—all true

Shared Sorrows   0% BS—all true

Scalping Columbus   0% BS—all true

The Curse of the Totem Pole   0% BS—all true

Now That's Brave   0% BS—all true

Farts Among Many   75% BS—25% true

Evil Spirits of Alcatraz   98% BS—2% true

General Fremont's Cannon   0% BS—all true

How I Saved Patty Hearst's Father from the SLA 0% BS—all true

Never Let a Good Deed Go Unpunished   0% BS—all true

The Saga of the Lahontan Valley Long-Legged Turtles   98% BS—2% true

Mark Your Territory   10% BS—90% true

Sonny Mosquito and the Chicken Dance   0% BS—all true

White Man Sweats Him   0% BS—all true

Tell Me Another Damn Indian Story, Grandpa   0% BS—all true

Alcatraz Is Not an Island   95% BS—5% true

Onward Christian Soldiers   0% BS—all true

Good Medicine   50% BS—50% true

Brokeback Boulder   0% BS—all true

Filipino Gold   0% BS—all true

Good Medicine II   100% BS

Italian Mill House   0% BS—all true

Peace and Friendship   0% BS—all true

The Goose Hunter   100% BS

Going Back   0% BS—all true

The Nickel Hunter   100% BS

Medicine Gift   0% BS—all true

Newt   100% BS

Walking Eagle Nation   100% BS

Jewish Indian   100% BS

Don't Take Chances   50% BS—50% true

The Four B.C.s   0% BS—all true

Twelve Disciples   100% BS

Two Tents   100% BS

This is a Mini-Joke, So You Give Me a Mini-Ha-Ha   0% BS—all true

Spiritual Leader, Shaman, Almost a Messiah   My opinion—100% BS

Indian Health (You're Gonna Die!)   50% BS—50% true

The Nine Lives of Fortunate Eagle   0% BS—all true